60   10-96

Morse's Greatest Mystery

and other stories

By the same author:

Last Bus to Woodstock

Last Seen Wearing

The Silent World of Nicholas Quinn

Service of All the Dead

The Dead of Jericho

The Riddle of the Third Mile

The Secret of Annexe 3

The Wench Is Dead

The Jewel That Was Ours

The Way Through the Woods

MORSE'S GREATEST MYSTERY

AND OTHER STORIES

COLIN DEXTER

CROWN PUBLISHERS, INC.
NEW YORK

Copyright © 1993 by Colin Dexter

All rights reserved. No part of this book may be reproduced or transmitted in
any form or by any means, electronic or mechanical, including photocopying,
recording, or by any information storage and retrieval system, without
permission in writing from the publisher.

Published by Crown Publishing, Inc., 201 East 50th Street,
New York, New York, 10022.
Member of the Crown Publishing Group.
Random House, Inc. New York, Toronto,
London, Sydney, Auckland

Originally published in Great Britain by Macmillan
London Ltd. in 1993

Crown is a trademark of Crown Publishers, Inc.

Manufactured in the United States of America

Library of Congress Cataloging-in-Publication Data is available upon request.

ISBN 0-517-79992-8

10 9 8 7 6 5 4 3 2 1

First American Edition

For my grandsons

Thomas and James

Contents

AS GOOD AS GOLD

Whereby are given unto us exceeding great and precious promises: that by these ye might be partakers of the divine nature, having escaped the corruption that is in the world.

(2 Peter, ch. 1, v. 4)

(i)

Admiring friend: 'My, that's a beautiful baby you have there!'
Mother: 'Oh, that's nothing—you should see his photograph.'

(Anon)

Chief Superintendent Strange took back the snapshot of Grandson Number One (two years, three months) and lovingly looked at the lad once more.

'Super little chap. You can leave him with anybody. As good as gold.'

He poured a little more of the Macallan into each of the glasses.

Birthdays were becoming increasingly important for Strange as the years passed by—fewer and ever fewer of them left, alas. And he thought he was enjoying the little early-evening celebration with a few of his fellow senior officers.

Only two of them remaining now, though.

Quite predictably remaining, one of the two.

Musing nostalgically, Strange elaborated on memories of childhood.

'Huh! One of the first things I ever remember as a kid, that. This woman was looking after me when my ol' mum had to go out somewhere—and when she came back she asked her whether I'd been a good boy while she'd been away and she'd been looking after me—and she said she could leave me with her any time she liked because I'd been as good as gold. Those were the very words — "As good as gold".'

3

There was a short silence, before he resumed, briefly.

'I'm not boring you by any chance, Morse?'

The white head across the desk jerked quickly to the vertical and shook itself emphatically. Seven—or was it eight?—'she's. With one or two 'her's thrown in for good measure? Yet in spite of the bewildering proliferation of those personal pronouns (feminine), Morse had found himself able to follow the story adequately, feeling gently amused as he pictured the (now) grossly overweight Superintendent as a podgy but obviously pious little cherub happily burbling to his baby-sitter.

All a bit nauseating, but . . .

'Certainly not, sir,' he said.

'You know the origin of the phrase, of course?'

Oh dear. Just a minute . . .

But Strange was already a furlong ahead of him.

'All to do with the Gold Standard, wasn't it? If you needed some gold—to buy something, say—well, it was going to be too heavy to cart around all the time—and there probably wasn't enough in the bank anyway. So they gave you a note instead—a bit o' paper promising to "pay the bearer" and all that sort of thing —and that bit o' paper was as *good* as gold. If you took that bit o' paper to the Bank of England or somewhere, you could bet your bottom dollar—well, not "dollar" perhaps—you know what I mean, though—you could get your gold-bar—if you really wanted it. You could have all the confidence in the *world* in that bit o' paper.'

Thank you, Mr Strange.

Clearly, in terms of frequency, the 'bit o' paper' had usurped the personal pronouns (feminine). But Morse was apparently unconcerned, and nodded his head encouragingly as the bottle, now at a virtually horizontal level, hovered over his empty glass.

'You're not driving yourself home, Morse, I hope?'

'Certainly not, sir.'

'Little more for you, Crawford?'

Strange turned to the only other person there in the room, seated at the desk beside Morse.

'No more for me, thank you, sir. I shall have to get back to the office.'

'Still some work to do—this time of day?'

'Just a bit, sir.'

'Ah—the Muldoon business! Yes. Going all right?'

Detective Inspector Crawford looked rather less confident than Strange's putative bearer of the promissory bank-note.

'We're making progress, sir.'

'Good! Fine piece of work that, Crawford. Aggregation, accumulation of evidence—that's what it's all about, isn't it? I know we've got a few smart alecs like Morse here who—you know, with all that top-of-the-head stuff . . . but real police work's just honest graft, isn't it? And I mean *honest*. We're winning back a lot of public support, that's for sure. We've taken a few knocks recently, course we have. Bad apples—one or two in every barrel; in every profession. Not here though! Not in our patch, eh, Morse?'

'Certainly not, sir.'

'Above suspicion—that's what *we've* got to be. Compromise on the slightest thing and you're on the slope, aren't you—on the slippery slope down to . . .'

Strange gulped back a last mouthful of Malt—clearly the name to be found at the bottom of the said slope temporarily eluding him. It was time to be off home. Almost.

'No, you can't afford to start on that.'

'Certainly not,' agreed Morse with conviction, happily unaware that he was becoming almost as repetitive as Strange.

'It's just like Caesar's wife, isn't it? "Caesar's wife must be above suspicion." You'll remember that, Morse. You were a Classics man.'

Morse nodded.

'What was her name?' asked Strange.

Oh dear. Just a minute . . .

Morse dredged his memory—unproductively. What *was* her name? She'd been accused (he remembered) of some extra-marital escapade, and Caesar had divorced her on the spot; not because he thought she was necessarily guilty, but because he couldn't afford to have a wife even suspected of double-dealing. Well, that's what *Caesar* said . . . Like as not he was probably just fed up with her; had some woman on the side himself . . . What *was* her name?

'Pomponia,' supplied Crawford.

Mentally Morse kicked himself. Of course it was.

'You all right, Morse?' Strange looked anxiously over his half spectacles, like a schoolmaster disappointed in a star pupil. 'Not had too much booze, have you?'

'Certainly not, sir.'

'You know,' Strange sat back expansively in his chair, fingers laced over his great paunch, 'you're a couple of good men, really. I know you may have cut a few corners here and there—by-passed a few procedures. Huh! But we've none of us ever lost sight of what it's really all about, have we? The Police Force? Integrity, fairness . . . honesty . . .'—then, after a deep breath, an impressive heptasyllabic finale—'incorruptibility.'

The Super had sounded fully sober now, and had spoken with a quiet, impressive dignity.

He rose to his feet.

And his fellow officers did the same.

In the corridor outside, as they walked away from Strange's office, Crawford was clearly agitated.

'Can I speak to you, Morse? It's very urgent.'

(ii)

'How did you get your wooden leg?'
    Silas Wegg replied, (tartly to this personal inquiry), 'In an accident.'

(Charles Dickens, *Our Mutual Friend*)

Oxford Prison, closed permanently a few years earlier, had recently been re-opened as a temporary measure. And with nothing in life quite so permanent as the temporary, the prison officers now temporarily posted there were fairly confidently expecting a permanent sojourn in Oxford.

On the evening of Strange's birthday, a wretched man sat wretchedly on his bed in a cell on A-Wing. From what he had gathered so far, he feared that his own temporary accommodation there would very soon be exchanged for a far more permanent tenancy in one of Her Majesty's top-security prisons somewhere else in the UK.

The man's name was Kieran Dominic Muldoon.

The question at stake was not really one of innocence or guilt, since there was universal consensus in favour of the latter. Even at the age of sixteen, Muldoon had been flirting with terrorism; and now, twenty years later, she had long been his permanent mistress.

That much was known.

It was now only a question of evidence—of sufficient evidence to shore up a case for a prosecuting counsel.

So far he'd been lucky, Muldoon knew that. Both in Belfast and in Birmingham, when he'd been detained, incriminatory links between people and places and plans had proved too difficult to substantiate; and the authorities had released him.

Had been compelled to release him.

This time, though, he'd surely been a bit *unlucky*?

He'd been conscious of that when they'd arrested him three days earlier from his Cowley Road bed-sit and taken him to St Aldate's Police Station in the City Centre, when with conspicuous confidence they'd straightaway charged him, and when the Magistrates' Court (immediately opposite) had granted a remand into custody without the slightest demur.

That, in turn, had been only a few hours after they'd discovered the explosive and the timers and the detonators out in the flat in Bannister Close on the Blackbird Leys Estate.

Jesus! What a mistake that had been to tell them he'd never been anywhere near the flat; didn't even know where the bloody block of flats *was*.

Why had they smiled at him?

Thinking back on things, he *had* felt uneasy that late afternoon a week ago when he'd gone along there—the *only* time he'd ever gone along there. He'd heard neither the clicks of any hidden camera nor the tell-tale whirr of a Camcorder; had seen no flashes; had spotted no suspicious unmarked van. No. It must have been someone in one of the council houses opposite—if they'd got some photographic evidence against him.

Because the police had got *something*.

So calm, this time. Especially that bugger Crawford.

So bloody cocky.

It couldn't be fingerprints, surely? As ever, the three of them had been almost neurotically finicky on that score; and the dozen or so cans of booze had been put into a black plastic bag and duly consigned (Muldoon had no reason to doubt) to one of the skips at the local Waste Reception Area.

But could they have been careless, and left something.

Because the police had got *something*.

Still, he'd kept his cool pretty well when they'd grilled him on names, addresses, train-journeys, stolen cars, money-transfers, weapons, explosives . . . For apart from a few regular protestations of ignorance and innocence, he'd answered little.

Or nothing.

It was at a somewhat lower level of anxiety that he worried about the ransacking of his bed-sit. They must have found them all by now.

The videos.

Ever since he could remember, Muldoon had been preoccupied with the female body, in which (as he well knew) he joined the vast majority of the human race, masculine, and some significant few of the human race, feminine. But in his own case the preoccupation was extraordinarily obsessive and intense; and intensifying as the years passed by—frequently satisfied (oh, yes!) yet ever feeding, as it were, upon its own satiety.

Only thirteen, he had been, when the hard-eyed woman had ushered him through into the darkened warmth of the cinema where, as he groped for a seat, his young eyes had immediately been transfixed upon the luridly pornographic exploits projected on the screen there, his whole being jerked into an incredible joy . . .

Since he'd been in Oxford—three months now—he'd learned that the boss of the Bodleian Library was entitled to receive a copy of every single book published in the UK. And in his own darkly erotic fancies, Muldoon's idea of Heaven was easily conceived: to be appointed Curator of some Ethereal Emporium receiving a copy of every hard-porn video passed by some Celestial Film Censor as 'Suitable Only For Advanced Voyeurs', with crates of Irish whiskey and trays of stout and cartons of cigarettes stacked double-deep all round his penthouse walls . . .

Jesus!

How could he even begin to cope if they put him inside for five—ten—years? Longer?

Please, God—no!

He'd not started off wanting too desperately to change the world; indeed not too troubled, in those early days, even about changing the borders of a divided Ireland. Certainly never *positively* wanting to kill civilians . . . women and children.

But he had done so. Twice now.

Or his bombs had.

He rose from his bed, lit another cigarette, and with the aid of an elbow-crutch stomped miserably around the small cell.

Sixteen years ago the accident had been, in Newry—when he'd crashed a stolen car at 96.5 mph (according to police evidence). Somehow a piece of glass had cut a neat slice from the top of his left ear; and the paramedics had had little option but to leave his right leg behind in the concertina'ed Cortina. All right, they'd given him an artificial leg; patiently taught him how to use it. But he'd always preferred the elbow-crutch; indoors, anyway. And no choice in the matter now, since the leg was back there in the bed-sit—in a cupboard—along with the videos.

Yes, they must have found them all by now.

And a few other things.

According to the solicitor fellow, they were still going through his room with a tooth-comb; still going through the flat in Bannister Close, too.

Jesus!

If they found him guilty—even on the possession of firearms and explosives charge . . .

Would he talk? Would he grass—if the police suggested some . . . some arrangement?

Course not!

He had a right to silence; he had a duty to silence.

Say nothing!

Let *them* do the talking.

He wouldn't.

Unless things became unbearable, perhaps . . .

Muldoon sat down on the side of his bed once more, conscious that just a tiny corner of his resolution was starting to crumble.

(iii)

You may not drive straight on a twisting lane.

(Russian proverb)

Twenty minutes later, Sergeant Lewis was still waiting patiently in the corridor outside the office of Detective Inspector Crawford. He could hear the voices inside: Morse's, Crawford's, and a third —doubtless that of Detective Sergeant Wilkins; but the general drift of the conversation escaped him. Only when (at last!) the door partially opened did individual words become recognizable —and those, Morse's:

'No!' (*fortissimo*) 'No!' (*forte*) 'And if you take *my* advice, you'll have nothing to do with it yourself, either. There are better ways of doing things than that, believe me.' (*mezzo piano*) '*Cleverer* ways, too.'

Looking unusually perturbed, his pale cheeks flushed, Morse closed the door behind him; and the words 'Christ Almighty!' (*pianissimo*) escaped his lips before he was aware of Lewis's presence.

'What the 'ell are you doing here?'

'The Super rang me, sir. You told him I was running you back home.'

'So what?'

'Well, I *wasn't*, was I?'

'What's that got to do with Strange?'

'He was just checking up, that's all.'

'Suspicious bugger!'

'He didn't think you should be driving yourself.'

'You get off home. I'm fine.'

'You're not, sir. You know you're not.'

About to expostulate, suddenly Morse decided to capitulate.

'What was all that about, then?' asked Lewis, as they walked along the endless corridors towards the car-park.

(iv)

Barring that natural expression of villainy which we all have, the man looked honest enough.

(Mark Twain)

Behind them, in Crawford's office, Sergeant Wilkins gave vent to his exasperation:

'A stuffed *prick*—that's what *he's* getting!'

'That's unfair,' said Crawford quietly.

'But he doesn't seem to understand. We're not really *planting* evidence at all, are we? We've *got* the bloody evidence. It was all there.'

'*Was* all there,' agreed Crawford, dejectedly.

'How bloody unlucky can you get in life!'

Crawford was silent.

'You—you still going ahead with things, sir?'

'Look. I'll *never* let Muldoon off the hook now. I'll do *anything* to see that murderous sod behind bars!'

'Me, too. You know that.'

'It's just that I'd have been happier in my own mind if Morse had been with us. He worries me, you see. "Cleverer ways," he said . . .'

'Seems to me he's more worried about keeping his nose clean than seeing justice done.'

'Got a pension to worry about, hasn't he? He's finishing with us soon.'

A sudden thought struck Sergeant Wilkins:

'He won't . . . he wouldn't *say* anything about it, would he?'

'Morse? Oh, no.'

'Some people blab a bit—especially when they've had a drop too much to drink.'

'Not Morse. He's never had too much to drink, anyway—not as *he* sees things.'

'Not much help, though, is he?'

'No. And I'm disappointed about that, but . . .'

'But what, sir?'

Crawford took a deep breath. 'It's just that—well, I found it *moving*, what he said just now—you know, what he thought about what was valuable, what was important in life. The Super was saying exactly the same thing really, but . . . I dunno, compared with Morse he sounded sort of all big words and bull-shit—'

'Instead of all little words and horse-piss!'

'You've got him wrong, you know. He's a funny bugger, I agree. But there's a big streak of integrity somewhere in Morse.'

'Perhaps so. Perhaps I'm being very unfair.'

Crawford rose to his feet. 'Not *very* unfair—don't be too hard on yourself. Let's just say he's a stuffed shirt, shall we? That'd be a bit fairer than, er, than what *you* just called him.'

(v)

The colleague may be exceptionally thick-headed, like Watson.

(Julian Symons, *Bloody Murder*)

The sole trouble with Malt Whisky, Morse maintained, was that it left one feeling rather thirsty; and he insisted that if Lewis really wished to learn what had transpired in Crawford's office, it would have to be over a glass of beer.

Thus it was that, ten minutes after being driven from Kidlington Police HQ, Morse sat drinking a Lewis-purchased pint at the King's Arms in Banbury Road, and spelling out Crawford's unhappy dilemma . . .

Following information received, a flat in Bannister Close had been under police surveillance for several weeks. Patience had been rewarded, gradatim; and a dossier of interesting, suggestive, and potentially incriminating evidence had been accumulated.

At intermittent periods the flat, it was believed, served in three separate capacities: first, as a meeting-house for members of a terrorist cell (suspected of being responsible for the two recent bombing incidents in Oxford); second, as a store-house for explosive and bomb-making equipment; third, as a safe-house for any other member of the group on the run from elsewhere in the UK.

For the police to rush in where hardened terrorists were so fearful of treading would have been to miss a golden opportunity of smashing an entire cell and of arresting its ring-leaders. But, perforce, this softly-softly policy had been rescinded on the specific orders of the Home Office, following hot intelligence that a big step-up in terrorist activity was scheduled for mainland Britain in the spring. 'Damage limitation'—that was the buzz-phrase now. All very well waiting patiently to net some of the big fish—very laudable too!—but no longer justifiable in terms of potential civilian casualties.

Hence the slightly precipitate actions taken: first the raiding of the flat, empty of people yet full enough of explosive materials, bombing equipment, and fingerprints; second, the arrest of Kieran Dominic Muldoon, the only one of the shadowed terrorists who had established himself as 'of fixed address' in the City of Oxford.

Not the best of outcomes, certainly, since the other birds had by now abandoned their nests; as they would have done in any case, unless they had been cornered en bloc . . . or unless Kieran Muldoon could now be 'persuaded' in some way . . . bribed, cajoled, decoyed, lured, trapped—into betraying the whereabouts of his fellow fanatics . . . For example, there were two other properties being watched: one in Jericho; one out on the Botley Road.

There had been some *little* disappointment about the contents of Muldoon's own small living-quarters in the Cowley Road: a technical manual on bomb-making, though, and some dozens of addresses, code-names, telephone numbers: *almost* enough evidence there, and all duly impounded and documented and despatched for forensic tests and all the rest of it—and finally, of course, to be exhibited.

And—*and*—in addition to all this, two little solidly connecting links between Muldoon's bed-sit and Bannister Close.

Two little beauties!

The first, a can of Beamish stout, found under a sofa in the flat at Bannister Close, with Muldoon's fingerprints daubed all over it. The second, a photograph of Muldoon himself, climbing the outside iron staircase leading up to the balconied first floor there: an unequivocal, unambiguous photograph—both of the place, yes, and of the man—with the left side of his face in profile; and a splendid view of that unmistakable ear, a segment sliced so neatly from the top.

In addition the police had a taped interview with Muldoon, as well as a signed statement—the latter containing a firm denial of his ever having been at the Blackbird Leys Estate, let alone in Bannister Close.

Every procedure had been scrupulously followed from the start: a comprehensive register of exhibits had been typed out and checked;

the key 'continuity' in the handling of these exhibits had been meticulously maintained; and the Exhibits Officer appointed was an
experienced man, fully conversant with his specific responsibilities.

'Everything hunky-dory, Lewis. Except . . .'

'Don't tell me they've lost something?'

'Not "they"; "he".'

'The photo?'

'*And* the can!'

'Bloody hell! Who was he? Who *is* he?'

'Watson. Detective Constable Watson.'

'Poor chap!'

Morse grinned feebly. 'Perhaps he never *should* have been a
detective—not with a name like that.'

'How did he come to lose—?'

'Ah! That's the good news, Lewis. He's not exactly lost them at
all, so he says.'

'What's the bad news, then?'

'The bad news is he can't find them. Nor can half a dozen other
people—who've been through everything umpteen times.'

Lewis, a man who swore very rarely, surprised his chief a second time:

'Bloody hell!'

'And Crawford, my colleague and *former* friend Crawford—
you'll never believe this!—is planning *to put them both back* on the
Exhibits Register: the can and the photo.'

'How on earth does he think—?'

'That's where he thought I might come in.'

'Well, you can't really blame him too much, perhaps.'

Morse looked up in amazement, his blue eyes penetratingly
fierce upon those of his subordinate. He spoke in a chilling hiss:

'What—did—you—say?'

Lewis sought to stand his ground: 'It's not—I mean, it's not as if
he was *fabricating* the evidence, is it, sir?'

Morse exploded now, and several other customers turned round
as they heard his furious rejoinder.

'What the hell *is* it, then—if it isn't fabrication? Come on, man! For Christ's sake tell me what *you* think it bloody well is!'

Lewis was badly taken aback. The blood had drained from his cheeks, and he could make no answer.

'*Facilis descensus Averno,*' mumbled Morse.

'Pardon, sir?'

'Forget it. And take me home!' Morse drained his beer and banged his glass down heavily on the table.

There was a supremely awkward silence between the two of them until the car pulled into Morse's parking-space outside his North Oxford flat. Then it was Lewis who spoke:

'Inspector Crawford,' he said slowly and quietly, 'was very kind to me when I first came to HQ—couple of years before I knew you. He's a good man. He wouldn't do *anything* that was basically unfair—I know that. So, if you will, sir, I want you to do me a big favour. I want you to go and see him, tell him that you told *me* about ... things, and tell him that if I can do anything—'

But Morse cut him viciously short. 'Look, my son! Don't you start giving *me* bloody orders, all right?'

'I wasn't really—'

'*Shut up!* And if you don't forget all this bloody nonsense—now!—you stop being my sergeant, is that clear? And you won't be anybody else's bloody sergeant, either—not while I'm in the Force! You'll be queuing up for your dole money, like plenty of other poor sods. Is that understood?'

Morse got out of the car and slammed the door shut with an almighty bang.

(vi)

U-turn: a turn made by a vehicle reversing into the direction of oncoming traffic, recommended only when there appear no signs of oncoming traffic.

(*Small's Enlarged English Dictionary*, 12th edition)

Next morning, with extreme reluctance, with deep distaste—and with considerable embarrassment—Morse called into Crawford's office, and did his sergeant's bidding.

(vii)

Television is more interesting than people. If it were not, we should have people standing in the corners of our rooms.

(Alan Coren, *The Times*)

He was being treated fairly well—better than he deserved or expected—Muldoon knew that. Even Crawford had been pretty reasonable: distanced, unsmiling, yes—but not *positively* unpleasant. Told him about his rights: his right to receive a few visitors (he didn't want any of *them*!); to wear his own clothes; to have food brought in to him—if he could afford it, if he wanted it; to share in the recreational facilities provided, including TV and snooker . . .

So tight, the supervision though—oppressive, constricting supervision. How he longed to be *out* somewhere: out in the streets, out in a car, out in a pub—out anywhere.

Oh, Jesus!

With naked lust he looked at a photograph of a naked model taken in the sun, in the *Sun*, when the door of his cell was unlocked and Crawford (again!) came in.

It was all about those houses (again!)—those other houses the police had been watching: the Jericho house—the 'safe-house', as Muldoon had always known it; and that (much dodgier) semi-detached, semi-derelict little property out on the Botley Road. Why did Crawford keep going on about those bloody houses?

Why?

'You stayed in either of them, Muldoon?'

'No.'

'Never?'

'Never.'

'Any of your friends ever stayed there?'

'Stayed where?'

'Well, let's talk about Jericho first, shall we?'

'Where?'

'Jericho.'

'I thought Jericho was near Jerusalem.'

'What about Botley Road?'

'Which road?'

'You know, just down past the station.'

'You mean the bus station?'

'No. The railway station.'

'Never bin down there. Don't think so.'

'All right. So why not come out with us? Just to have a look, that's all.'

'No chance.'

'Might jog the memory, you never know.'

'No memory to jog, is there?'

'You *said* you'd never been to Blackbird Leys.'

'So?'

'We've got a photo of you there.'

'So you say.'

'Why not come out and have a quick look at these other places, that's all we ask?'

'No point, is there?'

Crawford half rose to his feet. 'Pity, you know. We could have made life that little bit easier for you, one way or another.'

'What's that s'posed to mean?'

'Look, Muldoon. We don't expect you to shop your mates. All I'm saying is this: if you agree to come out and make a couple o' statements—even if they're a load of rubbish . . .'

Muldoon not only looked puzzled; he *was* puzzled.

'What's it you're *after*? How the hell's it going to help you if—'

But Crawford, risen to his feet, now brusquely cut short Muldoon's protestations.

'No! You're right. It's not going to help much at all, is it? It was just that . . .'

'Yeah? Just *what?*' Muldoon leaned forward, interested in spite of himself; and Crawford slowly sat down again on the hard, upright chair.

'Look, lad! Let me put my cards on the table. It's going to be bloody difficult for you to stay out of prison—this time. *I* know that—*you* know that. And shall I tell you something else? It's one helluva job—even for *me*—to get you out of this place, even for an hour or two; even to buy you a ride on one of the Tourist Buses. D'you know how many signatures I'd need for that—apart from the Governor's?'

Jesus!

Muldoon looked down at the floor as Crawford continued.

'There's only two ways we can give you any little outing. One's if you get transferred somewhere—up to Bullingdon Prison, say. Not very likely that, though, for a few weeks yet. And the other's if you'd agree to . . . But I'm wasting my breath. Pity though! As I say, we could have made it worth your while—*well* worth your while . . .'

Muldoon suddenly squared his mouth, and bared a set of ugly, deeply nicotined teeth.

'Come on! Spill it, Crawford. What's in it for *me?*'

'Not much. We couldn't afford to give you a season-ticket at the local knocking-shop, but . . .'

'But *what?*'

'Next best thing, perhaps?'

'Yeah? And what's that s'posed to mean?'

Crawford sighed. 'I can't make any marvellous promises—you know that. But if you agreed to keep your mouth shut—like *we* would . . .'

'Go on!'

'Well, what do you want? Fags? Booze? Money? Sex-videos? . . .'

Muldoon shook his head, albeit indecisively.

'OK. Well, that settles it, then.' Crawford rose quickly to his feet now, this time with a purposiveness heralding an imminent departure.

But Muldoon was on his feet too.

'When d'you reckon—when could this have bin? With the videos, say?'

Crawford shrugged indifferently. 'Tomorrow? Day after? Not quite sure, really. It's just that we got some pretty hot stuff in last week—from Denmark—and one or two of the lads thought they ought just to give it, you know, give it the once-over.'

'How long would they be? Watching that stuff?'

'Dunno, really. Couple of hours? Bit longer? Till the booze runs out? Some of 'em tell me they get a little bit bored—after a while. But I don't reckon they're going to get bored too quickly with this little lot.'

Muldoon sat silent for a while.

Muldoon sat silent for a considerable while.

Finally he breathed in deeply, held his breath—and exhaled, noisily.

Then he lit yet another cigarette.

And another little corner of his resolution was collapsing. Had collapsed.

'Tomorrow, you say?'

Phew!

Outside the re-locked room, Inspector Crawford also exhaled, though silently. And to Sergeant Wilkins, standing at the far end of the corridor, he gave a faint smile, and raised his right fist to shoulder-level, the thumb upstandingly proud like some *membrum virile* blessed with a joyous erection.

(viii)

The fastest recorded time for completing *The Times* crossword under test conditions is 3 minutes 45 seconds, by Mr Roy Dean, of Bromley, Kent.

(*The Guinness Book of Records*)

After returning from Inspector Crawford's room late that same afternoon, Sergeant Lewis found Morse seated at his desk, *The*

Times in front of him, looking grim—and smoking a cigarette. It seemed to Lewis, in view of the tight-lipped taciturnity hitherto observed between the pair of them throughout the day, that it was the latter activity which afforded the more promising ice-breaker.

'I thought you'd given up, sir?'

'I have—many times. In fact I've given up smoking more often than anyone else in the history of the habit. By rights I should have a paragraph all to myself in *The Guinness Book of Records.*'

The tone of Morse's words was light enough, perhaps, but the underlying mood was sombre.

And Lewis, too, as he sat down, looked far from happy with himself.

'You told me off good and proper last night, didn't you, sir? *And* I deserved it. You were right. To be truthful, I wish I'd taken a bit more notice of you.'

'Why this sudden change of heart?'

'Well, it's getting . . . it's getting all a bit involved and underhand—'

'Dishonest.'

'Yes . . . and *messy.*'

The hard lines on Morse's face relaxed somewhat. 'You can hardly expect the sort of classical economy and purity of line you get when you're working with me! Crawford's a cretin—that's common knowledge, isn't it?'

'No he's not! It's just that—well, I don't honestly think he's *all that* bright.'

'Your judgement is reasserting itself, Sergeant.'

Lewis was silent.

'Come on. You know you're dying to tell me all about it.'

'I thought you didn't want anything to do with it.'

'How right you are!' snapped Morse bitterly.

He got up and took his mackintosh off its peg.

A persistent drizzle had stippled the window that looked out over the car-park—a window through which Lewis had so often seen Morse gazing as he grappled in his mind with the problems of a case.

Saw him so gazing now; but only for a few seconds, before he put on his mackintosh and walked to the door.

'Make sure you lock up! If there's some crook around prepared to pinch an empty can of Beamish, what the hell's he going to do with my Glenfiddich? Goo' night!'

The door slammed, and Morse was gone.

But Lewis heard no footsteps along the corridor; and twenty seconds later the door re-opened slowly, and Morse stepped back into his office.

'It *would* help, Lewis, wouldn't it, if you told me what's worrying you.'

'Yes,' replied Lewis simply.

'You should have told me earlier.'

'You looked, well, pretty grim, sir.'

'What? Oh, that! That was just *me*—not you. Six minutes—to the second almost—with the crossword! Would have been just about the record—except for one clue: I couldn't do 14 across. *Still* can't do bloody 14 across.'

'Shall *I* have a look at it?'

'You? Fat lot o' use that'd be!'

Lewis looked down at the threadbare patch of off-white carpet on his own side of Morse's desk.

'If you *could* spare five minutes, sir—I'd feel a lot happier.'

Morse took off his mackintosh, replaced it on its peg, and resumed his seat in the black-leather armchair behind his desk.

(ix)

Now faith is the substance of things hoped for, the evidence of things not seen.

(Hebrews, ch. 11, v. 1)

As Morse now began to see, Crawford's scheme hardly matched the strategic genius of Napoleon at Austerlitz, or NASA in planning one of its moon missions . . .

At 20.30, an hour after lighting-up time, on Thursday, 31 March, Muldoon, handcuffed to a police officer, his head concealed from any inquisitive public or press intrusion beneath a grey prison blanket, would be taken from Oxford Prison in an unmarked police van. The outing had already been sanctioned (no problem) 'in pursuance of corroborative or associative evidence'. No one had ever understood this long-winded phrase, yet it had the merit of sounding most impressive.

The prisoner would be taken first to Jericho, then to Botley; shown over the two properties in question; and invited, on each occasion, to make a brief statement. This, in truth, in the interests of verisimilitude only. Yet (as Crawford maintained) there was always just the possibility that Muldoon *would* say something of value. Prisoners had grassed in the past; prisoners would grass in the future.

Thereafter things would become a little more complicated.

Muldoon would then be informed that the reward for his co-operation lay some ten miles away, along the A40, in a police-house in Witney. In fact, the van would be driven out from Botley on to the western Ring Road; and, after a suitably convincing 'ten-mile' detour, would land up in the Blackbird Leys Estate, on the eastern side of Oxford, beyond the Rover car-plant at Cowley.

At which point, Crawford's careful, albeit clumsy, planning would enter its critical phase.

The outward appearance of Bannister Close might well be fairly familiar to Muldoon. Although he had visited the flat only once (as it appeared) there was the real possibility that he might recognize some aspect of the block—its architectural style, its black-painted balcony, the colours of its doors and windows—even in semi-darkness. And no risks could be taken.

Therefore . . .

Muldoon, still handcuffed, would be dropped off at the *rear* of the block, where a main road ran behind the back of the properties. In the interests of public safety a five-foot fence of vertical wooden slats had been erected to separate this road from Bannister Close. But as in so many parts of the Estate, vandals had been at work here too, and several irregular gaps had been kicked through the fencing; and (Crawford had done his homework) there was a most convenient opening, two or three feet wide, in the stretch almost immediately behind Number 14.

Easy.

And since a fairly steep grassy slope led down from the fence to the concreted path running beside the rear entrance to the flats, it seemed wholly unlikely that a man with only one leg was going to be too deeply engrossed in his environment.

The flat originally raided was on the first floor, with access only via an external stairway, one at each end of the block. But by a stroke of good fortune, the flat beneath it, on the ground floor, was empty; had been empty for several months—the For Sale notice stuck into the scratty patch of weedy waste which passed itself off in the property's specification as 'a small front garden'. And it was to be in the living-room of *this* flat (Crawford had decreed) that the scene was to be set: off screen, and on screen, as it were.

One of Crawford's old colleagues, now a senior member of the Obscene Publications Squad—a man with the not inappropriate name of Cox—would be providing an outsize TV screen, together with a veritable feast of video-sex for the viewers. Only five viewers though: Cox himself, Crawford, Wilkins, Lewis—and Muldoon.

An inviting tray of Beamish stout would be available, and the four police officers would each nonchalantly help themselves from it, drinking straight from the cans—no glasses! And a man who had tasted no alcohol for a week—and an Irishman, to boot— would surely speedily succumb.

And if he didn't? Well, no real worry.

Quite a few props would be required to set the stage and—wait for it!—behold now Crawford's *coup de grâce*! A ridiculously oversized furniture-van had been hired to convey a carpet, four chairs, a settee, a table, a large TV set . . .

Wait!

. . . and this van would *still* be parked outside the property when, after the final curtain, Muldoon would emerge—*through the front door*. And there, bang in front of him, instead of a potentially recognizable prospect, would stand the great pantechnicon, blocking anything and everything—particularly the council houses opposite.

And now—O Napoleon!—mark a stroke of rare genius. Not only would the van serve to bring the props; not only would it conceal the view over that unlovely neighbourhood; *it would also house the photographer*, who would once more capture Muldoon on film outside the very place of which earlier he had so vehemently denied all knowledge. This time, though, from much closer quarters—from behind a grille (removed) in the side of the van, with a camera loaded with 1000 ASA film, and positioned on a tripod to prevent any shake.

And that would be that. A whole *series* of shots this time. *And* (Crawford had averred) if DC Watson or some other incompetent idiot lost *those*, then good luck to Muldoon and his co-criminals! The police wouldn't deserve to catch, or the courts to convict them.

But that wouldn't happen again.

For Muldoon it would be back to Oxford. Back to prison. And very soon, if there were any justice in life, back to prison *for* life. For whatever the dishonesty of the scheme devised against him, Muldoon was a cruel and murderous bastard.

There could be no mistake on that score.

(x)

If I repent of anything, it is very likely to be my good behaviour.

(Henry David Thoreau)

Such was Lewis's account—of Crawford's account—itself, in turn, transmuted in Morse's mind to the heightened version presented to the reader in the preceding paragraphs.

When it was finished, Morse looked almost as puzzled as (apparently) the prisoner himself had looked earlier.

'Has Muldoon got any idea that things have gone missing?'

'Seems not, sir.'

'He must be suspicious, though—about being offered something for nothing? It's surely very improbable, isn't it, that he's going to spill any beans?'

'We *do* get informers, though. *And* they get paid.'

'Unusual currency—sex-videos.'

'Well, that's his particular taste, according to Crawford. They found dozens of 'em in his room. Not natural, is it?'

'Not all that *un*-natural, would you say?'

'Have you *seen* some of these videos?'

'No, Lewis. Unlike you, I've lived a very sheltered life. I have *tried* to get invited along to one of these porno-parties, but everybody seems to think I'm above such things.'

'You wouldn't enjoy 'em, sir. They make you feel—well, cheap, somehow.'

'Perhaps most of us *are* cheap.'

Lewis shook his head. 'And goodness knows what the missus would say if she knew.'

'*Need* she know?'

'You'd understand better if you were married, sir.'

Morse was silent for a short while before continuing. 'I'll tell you one thing: I wish I could understand *Crawford* better. Why doesn't he do things a bit more *simply*?'

'What are you thinking of?'

'Well, if he's lost a beer-can, why doesn't he just give the fellow *another* beer-can—and then stick it in the exhibits locker?'

'I'm not sure. But I think he feels it'll salve his conscience a bit if it comes from Blackbird Leys, you know—not from the prison.'

'What's the difference? It's dishonest either way.'

'You'd have to ask Crawford that. I don't know.'

'And why not just *fiddle* the photo? I know a Spanish chap—name of McSevich—'

'Spanish? With a name like that?'

'Like you, Lewis, I am not privy to some of the greater mysteries in life. All I know is that this chap's a wizard with a camera. He
can stick a ghost in the middle of a group-photograph—all that
sort of fake stuff. He can probably let you have a snap of the Home
Secretary outside a strip-club—in his jock-strap.'

'In the dark.'

Morse grinned. 'No problem.'

'That would be even *more* dishonest, though.'

'What? What are you talking about?'

'I think—I *think* I understand why Crawford's doing it this way.'

'You *do*? Well, tell me. Come on! Come on, Lewis! Try!'

Lewis took a deep breath. It was going to be difficult—but he
would try.

'Look at it this way, sir. If I—let's say I was being unfaithful to
the missus and going off somewhere with a lady-friend. Let's say
I'd told the missus I was going by train—but I wasn't really going
by train at all, because this lady-friend was going to pick me up in
her car somewhere, all right?'

'Lewis, I look at you in a completely new light!'

'It's just that I'd rather have a taxi actually *take* me to the station,
and get picked up *there*—rather than meet in St Giles' or somewhere. I know you wouldn't understand something like that,
but . . .'

'But I do,' said Morse quietly. 'I know exactly what you mean.'

Lewis felt encouraged to add a gloss: 'It's as if Crawford's only
prepared to be dishonest in an honest sort of way.'

Morse recited the couplet that had been going through his
mind:

'Honour rooted in Dishonour stood,
And Faith, unfaithful, kept him falsely true.'

'Who wrote that, sir?'

'Forget.'

Morse rose from his desk, a final thought striking him.

'You know, if your prisoner's going to be handcuffed all the while, it's bound to be a funny old photo, isn't it? Won't it give the game away?'

'No. He's only got one leg. And he couldn't scarper if he wanted to. Even *you* could catch him if he tried anything on, sir.'

'Thank you very much!'

Lewis too rose from his chair, reluctantly, unhappily—and made his decision.

'I'm going back to see Inspector Crawford. I'm not having anything to do with it. I'm letting him down, I know—after what I told him. But I—it's just not on. I can't do it. He'll have to find somebody else.'

Morse came round the desk and placed a hand on Lewis's shoulder.

'You get off home and see the missus. Leave all this to me. I'll go along and see Crawford myself. Have no fears!'

'You're sure, sir?'

'Absolutely. There'll be no trouble finding somebody to take your place.'

After Lewis had gone, Morse walked over to the window, and spent several minutes gazing out across the car-park.

(xi)

All men are tempted. There is no man that lives that can't be broken down, provided it is the right temptation, put in the right spot.

(Henry Ward Beecher, *Proverbs from a Plymouth Pulpit*)

When, after Muldoon, he had squeezed himself through the gap in the fencing, Morse stood beside his charge and unlocked the hand-cuffs—almost immediately to realize that the man with only one leg and an elbow-crutch was considerably more nimble than he in negotiating the grassy slope at the rear of the Bannister Close flats.

But Muldoon was patiently waiting for his escort, on the concreted path, when Morse finally effected his descent, the palm of his left hand ever reaching out for support to the side wall of a row of sheds in which the residents of the block doubtless stored bicycles, and old lawnmowers, and (inevitably) virtually empty pots of house-paint.

The ground here was liberally littered with crisp and cigarette packets and all the usual detritus of a run-down neighbourhood: a circumstance most grievous to Chief Inspector Morse. But the first part of the operation had been accomplished successfully, and sufficient light was thrown from the lace-curtained, white-painted windows there for Morse to see exactly where they were. Behind the kitchen window of Number 13, beside a carton of Persil washing-powder, was a 'Vote Conservative' poster, propped upside-down against a broken pane.

Morse had done his homework too.

'Sh!'

Morse raised a finger to his lips, then pointed across to the right —towards the far end of the flats. He spoke very quietly:

'Let me know if you hear a whistle. That'll be Sergeant Wilkins, giving us the all-clear.'

Muldoon nodded.

'Or if you hear anything else for that matter,' mumbled Morse, moving over to Muldoon's right.

For half a minute or so, the two men stood there side by side, unmoving, silent.

No noise.

Then, all of a sudden, to the left, at some point at the side of the sheds, there was the sound of a metal dust-bin lid, as if blown off its base in a gust of wind and now rumbling in a decelerating circle.

Muldoon whipped himself round immediately to face the direction whence the rattle had originated, crouching down instinctively, and remaining frozen for several seconds—both he and Morse (the latter still facing the opposite way) experiencing a frisson of fear, though each for a different reason.

'Wha's tha'?' whispered Muldoon.

But Morse made no answer, and the night, beneath the darkly overcast sky, was wholly still once more.

No more noise at all, in fact; and if there had been a low whistle from the far end of the block, it was heard by neither escort nor prisoner.

Instead, Inspector Crawford now appeared at the double-fronted glass doors slightly further along; and first Muldoon, then Morse, stepped over the threshold into the living-room of Number 13 Bannister Close.

(xii)

High definition is the state of being well filled with data. A photograph is, visually, 'high definition'.

(Marshal McLuhan, Understanding Media)

Although he had lost his religious faith many years since, Morse still retained a sort of residual religiosity; and two days after the bizarre incidents just described, he was seated, in mid-morning, in his North Oxford flat, listening with awesome reverence to the Fauré *Requiem*—when the door-bell rang.

'Can I come in, Morse?' Ill-at-ease, on the doorstep, stood Inspector Crawford.

'Look,' he began, seated a minute later opposite Morse in the lounge. 'I just want to thank you for your help, that's all. I know you didn't approve of what I did, but . . .'

'What's gone wrong?' asked Morse, reluctantly switching off the CD player.

Crawford shook his head sadly. '*Every* bloody thing—that's what! You remember that Beamish we had—'

'Much appreciated!'

'—it was a new thing of theirs. "Cask Pour", they call it.'

Morse knew all about such things: 'All the flavour from a can you'd normally expect from a barrel—that's the idea.'

'Yes, but *that* particular product only came onto the market on the 28th March—*last Monday*—you couldn't get it before then. Big launch on the telly, in the papers . . .'

'So . . . so the can with Muldoon's fingerprints on it . . .?'

'Yes! Couldn't *possibly* have come from the flat at the time we raided it.'

'Will anybody notice, though?'

'Watson noticed.'

'Not PC Watson?'

'PC Watson!'

Morse raised his eyebrows. 'I see what you mean,' he said slowly. 'Not exactly an Einstein, is he?'

'And if *he* noticed it . . .'

'Ye-es.'

'All that palaver, Morse—and I go and act like a greenhorn.'

'Never mind. You've got your photographs.'

'No! They're no bloody good either!'

'Don't tell me your fellow forgot to put film in the camera?'

'Oh no. He took some fine photos. Marvellously clear—too bloody clear. You see, Muldoon almost *never* ventured out and about with his elbow-crutch—I'd forgotten that. And the original photo we took showed him with an artificial leg. Course it bloody did!'

'Oh dear! Did, er, did Watson spot that as well?'

'He did.'

'You know, if that fellow could only stop losing things, he'd probably make "inspector".'

'He can have my job any time he likes!'

'Can't you just cut the bottom off the photos?' suggested Morse.

'Trouble is, I'd cut off the flat numbers as well if I did that—the way they've turned out; then they might just as well have been taken in Timbuktu as in Bannister Close.'

'I take your point,' said Morse.

'Anyway, I didn't come here to burden you with my troubles. As I say, I just wanted to thank you—in person. I didn't want to say anything over the blower—can't be too careful. So—if we can . . . if we can just, well, draw a veil over things? And I'm sorry I've been such a cretin.'

Morse got to his feet and stood in front of Crawford.

'Don't say that.' He spoke in a kindly fashion, oblivious (it appeared) that this was the self-same word he'd used so recently himself to describe his fellow officer. 'You could do with a drink.'

'I could do with *two*,' corrected Crawford.

Morse went to his drinks-cabinet and took out the Glenfiddich, at the same time switching on again, albeit softly, the 'In Paradisum' from the Fauré *Requiem*.

(xiii)

I am a camera with its shutter open, quite passive, recording, not thinking.

(Christopher Isherwood, *Goodbye to Berlin*)

Four days later, on Wednesday 6 April, an oblong buff envelope ('Please Do Not Bend') arrived by Registered Delivery at the Thames Valley Police HQ, addressed to Chief Inspector Morse.

Inside the envelope, together with two very glossy black-and-white photographs, was an invoice—and a letter:

Morse, old boy,

Sorry about the delay—Easter post and all that. Not bad, are they? Cheque please, as per invoice, asap. No extra fee charged for knocking over that bloody dust-bin! What will you think of next?

Pity I couldn't get the crutch in—he'd turned too far round. Interesting configuration of the left ear, though. I trust you'll approve of the 'topographically recognizable setting' (your specification). In fact the capsized Tory poster is a nice little prop, don't you reckon?

By the way, what the hell are they doing voting Tory down there?

Yours aye,

Manuel (McS)

PS Did I mention the cheque—asap?

Morse looked at the two photographs; and like the Almighty surveying one of his acts of Creation, he saw that they were good.

He reached for the phone and rang Inspector Crawford to tell him of his eleventh-hour reprieve—soon learning from Sergeant Wilkins that Crawford had just been called in to see Strange. He'd pass the message on, though.

(xiv)

Confessions are good for the soul but bad for the reputation.

(Thomas Robert Dewar)

When, half an hour later, Crawford came in, Morse reached into a drawer for the envelope. But it was Crawford, looking preternaturally pleased with himself, who immediately seized the initiative.

'I was just going to call *you*. You'll never guess what's happened.'

'Watson's unearthed his lost exhibits?'

'Better than that.'

'They've just appointed PC Watson Chief Constable?'

Crawford blurted it out: 'Muldoon! He's changed his plea— through his lawyer. He's pleading guilty as charged on all counts. *And* he's come clean on the Jericho and Botley places. *Very* interesting what he's told us about *them*. Complete change of heart, that's what he's had, Muldoon—with the, er, encouragement of some, you know—one or two little privileges.'

'Well done!' said Morse, quietly slipping the envelope back into its drawer.

'And *Strange*? He's over the moon.'

'Everybody'll be pleased.'

'Lucky though, wasn't I?' said Crawford reflectively.

'We all deserve a little bit of luck now and then,' said Morse.

After Crawford had gone, Morse once more took the photographs from their envelope, and looked at them briefly again—especially at that neatly sliced left ear—before slowly tearing them up and dropping the pieces into his waste-paper basket.

Then he wrote out a cheque, and addressed an envelope to Manuel McSevich, Esquire, The Studio, High St., Abingdon, Oxon. It seemed to Morse a quite disproportionate sum to pay; yet, perhaps, not totally exorbitant—considering the nature of the entertainment which that most unusual of evenings had provided.

(xv)

If children grew up according to early indications, we should have nothing but geniuses.

(Johann Wolfgang von Goethe)

Only very occasionally did Superintendent Strange patronize the canteen at HQ. But that lunchtime, as the solitary Morse sat at a corner table, his back to his colleagues, rather dejectedly sipping a bowl of luke-warm leek soup, he felt a hand on his shoulder.

'Can I join you?'

Morse nodded a supererogatory 'yes', as Strange unloaded from his tray a vast plateful of steak-and-kidney pie, two bread rolls, and a substantial wodge of treacle-tart covered—nay smothered—with custard.

'You heard about Muldoon, Morse?'

'Inspector Crawford told me the good news.'

Strange rubbed his hands gleefully. 'Excellent, isn't it? Excellent! Not the slightest suspicion of any undue police pressure either—you know that!'

'So I understand, sir.'

'*Above* suspicion, eh? Like Caesar's wife.'

'Let's hope so.'

'*You* couldn't remember her name, could you?'

'No.'

'Crawford could, though.'

Morse nodded. Crawford was clearly the flavour of the month.

So be it.

'You're not eating much?' queried Strange, forking another great gobbet of meat into his mouth.

'I'm not very hungry today.'

'It's a wonder you're not in the pub, then. You're usually *thirsty* enough.'

The reminder did little to lighten Morse's mood; and in sycophantic fashion he quickly sought to change the drift of the conversation.

'How's that little grandson of yours, sir?'

'Fine. Absolutely fine! Did I show you his latest photo?'

Morse nodded, hurriedly. 'Still behaving himself?'

For a few seconds, Strange looked slightly uneasy—before leaning over the almost empty plate of treacle-tart, a mischievous glint in his eye.

'To tell you the truth, Morse, his mother rang us only last night. Seems she left him with a baby-sitter when she went to church for Easter-morning service. And d'you know what the little bugger did? He went and bit the bloody baby-sitter's hand!'

'Just a temporary lapse,' suggested Morse.

'Course it was! We can't be good *all* the time, can we? None of us can.'

Morse nodded slowly. 'No, sir. We all have the occasional moment when we're not—we're not particularly proud of ourselves.'

Strange appeared gratified by this latter sentiment; and after spooning up his last mouthful of custard he sat back, replete and relaxed. Taking out his wallet, he extracted, just as he had done a week earlier, the latest snapshot of Grandson Number One (two years, three months).

'Super little chap, Morse. You can leave him with anybody—well, *almost* anybody! As good as gold, almost.'

As if with mutual understanding, the two policemen looked at each other then.

And smiled.

MORSE'S
GREATEST MYSTERY

'Hallo!' growled Scrooge, in his accustomed voice as near as he could feign it. 'What do you mean by coming here at this time of day?'

(Dickens, A Christmas Carol)

He had knocked diffidently at Morse's North Oxford flat. Few had been invited into those book-lined, Wagner-haunted rooms: and even he—Sergeant Lewis—had never felt himself an over-welcome guest. Even at Christmas time. Not that it sounded much like the season of good-will as Morse waved Lewis inside and concluded his ill-tempered conversation with the bank manager.

'Look! If I keep a couple of hundred in my current account, that's *my* look-out. I'm not even asking for any interest on it. All I *am* asking is that you don't stick these bloody bank charges on when I go—what? once, twice a year?—into the red. It's not that I'm mean with money'—Lewis's eyebrows ascended a centimetre—'but if you charge me again I want you to ring and tell me *why*!'

Morse banged down the receiver and sat silent.

'You don't sound as if you've caught much of the Christmas spirit,' ventured Lewis.

'I don't like Christmas—never have.'

'You staying in Oxford, sir?'

'I'm going to decorate.'

'What—decorate the Christmas cake?'

'Decorate the kitchen. I don't like Christmas cake—never did.'

'You sound more like Scrooge every minute, sir.'

'*And* I shall read a Dickens novel. I always do over Christmas. *Re*-read, rather.'

'If I were just *starting* on Dickens, which one—?'

'I'd put *Bleak House* first, *Little Dorrit* second—'

The phone rang and Morse's secretary at HQ informed him that he'd won a £50 gift-token in the Police Charity Raffle, and this time Morse cradled the receiver with considerably better grace.

'"Scrooge", did you say, Lewis? I'll have you know I bought five tickets—a quid apiece!—in that Charity Raffle.'

'I bought five tickets myself, sir.'

Morse smiled complacently. 'Let's be more charitable, Lewis! It's *supporting* these causes that's important, not *winning*.'

'I'll be in the car, sir,' said Lewis quietly. In truth, he was beginning to feel irritated. Morse's irascibility he could stomach; but he couldn't stick hearing much more about Morse's selfless generosity!

Morse's old Jaguar was in dock again ('Too mean to buy a new one!' his colleagues claimed) and it was Lewis's job that day to ferry the chief inspector around; doubtless, too (if things went to form) to treat him to the odd pint or two. Which indeed appeared a fair probability, since Morse had so managed things on that Tuesday morning that their arrival at the George would coincide with opening time. As they drove out past the railway station, Lewis told Morse what he'd managed to discover about the previous day's events . . .

The patrons of the George had amassed £400 in aid of the Littlemore Charity for Mentally Handicapped Children, and this splendid total was to be presented to the Charity's Secretary at the end of the week, with a photographer promised from *The Oxford Times* to record the grand occasion. Mrs Michaels, the landlady, had been dropped off at the bank in Carfax by her husband at about 10.30 a.m., and had there exchanged a motley assemblage of coins and notes for forty brand-new tenners. After this she had bought several items (including grapes for a daughter just admitted to hospital) before catching a minibus back home, where she had arrived just after midday. The money, in a long white envelope, was in her shopping bag, together with her morning's purchases. Her husband had not yet returned from the Cash and Carry Stores, and on re-entering the George via the saloon bar, Mrs Michaels had heard the telephone ringing. Thinking that it was probably the hospital (it was) she had dumped her bag on the bar counter and rushed to answer it. On her return, the envelope was gone.

At the time of the theft, there had been about thirty people in the saloon bar, including the regular OAPs, the usual cohort of pool-playing unemployables, and a pre-Christmas party from a local firm. And—yes!—from the very beginning Lewis had known that the chances of recovering the money were virtually nil. Even so, the three perfunctory interviews that Morse conducted appeared to Lewis to be sadly unsatisfactory.

After listening a while to the landlord's unilluminating testimony, Morse asked him why it had taken him so long to conduct his business at the Cash and Carry; and although the explanation given seemed perfectly adequate, Morse's dismissal of this first witness had seemed almost offensively abrupt. And no man could have been more quickly or more effectively antagonized than the temporary barman (on duty the previous morning) who refused to answer Morse's brusque enquiry about the present state of his overdraft. What then of the attractive, auburn-haired Mrs Michaels? After a rather lop-sided smile had introduced Morse to her regular if slightly nicotine-stained teeth, that distressed lady had been unable to fight back her tears as she sought to explain to Morse why she'd insisted on some genuine notes for the publicity photographer instead of a phonily magnified cheque.

But wait! Something dramatic had just happened to Morse, Lewis could see that: as if the light had suddenly shined upon a man that hitherto had sat in darkness. He (Morse) now asked— amazingly!—whether by any chance the good lady possessed a pair of bright green, high-heeled leather shoes; and when she replied that, yes, she did, Morse smiled serenely, as though he had solved the secret of the universe, and promptly summoned into the lounge bar not only the three he'd just interviewed but all those now in the George who had been drinking there the previous morning.

As they waited, Morse asked for the serial numbers of the stolen notes, and Lewis passed over a scrap of paper on which some figures had been hastily scribbled in blotchy Biro. 'For Christ's sake, man!' hissed Morse. 'Didn't they teach you to write at school?'

Lewis breathed heavily, counted to five, and then painstakingly rewrote the numbers on a virginal piece of paper: 773741–773780. At which numbers Morse glanced cursorily before sticking the paper in his pocket, and proceeding to address the George's regulars.

He was *virtually* certain (he said) of who had stolen the money. What he was *absolutely* sure about was exactly where that money was *at that very moment*. He had the serial numbers of the notes—but that was of no importance whatsoever now. The thief might well have been tempted to spend the money earlier—but not any more! And why not? Because at this Christmas time that person *no longer had the power to resist his better self*.

In that bar, stilled now and silent as the grave itself, the faces of Morse's audience seemed mesmerized—and remained so as Morse gave his instructions that the notes should be replaced in their original envelope and returned (he cared not by what means) to Sergeant Lewis's office at Thames Valley Police HQ *within the next twenty-four hours*.

As they drove back, Lewis could restrain his curiosity no longer. 'You really *are* confident that—?'

'Of course!'

'I never seem to be able to put the clues together myself, sir.'

'Clues? What clues, Lewis? I didn't know we had any.'

'Well, those shoes, for example. How do they fit in?'

'Who said they fitted in anywhere? It's just that I used to know an auburn-haired beauty who had six—*six*, Lewis!—pairs of bright green shoes. They suited her, she said.'

'So . . . they've got nothing to do with the case at all?'

'Not so far as I know,' muttered Morse.

❖

The next morning a white envelope was delivered to Lewis's office, though no one at reception could recall when or whence it had arrived. Lewis immediately rang Morse to congratulate him on the happy outcome of the case.

'There's just one thing, sir. I'd kept that scrappy bit of paper with the serial numbers on it, and these are brand-new notes all right—but they're not the same ones!'

'Really?' Morse sounded supremely unconcerned.

'You're not worried about it?'

'Good Lord, no! You just get that money back to ginger-knob at the George, and tell her to settle for a jumbo-cheque next time! Oh, and one other thing, Lewis. I'm on *leave*. So no interruptions from anybody—understand?'

'Yes, sir. And, er . . . Happy Christmas, sir!'

'And to you, old friend!' replied Morse quietly.

The bank manager rang just before lunch that same day. 'It's about the four hundred pounds you withdrew yesterday, Inspector. I did promise to ring about any further bank charges—'

'I explained to the girl,' protested Morse. 'I needed the money quickly.'

'Oh, it's perfectly all right. But you did say you'd call in this morning to transfer—'

'Tomorrow! I'm up a ladder with a paint brush at the moment.'

Morse put down the receiver and again sank back in the arm-chair with the crossword. But his mind was far away, and some of the words he himself had spoken kept echoing around his brain: something about one's better self . . . And he smiled, for he knew that this would be a Christmas he might enjoy almost as much as the children up at Littlemore, perhaps. He had solved so many mysteries in his life. Was he now, he wondered, beginning to glimpse the solution to the greatest mystery of them all?

EVANS TRIES
AN O-LEVEL

Dramatis Personae

The Secretary of the Examinations Board

The Govenor of HM Prison, Oxford

James Evens, a prisoner

Mr Jackson, a prison officer

Mr Stephens, a prison officer

The Reverend S. McLeery, an invigilator

Detective Superintendent Carter

Detective Chief Inspector Bell

The unexamined life is not worth living.

(Plato)

It was in early March when the Secretary of the Examinations Board received the call from Oxford Prison.

'It's a slightly unusual request, Governor, but I don't see why we shouldn't try to help. Just the one fellow, you say?'

'That's it. Chap called Evans. Started night classes in O-level German last September. Says he's dead keen to get some sort of academic qualification.'

'Is he any good?'

'He was the only one in the class, so you can say he's had individual tuition all the time, really. Would have cost him a packet if he'd been outside.'

'We-ell, let's give him a chance, shall we?'

'That's jolly kind of you. What exactly's the procedure now?'

'Oh, don't worry about that. I'll be sending you all the forms and stuff. What's his name, you say? Evans?'

'James Roderick Evans.' It sounded rather grand.

'Just one thing, Governor. He's not a violent sort of fellow, is he? I don't want to know his criminal record or anything like that, but—'

'No. There's no record of violence. Quite a pleasant sort of chap, they tell me. Bit of a card, really. One of the stars at the Christmas concert. Imitations, you know the sort of thing: Mike Yarwood stuff. No, he's just a congenital kleptomaniac, that's all.' The Governor was tempted to add something else, but he thought better of it. He'd look after *that* particular side of things himself.

'Presumably,' said the Secretary, 'you can arrange a room where—'

'No problem. He's in a cell on his own. If you've no objections, he can sit the exam in there.'

'That's fine.'

'And we could easily get one of the parsons from St Mary Mags to invigilate, if that's—'

'Fine, yes. They seem to have a helluva lot of parsons there, don't they?' The two men chuckled good-naturedly, and the Secretary had a final thought. 'At least there's one thing. You shouldn't have much trouble keeping him *incommunicado*, should you?'

The Governor chuckled politely once more, reiterated his thanks, and slowly cradled the phone.

Evans!

'Evans the Break' as the prison officers called him. Three times he'd escaped from prison, and but for the recent wave of unrest in the maximum-security establishments up north, he wouldn't now be gracing the Governor's premises in Oxford; and the Governor was going to make absolutely certain that he wouldn't be *dis*gracing them. Not that Evans was a *real* burden: just a persistent, nagging presence. He'd be all right in Oxford, though: the Governor would see to that—would see to it personally. And besides, there was just a possibility that Evans was genuinely interested in O-level German. Just a slight possibility. Just a very slight possibility.

At 8.30 p.m. on Monday 7 June, Evans's German teacher shook him by the hand in the heavily guarded Recreational Block, just across from D Wing.

'*Guten Glück*, Herr Evans.'

'Pardon?'

'I said, "Good luck". Good luck for tomorrow.'

'Oh. Thanks, er, I mean, er, *Danke schön*.'

'You haven't a cat in hell's chance of getting through, of course, but—'

'I may surprise everybody,' said Evans.

❧

At 8.30 the following morning, Evans had a visitor. Two visitors, in fact. He tucked his grubby string-vest into his equally grubby trousers, and stood up from his bunk, smiling cheerfully. 'Mornin', Mr Jackson. This is indeed an honour.'

Jackson was the senior prison officer on D Wing, and he and Evans had already become warm enemies. At Jackson's side stood Officer Stephens, a burly, surly-looking man, only recently recruited to the profession.

Jackson nodded curtly. 'And how's our little Einstein this morning, then?'

'Wasn't 'e a mathematician, Mr Jackson?'

'He was a bloody Kraut,' snapped Jackson. Evans's quiet voice always riled him, and Evans's present insight into his own vast ignorance riled him even more.

'I think 'e was a Jew, Mr Jackson.'

'I don't give a monkey's fuck what he was, you scruffy sod.'

'Scruffy' was, perhaps, the right word. Evans's face was unshaven, and he wore a filthy-looking red-and-white bobble hat upon his head. 'Give me a *chance*, Mr Jackson. I was just goin' to shave when you bust in.'

'Which reminds me.' Jackson turned his eyes on Stephens. 'Make sure you take his razor out of the cell when he's finished scraping that ugly mug of his. Clear? One of these days he'll do us all a favour and cut his bloody throat.'

For a few seconds Evans looked thoughtfully at the man standing ramrod straight in front of him, a string of Second World War medals proudly paraded over his left breast-pocket. 'Mr Jackson? Was it *you* who took me nail-scissors away?' Evans had always worried about his hands.

'*And* your nail-file, you poncy twit.'

'Look!' For a moment Evans's eyes smouldered dangerously, but Jackson was ready for him.

'Orders of the Governor, Evans.' He leaned forward and leered, his voice dropping to a harsh, contemptuous whisper. 'You want to *complain*?'

Evans shrugged his shoulders lightly. The crisis was over.

'You've got half an hour to smarten yourself up, Evans—and take that bloody hat off!'

'Me 'at? Huh!' Evans put his right hand lovingly on top of the filthy woollen, and smiled sadly. 'D'you know, Mr Jackson, it's the only thing that's ever brought me any sort o' luck in life. Kind o' lucky charm, if you know what I mean. And today I thought— well, with me exam and all that . . .'

Buried somewhere in Jackson, beneath all the bluster and the bullshit, was a tiny core of compassion; and Evans knew it.

'Just this once, then, Shirley Temple.' (If there was one thing that Jackson genuinely loathed about Evans it was his long, wavy hair.) 'And get bloody shaving!'

At 8.45 the same morning the Reverend Stuart McLeery left his bachelor flat in Broad Street and stepped out briskly towards Carfax. The weatherman reported temperatures considerably below the normal for early June, and a long black overcoat and a shallow-crowned clerical hat provided welcome protection from the steady drizzle which had set in half an hour earlier and which now spattered the thick lenses of his spectacles. In his right hand he was carrying a small brown suitcase, which contained all that he would need for his morning duties, including a sealed question-paper envelope, a yellow invigilation form, a special 'authentication' card from the Examinations Board, a paper-knife, a Bible (he was to speak to the Women's Guild that afternoon on the book of Ruth), and a current copy of *The Church Times*.

The two-hour examination was scheduled to start at 9.15 a.m.

Evans was lathering his face vigorously when Stephens brought in two small square tables, and set them opposite each other in the

narrow space between the bunk on the one side and on the other
the distempered stone wall, plastered at eye-level with a proud row
of naked women, vast-breasted and voluptuous. Next, Stephens
brought in two hard chairs, the slightly less battered of which he
placed in front of the table which stood nearer the cell door.

Jackson put in a brief final appearance. 'Behave yourself, laddy!'

Evans turned and nodded.

'And these' (Jackson pointed to the pin-ups) 'off!'

Evans turned and nodded again. 'I was goin' to take 'em down
anyway. A minister, isn't 'e? The chap comin' to sit in, I mean.'

'And how did you know that?' asked Jackson quietly.

'Well, I 'ad to sign some forms, didn't I? And I couldn't 'elp—'

'You sneaky little bastard.'

Evans drew the razor carefully down his left cheek, and left a
neat swath in the white lather. 'Can I ask you something, Mr Jackson? Why did they 'ave to bug me bloody cell?' He nodded his
head vaguely to a point above the door.

'Not a very neat job,' conceded Jackson.

'They're not—they don't honestly think I'm goin' to try to—'

'They're taking no chances, Evans. Nobody in his bloody senses
would take any chances with *you*.'

'Who's goin' to listen in?'

'I'll tell you who's going to listen in, laddy. It's the Governor
himself, see? He don't trust you a bloody inch—and nor do I. I'll
be watching you like a bleedin' hawk, Evans, so keep your nose
clean. Clear?' He walked towards the door. 'And while we're on
the subject of your nose, Evans, it's about time you changed that
filthy snot-rag dangling from your arse pocket. Clear?'

Evans nodded. He'd already thought of that, and Number Two
Handkerchief was lying ready on the bunk—a neatly folded
square of off-white linen.

'Just one more thing, Einstein.'

'Ya? Wha's 'at?'

'Good luck, old son.'

❖

In the little lodge just inside the prison's main gates, the Reverend S. McLeery signed his name neatly in the visitors' book, and thence walked side by side with a silent prison officer across the exercise yard to D Wing, where he was greeted by Jackson. The Wing's heavy outer door was unlocked, and locked behind them, the heavy inner door the same, and McLeery was handed into Stephens's keeping.

'Get the razor?' murmured Jackson.

Stephens nodded.

'Well, keep your eyes skinned. Clear?'

Stephens nodded again; and McLeery, his feet clanging up the iron stairs, followed his new guide, and finally stood before a cell door, where Stephens opened the peep-hole and looked through.

'That's him, sir.'

Evans, facing the door, sat quietly at the farther of the two tables, his whole attention riveted to a textbook of elementary German grammar. Stephens took the key from its ring, and the cell lock sprang back with a thudded, metallic twang.

It was 9.10 a.m. when the Governor switched on the receiver. He had instructed Jackson to tell Evans of the temporary little precaution—that was only fair. (As if Evans wouldn't spot it!) But wasn't it all a bit theatrical? Schoolboyish, almost? How on earth was Evans going to try anything on today? If he was so anxious to make another break, why in heaven's name hadn't he tried it from the Recreational Block? Much easier. But he hadn't. And there he was now—sitting in a locked cell, all the prison officers on the alert, two more locked doors between his cell and the yard, and a yard with a wall as high as a haystack. Yes, Evans was as safe as houses . . .

Anyway, it wouldn't be any trouble at all to have the receiver turned on for the next couple of hours or so. It wasn't as if there was going to be anything to listen to, was it? Amongst other things, an invigilator's duty was to ensure that the strictest silence was observed. But . . . but still that little nagging doubt! Might Evans try to take advantage of McLeery? Get him to smuggle in a chisel or two, or a rope-ladder, or—

The Governor sat up sharply. It was all very well getting rid of any potential weapon that *Evans* could have used; but what about *McLeery?* What if, quite unwittingly, the innocent McLeery had brought in something himself? A jack-knife, perhaps? And what if Evans held him hostage with such a weapon? Sort of hi-jack-knifed him?

The Governor reached for the phone. It was 9.12 a.m.

The examinee and the invigilator had already been introduced by Stephens when Jackson came back and shouted to McLeery through the cell door. 'Can you come outside a minute, sir? You, too, Stephens.'

Jackson quickly explained the Governor's worries, and McLeery patiently held out his arms at shoulder level whilst Jackson lightly frisked his clothes. 'Something hard here, sir.'

'Ma reading glasses,' replied McLeery, looking down at the spectacle case.

Jackson quickly reassured him, and bending down on the landing thumb-flicked the catches on the suitcase. He picked up each envelope in turn, carefully passed his palms along their surfaces— and seemed satisfied. He riffled cursorily through a few pages of Holy Writ, and vaguely shook *The Church Times*. All right, so far. But one of the objects in McLeery's suitcase was puzzling him sorely.

'Do you mind telling me why you've brought this, sir?' He held up a smallish semi-inflated rubber ring, such as a young child with a waist of about twelve inches might have struggled into. 'You thinking of going for a swim, sir?'

McLeery's hitherto amiable demeanour was slightly ruffled by this tasteless little pleasantry, and he answered Jackson somewhat sourly. 'If ye must know, I suffer from haemorrhoids, and when I'm sitting down for any length o' time—'

'Very sorry, sir. I didn't mean to, er . . .' The embarrassment was still reddening Jackson's cheeks when he found the paper-knife at the bottom of the case. 'I think I'd better keep this though, if you don't mind, that is, sir.'

It was 9.18 a.m. before the Governor heard their voices again, and it was clear that the examination was going to be more than a little late in getting under way.

McLeery:	'Ye've got a watch?'
Evans:	'Yes, sir.'
McLeery:	'I'll be telling ye when to start, and again when ye've five minutes left. A' right?'
	Silence.
McLeery:	'There's plenty more o' this writing paper should ye need it.'
	Silence.
McLeery:	'Now. Write the name of the paper, 021–1, in the top left-hand corner.'
	Silence.
McLeery:	'In the top right-hand corner write your index num-ber—313. And in the box just below that, write your centre number—271. A' right?'
	Silence. 9.20 a.m.
McLeery:	'I'm now going to—'
Evans:	"E's not goin' to stay 'ere, is 'e?'
McLeery:	'I don't know about that. I—'
Stephens:	'Mr Jackson's given me strict instructions to—'
Evans:	"Ow the 'ell am I supposed to concentrate on me exam with a bleedin' screw breathin' down me neck? Christ! Sorry, sir, I didn't mean—'

The Governor reached for the phone. 'Jackson? Ah, good. Get Stephens out of that cell, will you? I think we're perhaps overdoing things.'

'As you wish, sir.'

The Governor heard the exchanges in the cell, heard the door clang to once more, and heard McLeery announce that the examination had begun at last.

It was 9.25 a.m.; and there was a great calm.

At 9.40 a.m. the Examinations Board rang through, and the Assistant Secretary with special responsibility for modern languages asked to speak to the Governor. The examination had already started, no doubt? Ah, a quarter of an hour ago. Yes. Well, there was a correction slip which some fool had forgotten to place in the examination package. Very brief. Could the Governor please . . .?

'Yes, of course. I'll put you straight through to Mr Jackson in D Wing. Hold the line a minute.'

Was this the sort of thing the Governor had feared? Was the phone call a fake? Some signal? Some secret message . . . ? But he could check on that immediately. He dialled the number of the Examinations Board, but heard only the staccato bleeps of a line engaged. But then the line *was* engaged, wasn't it? Yes. Not very intelligent, that . . .

Two minutes later he heard some whispered communications in the cell, and then McLeery's broad Scots voice:

'Will ye please stop writing a wee while, Mr Evans, and listen carefully. Candidates offering German, 021–1, should note the following correction. "On page three, line fifteen, the fourth word should read *goldenen*, not *goldene*; and the whole phrase will therefore read *zum goldenen Löwen*, not *zum goldene Löwen*." I will repeat that . . .'

The Governor listened and smiled. He had taken German in the sixth form himself, and he remembered all about the agreements of adjectives. And so did McLeery, by the sound of things, for the minister's pronunciation was most impressive. But what about Evans? *He* probably didn't know what an adjective *was*.

The phone rang again. The Magistrates' Court. They needed a prison van and a couple of prison officers. Remand case. And within two minutes the Governor was wondering whether *that* could be a hoax. He told himself not to be so silly. His imagination was beginning to run riot.

Evans!

For the first quarter of an hour Stephens had dutifully peered through the peep-hole at intervals of one minute or so; and after that, every two minutes. At 10.45 a.m. he nipped off to the gents', and was in such a hurry to get back that he found he'd dribbled down his trousers. But everything was still all right as he looked through the peep-hole once more. It took four or five seconds—no more. What was the point? It was always more or less the same. Evans, his pen between his lips, sat staring straight in front of him towards the door, seeking—it seemed—some sorely needed inspiration from somewhere. And opposite him McLeery, seated slightly askew from the table now: his face in semi-profile; his hair (as Stephens had noticed earlier) amateurishly clipped pretty closely to the scalp; his eyes behind the pebble lenses peering short-sightedly at *The Church Times*; his right index finger hooked beneath the narrow clerical collar; and the fingers of the left hand, the nails meticulously manicured, slowly stroking the short black beard.

At 10.50 a.m. the receiver crackled to life and the Governor realized he'd almost forgotten Evans for a few minutes.

Evans: 'Please, sir!' (A whisper)
Evans: 'Please, sir!' (Louder)
Evans: 'Would you mind if I put a blanket round me shoulders, sir? It's a bit parky in 'ere, isn't it?'

	Silence.
Evans:	'There's one on me bunk 'ere, sir.'
McLeery:	'Be quick about it.'
	Silence.

At 10.51 a.m. Stephens was more than a little surprised to see a grey regulation blanket draped round Evans's shoulders, and he frowned slightly and looked at the examinee more closely. But Evans, the pen still between his teeth, was staring just as vacantly as before. Blankly beneath a blanket . . . Should Stephens report the slight irregularity? Anything at all fishy, hadn't Jackson said? Mm. He looked through the peep-hole once again, and even as he did so Evans pulled the dirty blanket more closely to himself. Was he planning a sudden batman leap to suffocate McLeery in the blanket? Don't be daft! There was never any sun on this side of the prison; no heating, either, during the summer months, and it could get quite chilly in some of the cells. Mm. Stephens decided to revert to his earlier every-minute observation.

At 11.20 a.m. the receiver once more crackled across the silence of the Governor's office, and McLeery informed Evans that only five minutes remained. The examination was almost over now, but something still gnawed away quietly in the Governor's mind. He reached for the phone once more.

At 11.22 a.m. Jackson shouted along the corridor to Stephens. The Governor wanted to speak with him—'*Hurry*, man!' Stephens picked up the phone apprehensively and listened to the rapidly spoken orders. Stephens himself was to accompany McLeery to the main prison gates. Understood? Stephens personally was to make absolutely sure that the door was locked on Evans after McLeery had left the cell. Understood?

Understood.

❖

At 11.25 a.m. the Governor heard the final exchanges.

McLeery: 'Stop writing, please.'

           Silence.

McLeery: 'Put your sheets in order and see they're correctly numbered.'

           Silence.

           Scraping of chairs and tables.

Evans: 'Thank you very much, sir.'

McLeery: 'A' right, was it?'

Evans: 'Not *too* bad.'

McLeery: 'Good . . . Mr Stephens!' (Very loud)

The Governor heard the door clang to for the last time. The examination was over.

'How did he get on, do you think?' asked Stephens as he walked beside McLeery to the main gates.

'Och. I canna think he's distinguished hissel, I'm afraid.' His Scots accent seemed broader than ever, and his long black over-coat, reaching almost to his knees, fostered the illusion that he had suddenly grown slimmer.

Stephens felt pleased that the Governor had asked *him*, and not Jackson, to see McLeery off the premises, and all in all the morn-ing had gone pretty well. But something stopped him from mak-ing his way directly to the canteen for a belated cup of coffee. He wanted to take just one last look at Evans. It was like a pro-gramme he'd seen on TV—about a woman who could never *really* convince herself that she'd locked the front door when she'd gone to bed: often she'd got up twelve, fifteen, sometimes twenty times to check the bolts.

He re-entered D Wing, made his way along to Evans's cell, and opened the peep-hole once more. *Oh, no!* CHRIST, NO! There, sprawled back in Evans's chair was a man (for a semi-second Stephens thought it must be Evans), a grey regulation blanket slipping from his shoulders, the front of his closely cropped, irregularly tufted hair awash with fierce red blood which had dripped already through the small black beard, and was even now spreading horribly over the white clerical collar and down into the black clerical front.

Stephens shouted wildly for Jackson: and the words appeared to penetrate the curtain of blood that veiled McLeery's ears, for the minister's hand felt feebly for a handkerchief from his pocket, and held it to his bleeding head, the blood seeping slowly through the white linen. He gave a long low moan, and tried to speak. But his voice trailed away, and by the time Jackson had arrived and despatched Stephens to ring the police and the ambulance, the handkerchief was a sticky, squelchy wodge of cloth.

McLeery slowly raised himself, his face twisted tightly with pain. 'Dinna worry about the ambulance, man! I'm a' right ... I'm a' right ... Get the police! I know ... I know where ... he ...' He closed his eyes and another drip of blood splashed like a huge red raindrop on the wooden floor. His hand felt along the table, found the German question paper, and grasped it tightly in his bloodstained hand. 'Get the Governor! I know ... I know where Evans ...'

Almost immediately sirens were sounding, prison officers barked orders, puzzled prisoners pushed their way along the corridors, doors were banged and bolted, and phones were ringing everywhere. And within a minute McLeery, with Jackson and Stephens supporting him on either side, his face now streaked and caked with drying blood, was greeted in the prison yard by the Governor, perplexed and grim.

'We must get you to hospital immediately. I just don't—'

'Ye've called the police?'

'Yes, yes. They're on their way. But—'

'I'm a' right. I'm a' right. Look! Look here!' Awkwardly he opened the German question paper and thrust it before the Governor's face. 'It's there! D'ye see what I *mean*?'

The Governor looked down and realized what McLeery was trying to tell him. A photocopied sheet had been carefully and cleverly superimposed over the last (originally blank) page of the question paper.

'Ye see what they've done, Governor. Ye see . . .' His voice trailed off again, as the Governor, dredging the layers of long-neglected learning, willed himself to translate the German text before him:

Sie sollen dem schon verabredeten Plan genau folgen. Der wichtige Zeitpunkt ist drei Minuten vor Ende des Examens . . . 'You must follow the plan already somethinged. The vital point in time is three minutes before the end of the examination but something something—something something . . . Don't hit him too hard—remember, he's a minister! And don't overdo the Scots accent when . . .'

A fast-approaching siren wailed to its crescendo, the great doors of the prison yard were pushed back, and a white police car squealed to a jerky halt beside them.

Detective Superintendent Carter swung himself out of the passenger seat and saluted the Governor. 'What the hell's happening, sir?' And, turning to McLeery: 'Christ! Who's hit *him*?'

But McLeery cut across whatever explanation the Governor might have given. 'Elsfield Way, officer! I know where Evans . . .' He was breathing heavily, and leaned for support against the side of the car, where the imprint of his hand was left in tarnished crimson.

In bewilderment Carter looked to the Governor for guidance. 'What—?'

'Take him with you, if you think he'll be all right. He's the only one who seems to know what's happening.'

Carter opened the back door and helped McLeery inside; and within a few seconds the car leaped away in a spurt of gravel.

❖

'Elsfield Way', McLeery had said; and there it was staring up at the Governor from the last few lines of the German text: 'From Elsfield Way drive to the Headington roundabout, where . . .' Yes, of course. *The Examinations Board was in Elsfield Way,* and someone from the Board must have been involved in the escape plan from the very beginning: the question paper itself, the correction slip . . .

The Governor turned to Jackson and Stephens. 'I don't need to tell you what's happened, do I?' His voice sounded almost calm in its scathing contempt. 'And which one of you two morons was it who took Evans for a nice little walk to the main gates and waved him bye-bye?'

'It was me, sir,' stammered Stephens. 'Just like you told me, sir. I could have sworn—'

'What? Just like I told you, you say? What the hell—?'

'When you rang, sir, and told me to—'

'When was that?' The Governor's voice was a whiplash now.

'You know, sir. About twenty past eleven, just before—'

'You blithering idiot, man! It wasn't *me* who rang you. Don't you realize—' But what was the use? He *had* used the telephone at that time, but only to try (unsuccessfully, once more) to get through to the Examinations Board.

He shook his head in growing despair and turned on the senior prison officer. 'As for you, Jackson! How long have you been pretending you've got a brain, eh? Well, I'll tell you something, Jackson. Your skull's *empty*. Absolutely bloody empty!' It was Jackson who had spent two hours in Evans's cell the previous evening; and it was Jackson who had confidently reported that there was nothing hidden away there—nothing at all. And yet Evans had somehow managed to conceal not only a false beard, a pair of spectacles, a dog-collar, and all the rest of his clerical paraphernalia, but also some sort of weapon with which he'd given McLeery such a terrible blow across the head. Aurrgh!

A prison van backed alongside, but the Governor made no immediate move. He looked down again at the last line of the German: '. . . to the Headington roundabout, where you go straight over and make your way to . . . to Neugraben.' 'Neugraben'? Where on earth—? 'New' something. 'Newgrave'? Never heard of it. There was a 'Wargrave', somewhere near Reading, but . . . No, it was probably a code word, or— And then it hit him. Newbury! God, yes! Newbury was a pretty big sort of place but—

He rapped out his orders to the driver. 'St Aldates Police Station, and step on it! Take Jackson and Stephens here, and when you get there ask for Bell. Chief Inspector Bell. Got that?'

He leaped the stairs to his office three at a time, got Bell on the phone immediately, and put the facts before him.

'We'll get him, sir,' said Bell. 'We'll get him, with a bit o' luck.'

The Governor sat back, and lit a cigarette. Ye gods! What a beautifully laid plan it had all been! What a clever sod Evans was! Careless leaving that question paper behind; but then, they all made their mistakes somewhere along the line. Well, *almost* all of them. That's why they were doing their porridge, and that's why very very shortly Mr clever-clever Evans would be back inside doing *his* once more.

The phone on his desk erupted in a strident burst, and Superintendent Carter informed him that McLeery had spotted Evans driving off along Elsfield Way; they'd got the number of the car all right and had given chase immediately, but had lost him at the Headington roundabout; he must have doubled back into the city.

'No,' said the Governor quietly. 'No, he's on his way to Newbury.' He explained his reasons for believing so, and left it at that. It was a police job now—not his. He was just another good-for-a-giggle, gullible governor, that was all.

'By the way, Carter. I hope you managed to get McLeery to hospital all right?'

'Yes. He's in the Radcliffe now. Really groggy, he was, when we got to the Examination offices, and they rang for the ambulance from there.'

The Governor rang the Radcliffe a few minutes later and asked for the accident department.

'McLeery, you say?'

'Yes. He's a parson.'

'I don't think there's anyone—'

'Yes, there is. You'll find one of your ambulances picked him up from Elsfield Way about—'

'Oh, *that*. Yes, we sent an ambulance all right, but when we got there, the fellow had gone. No one seemed to know where he was. Just vanished! Not a sign—'

But the Governor was no longer listening, and the truth seemed to hit him with an almost physical impact somewhere in the back of his neck.

A quarter of an hour later they found the Reverend S. McLeery, securely bound and gagged, in his study in Broad Street. He'd been there, he said, since 8.15 a.m., when two men had called and . . .

Enquiries in Newbury throughout the afternoon produced nothing. Nothing at all. And by tea-time everyone in the prison knew what had happened. It had not been Evans, impersonating McLeery, who had walked *out*; it had been Evans, impersonating McLeery, who had stayed *in*.

The fish and chips were delicious, and after a gentle stroll round the centre of Chipping Norton, Evans decided to return to the hotel and have an early night. A smart new hat concealed the wreckage of his closely cropped hair, and he kept it on as he walked up to the reception desk of the Golden Lion. It would take a good while for his hair to regain its former glories—but what the hell did *that* matter. He was *out* again, wasn't he? A bit of bad

luck, that, when Jackson had pinched his scissors, for it had meant
a long and tricky operation with his only razor blade the previous
night. Ah! But he'd had his good luck, too. Just think! If Jackson
had made him take his bobble hat off! Phew! That really *had* been
a close call. Still, old Jackson wasn't such a bad fellow ... One of
the worst things—funny, really!—had been the beard. He'd
always been allergic to sticking plaster, and even now his chin was
irritatingly sore and red.

The receptionist wasn't the same girl who'd booked him in, but
the change was definitely for the better. A real honey, this one. As
he collected his key, he gave her his sexiest smile, told her he
wouldn't be bothering with breakfast, ordered the *Daily Express*,
and asked for an early-morning call at 6.45 a.m. Tomorrow was
going to be another busy day.

He whistled softly to himself as he walked up the broad stairs
... He'd sort of liked the idea of being dressed up as a minister—
dog-collar and everything. Yes, it had been a jolly good idea for
'McLeery' to wear *two* black fronts, *two* collars. But that top collar!
Phew! It had kept on slipping off the back stud; and there'd been
that one panicky moment when 'McLeery' had only just got his
hand up to his neck in time to stop the collars springing apart
before Stephens ... Ah! They'd got *that* little problem worked out
all right, though: a pen stuck in the mouth whenever the evil eye
had appeared at the peep-hole. Easy! But all that fiddling about
under the blanket with the black front and the stud at the back of
the collar—that had been far more difficult than they'd ever bar-
gained for ... Everything else had gone beautifully smoothly,
though. In the car he'd found everything they'd promised him:
soap and water, clothes, the map—yes, the *map*, of course. The
Ordnance Survey Map of Oxfordshire ... He'd got some good
friends; some very clever friends. Christ, ah!

He unlocked his bedroom door and closed it quietly behind him
—and then stood frozen to the spot, like a man who has just
caught a glimpse of the Gorgon.

Sitting on the narrow bed was the very last man in the world that Evans had expected—or wanted—to see.

'It's not worth trying anything,' said the Governor quietly, as Evans's eyes darted desperately around the room. 'I've got men all round the place.' (Well, there were only *two*, really: but Evans needn't know that.) He let the words sink in. 'Women, too. Didn't you think the blonde girl in reception was rather sweet?'

Evans was visibly shaken. He sat down slowly in the only chair the small room could offer, and held his head between his hands. For several minutes there was utter silence.

Finally, he spoke. 'It was that bloody correction slip, I s'pose.'

'We-ell' (the Governor failed to mask the deep satisfaction in his voice) 'there *are* a few people who know a little German.'

Slowly, very slowly, Evans relaxed. He was beaten—and he knew it. He sat up at last, and managed to smile ruefully. 'You know, it wasn't *really* a mistake. You see, we 'adn't been able to fix up any 'otel, but we could've worked that some other way. No. The really important thing was for the phone to ring just before the exam finished—to get the screws out of the way for a coupla minutes. So we 'ad to know exactly when the exam *started*, didn't we?'

'And, like a fool, I presented you with that little piece of information on a plate.'

'Well, *somebody* did. So, you see, sir, that correction slip killed two little birds with a single stone, didn't it? The name of the 'otel for *me*, and the exact time the exam started for, er, for, er . . .'

The Governor nodded. 'It's a pretty common word, though, "Löwe". It's on the beer labels for a start.'

'Good job it *is* pretty common, sir, or I'd never 'ave known where to come to, would I?'

'Nice name, though: *zum goldenen Löwen*.'

''Ow did you know which Golden Lion it was? There's 'undreds of 'em.'

'Same as you, Evans. Index number 313; Centre number 271.

Remember? Six figures? And if you take an Ordnance Survey Map for Oxfordshire, you find that the six-figure reference $^{313}/_{271}$ lands you bang in the middle of Chipping Norton.'

'Yea, you're right. Huh! We'd 'oped you'd bugger off to Newbury.'

'We did.'

'Well, that's something, I s'pose.'

'That question paper, Evans. Could you really understand all that German? I could hardly—'

'Nah! Course I couldn't. I knew *roughly* what it was all about, but we just 'oped it'd throw a few spanners in the works—you know, sort of muddle everybody a bit.'

The Governor stood up. 'Tell me one thing before we go. How on earth did you get all that blood to pour over your head?'

Evans suddenly looked a little happier. '*Clever*, sir. Very clever, that was—'ow to get a couple o' pints of blood into a cell, eh? When there's none there to start off with, and when, er, and when the "invigilator", shall we say, gets searched before 'e comes in. Yes, sir. You can well ask about that, and I dunno if I ought to tell you. After all, I might want to use that particular—'

'Anything to do with a little rubber ring for piles, perhaps?'

Evans grinned feebly. 'Clever, though, wasn't it?'

'Must have been a tricky job sticking a couple of pints—'

'Nah! You've got it wrong, sir. No problem about *that*.'

'No?'

'Nah! It's the *clotting*, you see. That's the big trouble. We got the blood easy enough. Pig's blood, it was—from the slaughter'ouse in Kidlington. But to stop it clotting you've got to mix yer actual blood' (Evans took a breath) 'with one tenth of its own volume of 3.8 per cent trisodium citrate! Didn't know that, did you, sir?'

The Governor shook his head in a token of reluctant admiration. 'We learn something new every day, they tell me. Come on, m'lad.'

Evans made no show of resistance, and side by side the two men walked slowly down the stairs.

'Tell me, Evans. How did you manage to plan all this business? You've had no visitors—I've seen to that. You've had no letters—'

'I've got lots of friends, though.'

'What's that supposed to mean?'

'Me German teacher, for a start.'

'You mean—? But he was from the Technical College.'

'*Was* 'e?' Evans was almost enjoying it all now. 'Ever check up on 'im, sir?'

'God Almighty! There's far more going on than I—'

'Always will be, sir.'

'Everything ready?' asked the Governor as they stood by the reception desk.

'The van's out the front, sir,' said the pretty blonde receptionist. Evans winked at her; and she winked back at him. It almost made his day.

A silent prison officer handcuffed the recaptured Evans, and together the two men clambered awkwardly into the back seat of the prison van.

'See you soon, Evans.' It was almost as if the Governor were saying farewell to an old friend after a cocktail party.

'Cheerio, sir. I, er, I was just wonderin'. I know your German's pretty good, sir, but do you know any more o' these modern languages?'

'Not very well. Why?'

Evans settled himself comfortably on the back seat, and grinned happily. 'Nothin', really. I just 'appened to notice that you've got some O-level Italian classes comin' up next September, that's all.'

'Perhaps you won't be with us next September, Evans.'

James Roderick Evans appeared to ponder the Governor's words deeply. 'No. P'r'aps I won't,' he said.

❧

As the prison van turned right from Chipping Norton on to the Oxford road, the hitherto silent prison officer unlocked the handcuffs and leaned forward towards the driver. 'For Christ's sake get a *move* on! It won't take 'em long to find out—'

'Where do ye suggest we make for?' asked the driver, in a broad Scots accent.

'What about Newbury?' suggested Evans.

DEAD AS A DODO

'Why,' said the Dodo, 'the best way to explain it is to do it.' (And as you might like to try the thing yourself, some winter day, I will tell you how the Dodo managed it.)

(Lewis Carroll, *Alice in Wonderland*)

I t was more from necessity than from kindliness, just after 5 p.m. on a rain-soaked evening in early February 1990, that Chief Inspector Morse of the Thames Valley Police leaned over and opened the Jaguar's near-side door. One of his neighbours from the North Oxford bachelor flats was standing at the bus stop, was getting very wet—and was staring hard at him.

'Most kind!' said Philip Wise, inserting his kyphotic self into the passenger seat.

Morse grunted a vague acknowledgement as the car made a few further slow yards up the Banbury Road in the red-tail-lighted queue, his wipers clearing short-lived swaths across the screen. Only three-quarters of a mile to go, but at this time of day twenty minutes would be par for the progressively paralytic crawl to the flats. Never an easy conversationalist himself—indeed, known occasionally to lapse into total aphasia when driving a car—Morse was glad that Wise was doing all the talking. 'Something quite extraordinary's happened to me,' said the man in the dripping mackintosh.

In retrospect, Morse was aware that he'd listened, at least initially, with no more than polite passivity. But listen he had done.

Philip Wise had gone up to Exeter College, Oxford, in October 1938; and in due course his linguistic abilities (particularly in German) had ensured for him, when war broke out a year later, a cushy little job in an Intelligence Unit housed on the outskirts of Bicester. For two years he had lived there in a disagreeable and draughty Nissen-hut; and when the chance came of his taking digs back in Oxford, he'd jumped at it. Thus it was that in October 1941 he had moved into Crozier Road, a sunless thoroughfare just off the west of St Giles'; and it was there that he'd first met Miss Dodo Whitaker ('Only the one "t", Inspector') who had a tiny top-floor bedsitter immediately above his own room in the grimy four-storey property that stood at number 14.

Why on earth she'd been saddled with a name like 'Dodo', he'd never discovered—nor enquired; but she was certainly a considerably livelier specimen than the defunct *Didus ineptus* of Mauritius. Although physically hardly warranting any second glance, especially in the wartime 'Utility' boiler-suit she almost invariably wore, she had the inestimable merit of being interesting. And sometimes, over half a glass of mild beer in the ill-lit bar at the rear of the Bird and Baby, her wonted nervousness would disappear, and in her rather deep, husky voice she would talk with knowledge, volubility, and wit, about the class-structure, about the progress of the war—and about music. Yes, above all about music. The pair of them had joined the Record Library, thereafter spending a few candle-lit evenings together in Dodo's room listening to everything from Vivaldi to Wagner. On one occasion, Wise had almost been on the verge of telling her of the Platonic-plus pleasure he was beginning to experience in her company.

Almost.

Dodo had a brother called Ambrose who now and then managed to get a weekend leave-pass and come to stay with Dodo, usually (though quite unofficially) sleeping on the floor of her single room. Almost immediately, Philip Wise and Ambrose Whitaker became firm friends, spending (somewhat to Dodo's annoyance) rather too many hours together drinking whisky—a commodity plentiful enough, if over-priced, in the Bird and Baby, but a rare one in the wilds of Bodmin, where Ambrose, with two stripes on each arm, spent his days initiating recruits into the mysteries of antiquated artillery pieces. He was a winsome, albeit somewhat raffish, sort of fellow whose attraction to alcohol apparently eclipsed even his love of music (Dodo spoke of Ambrose, amongst other things, as a virtuoso on the piano). Those weekends had flashed by, with Wise far too soon finding himself walking across Gloucester Green to see his friend off at the Great Western station late on Sunday afternoons.

Brother and sister—what an engaging couple they were!

Rich, too—at least their parents were.

Dodo, in particular, made no secret of her parents' extremely comfortable lifestyle, which Wise himself had once (and only once) experienced at first hand, when Dodo had suggested—on his having to spend a week in Bristol in February 1942—that he stay with them; had even loaned him a key to the family mansion in case they were out when he arrived. Wise had already known that Dodo's parents lived in Bristol, since he'd noticed the postmark on the letter (doubtless from Mummy) that lay each week on the undusted mahogany table in the small entrance hall of number 14—her name in the address, incidentally, always prefixed by the letter 'A'. Alice? Angela? Anne? Audrey?—Wise had never been told and, again, had never enquired. But that little fact was something else he'd known earlier, too, since he was with her when, with a practised flourish of those slim and sinewy fingers, she'd signed her membership card at the Record Library. As for the parents, they turned out to be a straight-laced, tight-faced pair who remained frigidly reserved towards their guest throughout his short stay, and who appeared less than effusively appreciative of Dodo—and almost embarrassingly dismissive of Ambrose. Oddly, Wise had not found a single fond memento of their talented offspring in the Whitakers' gauntly luxurious villa, and not a single family photograph to grace the daily-dusted mantelpieces.

⚜

It was three weeks after his return from this ill-starred visit that Dodo left Oxford, her wartime work (something 'hush-hush', it was understood) necessitating a move to Cheltenham. Only about forty miles away—and she'd keep in touch, she said.

But she hadn't.

'Forty-eight years ago, this was, Inspector. Forty-eight! I was twenty-three myself, and she must have been about the same. Year or two older, perhaps—I'm not sure. You see, I never even asked her how old she was. Pretty spineless specimen, wasn't I?'

In the darkness, Morse nodded his silent assent, and the Jaguar finally turned into the Residents Only parking area.

Wise contrived to keep talking as the two men dashed through the rain to the entrance hall. 'I'd be glad to give you a cup of tea . . . or something . . . You see, I haven't really told you anything yet.'

As they sat opposite each other in the living area, Wise passed across a white, six-page booklet containing details of 'A Service of Thanksgiving for the Life of AMBROSE WHITAKER, MA (Cantab.), FRAM 1917–1989', and Morse glanced cursorily at the contents: music; hymn; lesson; music; address; prayers; hymn; music; blessing; music; more music. Observing only that if he ever had a voice in his own funeral arrangements he would join Whitaker in choosing the 'In Paradisum' from the Fauré *Requiem*, Morse handed the leaflet back.

'The thing is this,' continued Wise. 'I saw an obituary in *The Times* in December, and I was sure it was the same man I'd known in the war. Quite apart from the pretty unusual Christian name, as well as the *very* unusual spelling of the surname, everything else fitted, too: born in Bristol, prodigy on the piano—everything! And I just couldn't help thinking back and wondering whether *she* was still alive—Dodo, that is. Anyway, a fortnight ago I read about this Memorial Service in Holborn, and I decided to go up and pay my last respects to an old friend—and perhaps . . .'

'Find some plump-bosomed old spinster—'

'Yes!'

'Did you find her?' asked Morse quietly.

Wise shook his head. 'There were an awful lot of important people from the musical world—I hadn't realized what a name Ambrose had made for himself. I got to the church early and stayed outside for a good while watching the people going in, including—pretty obvious who she was—Ambrose's wife, who drew up in a chauffeur-driven Rolls—registration AW 1! But I didn't see the woman I was looking for—and she wasn't in the church, either. I'd have spotted her straightaway if she had been. She was smallish, stockily built—just like her mother. And there was something else. She had a nasty little red scar—well, a nasty *big* scar really—just across the left-hand side of her jaw: a bicycle accident when she was a youngster, I think. She was awfully conscious of it and always used a lot of face-powder to try to cover it up a bit. But it was still pretty noticeable, I'm afraid. Well, to cut a long story a bit shorter, I went up to Ambrose's wife after the service and told her I'd known her husband in the war and said how sorry I was and all the rest of it. She was pleasant enough, but she seemed a bit strained, and there were other people waiting to have a word with her. So I didn't say much more except to mention that I'd known her husband's sister as well.' Wise paused a second or two before continuing.

'Do you know what happened then, Inspector? Ambrose's wife pointed to a grey-haired woman in a black dress standing with her back to us, a woman very much the same height and build as Dodo had been. "This gentleman here says he used to know you, Agnes . . ."'

'Agnes!'

'But I didn't hear any more—I just didn't know what to do—or say. You see, the woman in black turned round and faced me, *and she wasn't Dodo Whitaker.'*

❖

It was Morse who broke the silence which followed. 'Ambrose only had the one sister?'

Wise nodded, a wry, defeated smile upon his face. 'Yes—Agnes. He never did have a sister named "Dodo"!'

Again the two men were silent.

'Well?' asked Wise, finally.

It had always appeared to Morse an undeniable fact that coincidence plays a far greater role in human affairs than is generally acknowledged. And here was yet another instance of it—it must be! Wise's tale was interesting enough—assuredly so: but it wasn't much of a *problem*, surely? Ostentatiously he drained his whiskey, gratefully witnessed the replenishment, and then pronounced judgement: 'There were two Ambrose Whitakers, both musical men, and both from Bristol, and the one you knew wasn't the one who died.'

'You think not?' The half-smile on Wise's face made Morse rather uncomfortably aware that a slightly more intelligent analysis had been expected of him.

'You don't think,' suggested Morse weakly, 'that Agnes might have had some plastic surgery or something?'

'No, no. It's just that there are far too many coincidences for *me* to swallow. *Everything* fitted—down to the last detail. For example, Dodo told me that she and Ambrose once got a bit morbid about the possibility of his being killed in the war and how he'd told her that he'd settle for a couple of bits of music when they buried him: the "In Paradisum"—'

'Lovely choice!' interjected Morse. 'I saw that in the Service.'

'—and the adagio from the Mozart Clarinet Concerto—'

'Ah yes! K662.'

'K622.'

'Oh!'

Morse knew that he wasn't scoring many points; knew, too, that Wise was perfectly correct in believing that the coincidences were getting way out of hand. But he had no time at all to develop the quite extraordinary possibility that suddenly leaped into his brain; because Wise himself was clearly most anxious to propound his own equally astonishing conclusions.

'What would you say, Inspector, if I told you that Dodo wasn't Ambrose Whitaker's sister at all—*she was his wife.*'

Morse's face registered a degree of genuine surprise, but he allowed Wise to continue without interruption.

'It would account for quite a few things, don't you think? For example, it always seemed a bit odd to me that when Ambrose got any leave he invariably came all the way from Cornwall here to Oxford—via *Bristol*, at that!—just to see his *sister*. You'd think he'd have called in on his parents once in a while, wouldn't you? They were much nearer than Dodo was; and well worth keeping the right side of, surely? But it wouldn't be surprising if he took every opportunity of coming all the way to Oxford to see his *wife*, would it? And that would certainly tie up with him sleeping in her room. You know, with all that family money he could have taken a suite in The Randolph if he'd wanted. Yet instead of that, he slept—or so he said—on Dodo's *floor*. Then again, it would probably account for the fact that she never once let me touch her physically—not even hold hands. She was fond of me, though—I know she was . . .'

Momentarily Wise stopped, nodding slowly to himself. 'For some reason the Whitakers must have disapproved of Ambrose's marriage and wanted as little as possible to do with his wartime bride—hence their cool reception of me, Inspector! There may have been talk of disinheriting him—I don't know. I don't *know* anything, of course. But I suspect she was probably pregnant underneath that boiler-suit of hers, and as her time drew nearer she just *had* to leave Oxford. Then? Your guess is as good as mine: she died—she was killed in an air-raid—she got divorced—anything. Ambrose remarried, and the woman I met at the Memorial Service was his *second* wife.'

'Mm.' Morse was looking decidedly dubious. 'But if this Dodo girl *was* his wife, and if his parents couldn't stand the sight or sound of her, why on earth did they write to her every week? And why did she think she had the right to invite *you* down to Bristol? To *have* a key, even—let alone to give *you* one.' Morse shook his head slowly. 'She must have been pretty sure she could take their good-will for granted, I reckon.'

'You think they *were* her parents, then,' said Wise flatly.

'I'm sure of it,' said Morse.

Wise shook his head in exasperation. 'What the hell *is* the explanation, then?'

'Oh, I don't think there's much doubt about that,' said Morse. But he spoke these words to himself, and not to Wise. And very soon afterwards, seeing little prospect of any further replenishment, he took his leave—with the promise that he would give the problem 'a little consideration'.

The following Monday morning, Morse stood beside the Traffic Comptroller at Kidlington Police HQ and watched as 'AW 1' was keyed into the Car Registration computer. Immediately, the VDU spelled out the information that the car was still registered under the name of Mr A. Whitaker, 6 West View Crescent, Bournemouth; and noting the address Morse walked thoughtfully back to his ground-floor office. After ringing Directory Inquiries, and getting the Bournemouth telephone number, he was soon speaking to Mrs Whitaker herself, who in turn was soon promising to do exactly as Morse had requested.

Then Morse rang the War Office.

Ten days later, Philip Wise returned from a week's holiday in Spain to find a long note from Morse.

> P. W.
> I've discovered a few more facts, but some of what follows may possibly be pure fiction. As you know, records galore got destroyed

in the last war, affording limitless opportunity for people to cover up their traces by means of others' identity-cards and so on, especially after a period of chaos and carnage when nobody knew who was who or which corpse was which.

After Dunkirk, for instance.

Gunner (as he then was) Whitaker was the only man of thirty on board who survived, quite miraculously, when the <u>Edna</u> (a flat-bottomed barge registered in Felixstowe) was blown out of the water by a German dive-bomber on May 30th, 1940. He was picked up, with only a pair of waterlogged pants and a wrist-watch to call his own, by the naval sloop <u>Artemis</u>, and was landed at Dover, along with tens of thousands of other soldiers from almost every regiment in the land. (My own imaginative faculties now come wholly into play.) In due course, he was put on a train and sent to a temporary rehabilitation camp—as it happened, the one here in Oxford up on Headington Hill.

The fact that he was in a state of profound shock, with his nerves half-shot to pieces, is probably sufficient to account for his walking out of this camp (quite literally) after only one night under canvas, and hitch-hiking down to Bristol. But he didn't walk out alone. He took a friend with him, a man from the same regiment; and they both quite deliberately got out of the camp before either could be re-documented and re-posted. This second man had only a mother and sister as close family, who were both killed in one of the very first air-raids on Plymouth; and for some (doubtless considerable) sum of money, donated by the protective Whitaker parents, this man agreed to leave on permanent record the official War Office version of his fate after Dunkirk—'Missing presumed killed'—and for the rest of the war to assume the name and role of Ambrose Whitaker. In short, my guess is that the man who came up from Bodmin to see Dodo <u>was not Ambrose Whitaker at all</u>.

Your own guess about things fitted some of the facts well enough; but those facts also fit into a totally different pattern. Just consider some of them again. First, there was the weekly letter from Bristol, from parents who seemingly didn't even want to acknowledge their daughter and who hid all the family photos when you stayed with them. Odd! Then, take this daughter of theirs, Dodo. No great shakes physically, and only just up to

attracting an impressionable young man after he'd had a few pints
(please don't think me unfair!) in a dim pub-lounge or a candle-lit
bedroom—yet she decided to hide whatever charms she'd got
under a baggy boiler-suit. Decidedly odd! What else did you tell
me about her? She was nervy; she had a deepish voice; she wore too
much face-powder; she knew a great deal about the war ...
(You've guessed the truth by now, I'm sure.) Her Christian name
began with 'A', and you saw her sign her name that way at the
Record Library—with the sinewy fingers of an executant musi-
cian. But that *wasn't* odd, was it? Her name *did* begin with 'A', and
Ambrose Whitaker, as we know, was himself a fine pianist. And so
it wasn't only the scar on her jaw she was anxious to conceal with
those layers of face-powder—it was the stubble of a beard that
grew there every day. Because Dodo Whitaker was a man! And
not just any tuppeny-ha'penny old man, either: he was <u>Ambrose
Whitaker</u>.

Two points remain to be cleared up. First, why was it necessary
for Ambrose Whitaker to pose as a woman? Second, what was the
relationship between Ambrose and the artillery corporal from Bodmin? On the first point, it's clear that if he wanted to avoid any further wartime traumas Ambrose couldn't stay in Bristol, where he
was far too well known. Even if he moved to a place where he wasn't
known, it wouldn't have been completely safe to move <u>as a man</u>;
because suspicious questions were always going to be asked in
wartime about a young fellow who looked as if he might well be
dodging the column. So he took out a double insurance on his
deception—for him a desperately needed deception—not only by
moving to Oxford, but also by dressing and living <u>as a woman</u>. On
the second point, we don't perhaps need to probe too deeply into
the reasons why the sensitive and effeminate Ambrose was happy
to take every opportunity of spending his nights with (forgive me!)
the rather crude, whisky-swilling opportunist you got to know in
the war. Such speculation is always a little distasteful, and I will say
no more about it.

I rang Ambrose's widow, asking for a wartime photograph of
her husband, and I gave her your address, telling her you are an
archivist working for the Imperial War Museum. You should hear

from her soon; and when you do you'll be as near as anyone is ever likely to be to knowing the truth about this curious affair.

    E. M.

It was two days later that a still-pyjamaed Wise took delivery of a stiff white envelope, in which he found a brief note, together with a photograph of a young man in army uniform—a photograph in which no attempt had been made to turn the left-hand side of the sitter's face away from the honesty of the camera lens, or to retouch the line of a cruel scar that stretched across the face's lower jaw. And as Philip Wise looked down at the photograph he saw staring back at him the familiar, faithless eyes of Dodo Whitaker.

AT THE
LULU-BAR MOTEL

'I am sorry I have not learnt to play at cards. It is very useful in life.'

(Samuel Johnson, as reported by Boswell in
Tour to the Hebrides)

I shall never be able to forget what Louis said—chiefly, no doubt, because he said it so often, a cynical smile slowly softening that calculating old mouth of his: 'People are so gullible!'—that's what he kept on saying, our Louis. And I've used those self-same words a thousand times myself—used them again last night to this fat-walleted coach-load of mine as they debussed at the Lulu-Bar Motel before tucking their starched napkins over their legs and starting into one of Louis' five-star four-coursers, with all the wines and a final slim liqueur. Yes, people are so gullible . . . Not *quite* all of them (make no mistake!)—and please don't misunderstand me. This particular manifestation of our human frailty is of only marginal concern to me personally, since occasionally I cut a thinnish slice of that great cake for myself—as I did just before I unloaded those matching sets of leather cases and hulked them round the motel corridors.

But let's get the chronology correct. All that hulking around comes right after we've pulled into the motel where—as always—I turn to all the good people (the black briefcase tight under my right arm) and tell them we're here, folks; here for the first-night stop on a wunnerful tour, which every single one o' you is goin' to enjoy real great. From tomorrow—and I'm real sorry about this, folks—you won't have me personally lookin' after you anymore; but that's how the operation operates. I'm just the first-leg man myself, and someone else'll have the real privilege of drivin' you out on the second leg post-breakfast. Tonight itself, though, I'll be hangin' around the cocktail bar (got that?), and if you've any problems about . . . well, about *anything*, you just come along and talk to me, and we'll sort things out real easy. One thing, folks. Just one small friendly word o' counsel to you all. There's one or two guys around these parts who are about as quick an' as slick an' as smooth as a well-soaped ferret. Now, the last thing I'd ever try to do is stop you enjoyin' your vaycaytions, and maybe one or two of you could fancy your chances with a deck o' cards against the deadliest dealer from here to Detroit. But . . . well, as I say, just a friendly word o' counsel, folks. Which is this: *some people are so gullible!*—and I just wouldn't like it if any o' you—well, as I say, I just wouldn't like it.

That's the way I usually dress it up, and not a bad little dressing up at that, as I think you'll agree. 'OK' (do I hear you say?) 'if some of them want to transfer their savings to someone else's account— so what? You can't live other folks' lives for them, now can you? You did your best, Danny boy. So forget it!' Which all makes good logical sense, as I know. But they still worry me a little—all those warm-hearted, clean-living folk, because—well, simply because they're so gullible. And if you don't relish reading about such pleasant folk who plop like juicy pears into the pockets of sharp-fingered charlatans—well, you're not going to like this story. You're not going to like it one little bit.

Most of them were in their sixties or early seventies (no children on the Luxi-Coach Package Tours), and as they filed past the old driving cushion they slipped me a few bucks each and thanked me for a real nice way to start a vaycaytion. After that it took a couple of hours to hump all that baggage around the rooms, and it was half-past eight before I got down to some of Lucy's chicken curry. Lucy? She's a honey of a girl—the sort of big-breasted blonde that most of my fellow sinners would willingly seek to seduce and, to be honest with you . . . But let me return to the theme.

The cocktail bar is a flashily furnished, polychrome affair, with deep, full-patterned carpet, orange imitation-leather seats, and soft wall-lighting in a low, pink glow; and by about half-past nine the place was beginning to fill up nicely. Quite a few of them I recognized from the coach: but there were others. Oh yes, there were a few others ...

He wasn't a big fellow—five-six, five-seven—and he wore a loud check suit just like they used to do in the movies. When I walked in he was standing by the bar, a deck of cards shuttling magically from hand to hand. 'Fancy a game, folks? Luke's the name.' He was pleasant enough, I suppose, in an ugly sort of way; and with his white teeth glinting in a broad-mouthed smile, you could almost stop disliking him. Sometimes.

It was just before ten when he got his first bite—a stocky, middle-aged fellow who looked as if he could take pretty good care of himself, thank you. So. So, I watched them idly as they sat opposite each other at one of the smooth-topped central tables, and it wasn't long before a few others began watching, too. It was a bit of interest—a bit of an incident. And it wasn't *their* money at stake.

Now Lukey loved one game above all others, and I'll have to bare its bones a bit if you're going to follow the story. (Be patient, please: we're running along quite nicely now.) First, it's a dollar stake in the kitty, all right? Then two cards are dealt to each of the players, the court cards counting ten, the ace eleven, and all the other cards living up to their marked face-value. Thus it follows, as day follows night and as luck follows Luke, that the gods are grinning at you if you pick up a ten and an ace—for that is vingt-et-un, my friends, whether you reckon by Fahrenheit or Centigrade, and twenty-one's the best they come. And so long as you remember not to break that twenty-one-mile speed limit, you can buy as many more cards as you like and ... but I don't think you're going to have much trouble in following things.

It was the speed with which hand followed hand that surprised all the on-lookers, since our challenger ('Call me Bart') was clearly no stranger to the Lukesberry rules and five or six hands were through every minute. Slap! A dollar bill in the kitty. Slap! A dollar bill on top. Flick, flick; flick, flick; buy; stick; bust. Dollar, dollar; flick, flick; quicker, ever quicker. Soon I'm standing behind

Barty and I can see his cards. He picks up a ten, and a four; and without mulling it over for a micro-second he says, 'Stick.' Then Lukey turns over a seven, and an eight—and then he flicks over another card for himself: a Jack. Over the top! And Barty pockets yet another kitty; and it's back to that dollar-dollar, flick-flicking again. And when Bart wins again, Luke asks him nicely if he'd like to deal. But Bart declines the kind offer. 'No,' he says. 'I'm on a nice li'l winnin' streak here, pal, so just you keep on dealing them pretty li'l beauties same as before—that's all I ask.'

So Lukey goes on doing just that; and by all that's supersonic what a sharp our Lukey is! I reckon you'd need more than a slow-motion replay to appreciate that prestissimo prestidigitation of his. You could watch those fingers with the eagle eye of old Cortes—and yet whether he was flicking the cards from the top or the middle or the bottom, I swear no one could ever tell. In spite of all this, though, Barty-boy is still advancing his winnings. Now he picks up a seven, and a four; and he decides to buy another card for ten dollars. So Lukey covers the ten dollars from his own fat roll, deals Barty a nine—and things are looking mighty good. Then Luke turns over his own pair (why he bothers, I can't really say, for he knows them all along): a six, and a nine, they are—and things look pretty bad. He turns over another card from the deck—an eight. And once more he's out of his dug-out and over the top.

'My luck'll change soon,' says Luke.

'Not with me, it won't,' says Bart, picking up the twenty-two dollars from the kitty.

'You quitting, you mean?'

'I'm quitting,' says Bart.

'You've played before, I reckon.'

'Yep.'

'You always quit when you're winning?'

'Yep.'

Luke says nothing for a few seconds. He just picks up the deck and looks at it sourly, as if something somewhere in the universe

has gone mildly askew. Then he calls on the power of the poets
and he quotes the only lines he's ever learned:

'Barty,' he says,

> '"If you can make one heap of all your winnings?
> And risk it on one turn of pitch and toss . . ."'

Remember that? What about it? You've taken seventy-odd dollars
off o' me, and I'm just suggestin' that if you put 'em in the middle
—and if I cover 'em . . . What do you say? One hand, that's all.'

The audience was about thirty strong now, and as many were
urging Barty *on* as were urging him *off*. And they were all pretty
committed, too—one way or the other. One of them in particular . . .

I'd seen him earlier at the bar, and a quaint little fellow he was,
too. By the look of him he was in his mid- or late-seventies, no
more than four-ten, four-eleven, in his built-up shoes. His face was
deeply tanned and just as deeply lined, and he wore a blazer
gaudily striped in red and royal blue. Underneath the blazer
pocket, tastelessly yet lovingly picked out in purple cotton, was the
legend: Virgil K. Perkins Jnr. Which made you wonder whether
Virgil K. Perkins Snr was still somewhere in circulation—
although a further glance at his senile son seemed to settle that particular question in the negative. Well, it's this old-timer who tries
pretty hard to get Barty to pocket his dollars and call it a night.
And for a little while it seemed that Barty was going to listen. But
no. He's tempted—and he falls.

'Okey doke,' says Barty. 'One more hand it is.'

It was Luke now who seemed to look mildly uneasy as he covered the seventy-odd dollars and squared up the deck. From other
parts of the room the crowd was rolling up in force again: forty,
fifty of them now, watching in silence as Luke dealt the cards.
Barty let his pair of cards lie on the table a few seconds and his
hands seemed half full of the shakes as he picked them up. A ten;
and a six. Sixteen. And for the first time that evening he hesitated,

as he fell to figuring out the odds. Then he said, 'Stick'; but it took him twice to say it because the first 'stick' got sort of stuck in his larynx. So it was Lukey's turn now, and he slowly turned over a six —and then a nine. Fifteen. And Luke frowned a long time at his fifteen and his right hand toyed with the next card on the top of the deck, quarter turning it, half turning it, almost turning it— and then putting it back.

'Fifteen,' he said.

'*Sixteen*,' says Barty, and his voice was vibrant as he grabbed the pile of notes in the middle.

Then he was gone.

The on-lookers were beginning to drift away as Luke sat still in his seat, the cards still shuttling endlessly from one large palm to the other. It was the old boy who spoke to him first.

'You deserve a drink, sir!' he says. 'Virgil K. Perkins Junior's the name, and this is my li'l wife, Minny.'

'We're from Omaha,' says Minny dutifully.

And so Virgil gets Luke a rye whiskey, and they start talking.

'You a card player yourself, Mr Perkins?'

'Me? No, sir,' says Virgil. 'Me and the li'l wife here' (Minny was four or five inches the taller) 'were just startin' on a vaycaytion together, sir. We're from Omaha, just like she says.'

But the provenance of these proud citizens seemed of no great importance to Luke. 'A few quick hands, Mr Perkins?'

'No,' says Virgil, with a quiet smile.

'Look, Mr Perkins! I don't care—I just don't *care*—whether it's winnin' or losin', and that's the truth. Now if we just—'

'No!' says Virgil.

'You musta heard of beginner's luck?'

'*No!*' says Virgil.

'You're from Omaha, then?' says Luke, turning all pleasant-like to Minny . . .

❦

I left them there, walked over to the bar, and bought an orange juice from Lucy, who sometimes comes through to serve about ten o'clock. She's wearing a lowly cut blouse, and a highly cute hairstyle. But she says nothing to me; just winks—unsmilingly.

Sure enough, when I returned to the table, there was Virgil K. Perkins 'just tryin' a few hands', as he put it; and I don't really need to drag you through all the details, do I? It's all going to end up exactly as you expect . . . but perhaps I'd better put it down, if only for the record; and I'll make it all as brief as I can.

From the start it followed the usual pattern: a dollar up; a dollar down. Nice and easy, take it gently; and soon the little fellow was beaming broadly, and picking up his cards with accelerating eagerness. But, of course, the balance was slowly swinging against him: twenty dollars down; thirty; forty . . .

'Lucky little run for me,' says Luke with a disarming smile, as if for two dimes he'd shovel all his winnings across the table and ease that ever-tightening look round Virgil's mouth. It was all getting just a little obvious, too, and surely someone soon would notice those nimble fingers that forever flicked those eights and nines when only fours and fives could save old Virgil's day. And someone did.

'Why don't you let the old fella deal once in a while?' asks one.

'Yeah, why not?' asks another.

'You wanna deal, pop?' concedes Luke.

But Virgil shakes his white head. 'I've had enough,' he says. 'I shouldn't really—'

'Come on,' says Minny gently.

'He can deal. Sure he can, if he wants to,' says Luke.

'He can't deal off the bottom, though!'

Luke was on his feet in a flash, looking round the room. 'Who said that?' he asked, and his voice was tight and mean. All conversation had stopped, and no one was prepared to own up. Least of all me—who'd said it.

'Well,' said Luke, as he resumed his seat, 'that does it, pop! If I'm bein' accused of cheatin' by some lily-livered coward who won't repeat such villainous vilification—then we'll have to settle the question as a matter of honour, I reckon. *You* deal, pop!'

The old man hesitated—but not for too long. 'Honour' was one of those big words with a capital letter, and wasn't a thing you could shove around too lightly. So he picked up the cards and he shuffled them, boxing and botching the whole business with an awkwardness almost unmatched in the annals of card-play. But somehow he managed to square the deck—and he dealt.

'I'll buy one,' says Luke, slipping a ten-dollar bill into the middle.

Virgil slowly covers the stake, and then pushes over a card.

'Stick,' says Luke.

Taking from his blazer pocket an inordinately large handkerchief, the old man mops his brow and turns his own cards over: a queen; and—an ace!

Luke merely shrugs his shoulders and pushes the kitty across. 'That's the way to do it, pop! Just you keep dealing yourself a few hands like that and—'

'No!' cries Minny, who'd been bleating her forebodings intermittently from the very beginning.

But Virgil lays a gentle hand on her shoulder. 'Don't be cross with me, old girl. And don't *worry*! I'm just a-goin' to deal myself one more li'l hand and . . .'

And another, and another, and another. And the gods were not smiling on the little man from Omaha: not the slightest sign of the meanest grin. Was it merely a matter of saving Face? Of preserving Honour? No, sir! It seemed just plain desperation as the old boy chased his losses round and round that smooth-topped table, with Minny sitting there beside him, her eyes tightly closed as if she was pinning the remnants of her hopes in the power of silent prayer. (I hitched the briefcase tighter under my right arm as I caught sight of Lucy behind the crowd, her eyes holding mine—again unsmilingly.)

By half-past ten Virgil K. Perkins Jnr had lost one thousand dollars, and he sat there crumpled up inside his chair. It wasn't as if he was short of friends, for the large audience had been behind him all along, just willing the old fellow to win. And it wasn't as if anyone could blame our nimble-fingered Lukey anymore, for it was Virgil himself who had long since been dealing out his own disasters.

Not any longer, though. He pushed the deck slowly across the table and stood up. 'I'm sorry, old girl,' he says to Minny, and his voice is all choked up. 'It was your money as much as mine . . .'

But Luke was leaning across and he put his mighty palm on the old boy's skinny wrist. And he speaks quietly. 'Look, pop! You've just lost yourself a thousand bucks, right? So I want you to listen to me carefully because I'm gonna tell you how we can put all that to rights again. Now, we'll just have one more hand—'

'NO!' (The little old lady's voice was loud and shrill this time.) 'He *won't*! He won't lay down another dollar, d'you hear me? He's just—he's just a poor old fool, can't you see that? He's just a gullible, poor old—' But the rest of her words were strangled in her throat, and Virgil sat down again and put his arm round her shoulder as she began to weep silently.

'Don't you *want* to get all your money back?' Luke's voice is quiet again, but everyone can hear his words.

'Don't listen to him!' shouts one.

'Call it a day, sir!' shouts another.

Says Luke, turning to all of them: 'Old pop, here, he's got one helluva sight more spunk in him than the rest o' you put together! And, what's more, not a single man jack o' you knows the proposition I'm proposin'. Well?' (Luke looks around real bold.) 'Well? *Do* you?'

It was all silence again now, as Luke looks across to Virgil and formulates his offer. 'Look, pop. I've been mighty lucky tonight, as I think you might agree. So, I'm going to give you the sort o' chance you'll never have again. And this is what we'll do. We'll have just one last hand and we'll take two points off my score. Got that? I pick up eighteen—we call it sixteen. And just the same whatever score it is. What do you say, pop?'

But old Virgil—he shakes his head. 'You're a good sport, Luke, but—'

'Let's make it *three* off then,' says Luke earnestly. 'I pick up twenty—we call it seventeen. OK? Look, pop!' (He leans across and grips the wrist again.) 'Nobody's *ever* gonna make you any better offer than that. *Nobody*. You know something? It's virtually *certain* you're gonna get all that lovely money right back into that wallet o' yours, now, isn't it?'

It was tempting. Ye gods, it was tempting! And it was soon clear that the audience was thinking it was pretty tempting, too, with a good many of them revising their former estimate of things.

'What d'you say?' asks Luke.

'No,' says Virgil. 'It's not just me—it's Minny here. I've made enough of a fool of myself for one night, haven't I, old girl?'

Then Minny looked at him, straight on, like. A surprising change had come over her tear-stained face, and her blue eyes blazed with a sudden surge of almost joyous challenge. 'You take him on, Virgil!' she says, with a quiet, proud authority.

But Virgil still sat there dejected and indecisive. His hands ran across that shock of wavy white hair, and for a minute or two he pondered to himself. Then he decided. He took most of the remaining notes from his wallet, and counted them with lingering affection before stacking them neatly in the centre of the table. 'Do you wanna count 'em, Luke?' he says. And it was as if the tide had suddenly turned; as if the old man sensed the smell of victory in his nostrils.

For a few seconds now it seemed to be Luke who was nervy and hesitant, the brashness momentarily draining from him. But the offer had been taken up, and the fifty or sixty onlookers were in no mood to let him forget it. He slowly counted out his own bills, and placed them on top of Virgil's.

Two thousand dollars—on one hand.

Luke has already picked up the deck, and now he's shuffling the spots with his usual, casual expertise.

'Why are *you* dealin'?'

Luke looks up, and stares me hard in the eye. 'Was that *you* just spoke, mister?'

I nod. 'Yep. It was me. And I wanna know why it is you think you got some goddam right to deal them cards—because you don't deal 'em straight, brother. You flick 'em off the top and you flick 'em off the bottom and for all I know you flick 'em—'

'I'll see you outside, mister, as soon as—'

'You'll do no such thing,' I replies quietly. 'I just ain't goin' to be outside no more tonight again—least of all for you, brother.'

He looked mighty dangerous then—but I just didn't care. The skin along his knuckles was growing white as he slowly got to his feet and moved his chair backwards. And then, just as slowly, he sat himself down again—and he surprises everybody. He pushes the deck over the table and he says: 'He's right, pop. *You* deal!'

Somehow old pop's shaking hands managed to shuffle the cards into some sort of shape; and when a couple of cards fall to the floor, it's me who bends down and hands them back to him.

'Cut,' says pop.

So Luke cuts—about halfway down the deck (though knowing Lukey I should think it was *exactly* halfway down). Miraculously, it seems, old Virgil's hands had gotten themselves rid of any shakes, and he deals the cards out firm and fine: one for Luke, one for himself; another for Luke, and another for himself. For a few moments each man left them lying there on the top of the table. Then Luke picks up his own—first the one, and then the other.

'Stick!' he says, and his voice is a bit hoarse.

Every eye in the room was now on Virgil as he turned over his first card—a seven; then the second card—a ten. Seventeen! And all you've got to do, my friends, is to add on three—and that's a handsome little twenty, and the whole room was mumbling and murmuring in approval.

Every eye now switches to Luke, and in the sudden tense silence the cards are slowly turned: first a king, and then—ye gods!—an ace! And as Lukey smiles down at that beautiful twenty-oner the audience groaned like they always do when its favourite show-jumper knocks the top off the last fence.

And where, my friends, do we go from there? Well, I'll tell you. It was Lucy who started it all immediately Luke had left. She pushed her way through the on-lookers and plunged her hand deep down between those glorious breasts of hers to clutch her evening's tips.

'Mr Perkins, isn't it? I know it isn't all that much; but—but if it'll help, please take it.' About seven or eight dollars, it was, no more—but, believe me, it bore its fruit two-hundred-fold. It was me who was next. I'd taken about thirty-five dollars on the coach and (once more hitching the old briefcase higher under my arm) I fished it all out of my back pocket and placed it a-top of Lucy's crumpled offerings.

'Mr Perkins,' I said sombrely. 'You should've been on *my* coach, old friend.' That's all I said.

As for Virgil, he said nothing. He just sat back all crumpled up like before, with Minny sobbing silently beside him. I reckon he looked as if he couldn't trust himself to say a single word. But it didn't matter. All the audience was sad and sullenly sympathetic—and, as I said, they'd had their fill of Louis' vintage wines. And I've got to hand it to them. Twenty dollars; another twenty dollars; a fifty; a few tens; another twenty; another fifty—I watched them all as these clean-living, God-fearing folk forked something from their careful savings. And I reckon there wasn't a single man-jack of them who didn't make his mark upon that ever-mounting pile. But still Virgil said nothing. When finally he stumbled his way to the exit, holding Minny in one hand and a very fat pile of other people's dollars in the other, he turned round as if he was going to say something to all his very good friends. But still the words wouldn't come, it seemed; and he turned once more and left the cocktail bar.

❧

I woke late the next morning, and only then because Luke was leaning over me, gently shaking me by the shoulder.

'Louis says he wants to see you at half-past ten.'

I lifted my left arm and focused on the wrist-watch: already five to ten.

'You all right, Danny?' Luke was standing by the door now (he must have had a key for that!) and for some reason he didn't look mightily happy.

'Sure, sure!'

'Half-past, then,' repeated Luke, and closed the door behind him.

I still felt very tired, and I was conscious that the back of my head was aching—and that's unusual for me. Nothing to drink the night before—well, only the odd orange juice that Lucy had ... orange juice ...? I fell to wondering slightly, and turned to look at the other side of the bed, where the sheet was neatly turned down in a white hypotenuse. Lucy had gone—doubtless gone early; but then Lucy was always sensible and careful about such things ...

I saw my face frowning as I stood in front of the shaving-mirror; and I was still frowning when I took the suit off the hanger in the wardrobe and noticed that the briefcase was gone. But I'd have been frowning even more if the briefcase *hadn't* gone; and as I dressed, my head was clearing nicely. I picked up the two thick sealed envelopes that had nestled all night under my pillow, put them, one each, into the pockets of my overcoat, and felt happy enough when I knocked on the door of Louis' private suite and walked straight in. It was ten thirty-two.

There were the usual six chairs round the oblong table, and four of them were taken already: there was Luke, and there was Barty; then there was Minny; and at the head of the table, Louis himself —a Louis still, doubtless, no more than four-ten, four-eleven in his built-up shoes, but minus that garishly striped blazer now; minus, too, that shock of silvery hair which the previous evening had covered that large, bald dome of his.

'You're late,' he says, but not unpleasantly. 'Sit down, Danny.' So I sat down, feeling like a little boy in the first grade. (But I usually feel like that with Louis.)

'You seen Lucy?' asks Minny, as Barty pours me a drop of Irish.

'Lucy? No—have you tried her room?'

But no one seemed much willing to answer that one, and we waited for a few minutes in silence before Louis spoke again.

'Danny,' he says, 'you'll remember that when we brought you into our latest li'l operation a few months back I figured we'd go for about a quarter of a million before we launched out on a new one?'

I nodded.

'Well, we're near enough there now as makes no odds—a fact perhaps you may yourself be not completely unaware of? After all, Danny, it was one o' your jobs to take my li'l Lucy down to the bank on Mondays, now wasn't it? And I reckon you've got a pretty clear idea of how things are.'

I nodded again, and kept on looking him straight in the eyes.

'Well, it was never no secret from any of us—was it?—that I'd be transferrin' this li'l investment o' mine over to Luke and Bartholomew here as soon as they—well, as soon as they showed me they was worthy.'

I was nodding slowly all the time now; but he'd left something out. 'Lucy was goin' to be in it, too,' I said.

'You're very fond of my Lucy, aren't you?' says Minny quietly.

'Yep. I'm very fond of her, Minny.' And that was the truth.

'It's not bin difficult for any of us to see that, old girl, now has it?' Louis turned to Minny and patted her affectionately on the arm. Then he focuses on me again. 'You needn't have no worries about my li'l daughter, Danny. No worries at all! Did it never occur to you to wonder just why I christened this latest li'l investment o' mine as the "Lulu-Bar Motel"?'

For a few seconds I must have looked a little puzzled, but my head was clearing nicely with the whiskey, and I suddenly saw what he meant. Yes! What a deep old devil our Louis was! The *Lu*-cy, *Lu*-ke, *Bar*-tholomew Motel . . .

But Louis was still speaking: 'I only asked you down this mornin', Danny, because I was hopin' to wind it all up here and now—and to let you know how much I've bin aware o' your own li'l contribution. But—well, it's all tied up in a way with Lucy, isn't it? And I reckon' (he looked at Luke and Bart) 'I reckon we'd better call another li'l meeting tonight? About eight? All right?'

It seemed all right to all of us, and I got up to go.

'You off to town, Danny?' asks Louis, eyeing the overcoat.

'Yep.' That's all I said. Then I left them there and caught the bus to the station.

I'd always noticed it before: whenever I'd felt a bit guilty about anything it was as if I sensed that other people somehow seemed to *know*. But that's behind us now. And, anyway, it had been Lucy's idea originally—not mine. She'd needed me, of course, for devising the cheque and forging Louis' signature—for though I'm about as ham-fisted with a deck of cards as an arthritic octopus, I got my own particular specialism. Yes, sir! And Lucy trusted me, too, because I'd been carrying all that lovely money—240,000 dollars of it!—all neatly stacked in five-hundred bills, all neatly enveloped and neatly sealed—why, I'd been carrying it all around with me in the old briefcase for two whole days! And Lucy—Lucy, my love!—we shall soon be meeting at the ticket barrier on number one platform—and then be drifting off together quietly in the twilight . . .

At a quarter to twelve I was there—standing in my overcoat and waiting happily. (Lucy had never been early in her life.) I lit another cigarette; then another. By twelve forty-five I was beginning to worry a little; by one forty-five I was beginning to worry a lot; and by two forty-five I was beginning to guess at the truth. Yet still I waited—waited and waited and waited. And, in a sense, I suppose, I've been waiting for Lucy ever since . . .

It was when the big hand on the station clock came round to four that I finally called it a day and walked over to look at the Departure Board. I found a train that was due for New York in forty-five minutes, and I thought that that had better be that. I walked into the buffet and sat down with a coffee. So? So, here was yet another of life's illusions lying shattered in the dust, and yet . . . Poor, poor, lovely Lucy! I nearly allowed myself a saddened little smile as I thought of her opening up those two big envelopes in the briefcase—and finding there those 480 pieces of crisp, new paper, each exactly the size of a 500-dollar bill. She must have thought I was pretty—well, pretty gullible, I suppose, when we'd both agreed that *she* should take away the briefcase . . .

A single to New York would cost about fifty or sixty dollars, I reckoned; and as I joined what seemed to be the shorter queue at the ticket office I took the bulky envelope from the right-hand pocket of the overcoat, opened it—and stood there stunned and gorgonized. Inside were about 240 pieces of crisp, new paper, each exactly the size of a 500-dollar bill; and my hands were trembling as I stood away from the queue and opened the other envelope. Exactly the same. Well, no—not *exactly* the same. On the top piece of blank paper there were three lines of writing in Louis' unmistakably minuscule hand:

> *I did my best to tell you Danny boy but you never did really understand that filosofy of mine now did you? It's just what I kept on telling you all along. People . . .*

By now, though, I reckon you'll know those last few words that Louis wrote.

I walked back across to the buffet and ordered another coffee, counting up what I had in my pockets: just ten dollars and forty cents; and I fell to wondering where it was I went from here. Perhaps . . . perhaps there were one or two things in my favour. At least I could spell 'philosophy'; and then there was always the pretty big certainty (just as Louis said so often) that somewhere soon I'd find a few nice, kindly, gullible folk.

But as I glance around at the faces of my fellow men and women in the station buffet now, they all look very mean, and very hard.

NEIGHBOURHOOD WATCH

Sed quis custodiet ipsos custodes?
(But what about the vigilantes? Who's going to watch after
them?)

(Juvenal, *Satires*)

We must never make the criminal the *hero*, though!' pro-
claimed Marcus Price, Fellow of All Souls, as he
drained his beer and put down his glass with the gesture of a man
announcing to the company that *he'd* bought the previous round
himself and whose turn, pray, was it now.

'What about old Raffles, though? Gentleman-burglar and all
that. Remember him?'

The speaker was another Oxford don, Denis Stockman, an
authority (*the* authority) on the Grand Duchy of Lithuania in the
fifteenth century.

'Stole the Crown Jewels or something,' Stockman continued,
'then took 'em back when he found out what they were. No
chivalry like that these days, eh, Morse?'

'Oh no,' mumbled Morse.

Oh dear! But Morse had only himself to blame. He'd meant to
nip into the King's Arms just briefly that Wednesday lunchtime;
and for a start things had looked promising. The one other cus-
tomer was a very attractive thirty-odd-year-old brunette with
sludgy green eyes. She had smiled momentarily as he'd sat down a
few feet from her—before turning her attention back to *The Times*
crossword puzzle, in which even as he took his first draught she
wrote another word, with her left hand, the middle fingernail
marked with a broad, white lateral line, as if she might have
trapped it in a door.

Yes, only himself to blame . . .

Almost as soon as they'd spotted him there they'd pounced.
How long is it? Mind if we *join* you? What are you *drinking*?

Morse should, of course, have pleaded urgency in some criminal pursuit. But he didn't. The prospect of a further pint gladdened his heart, and he heard himself saying, 'Best Bitter.'

It was the fourth member of the quartet who now volunteered to get in the second round of drinks—a small, bald-headed man with a beer-belly and an NHS hearing-aid in his right ear. Morse had met him once or twice before and recalled that he'd been a refugee from pre-war Germany who now lived (very near Morse, wasn't it?) in a large North Oxford property reputedly stuffed with eminently collectable furniture and ornaments. Yes! Dr Eric Ullman—that was his name! A bachelor—like Morse.

'Good health, gentlemen!' Ullman's diction was precise, pedantic almost, as he raised his glass and toasted his two university acquaintances—and the chief inspector. 'And please forgive me perhaps if I tell you something—well, something that may surprise you a little?'

If any of the three pairs of eyebrows raised themselves, it was by little more than a millimetre.

'You're wrong, I think,' began Ullman, 'about there being no honour among thieves these days. Please let me explain. Last Friday I went to see *Così fan Tutte* at the Apollo Theatre here in Oxford. The Welsh National were doing it—doing it this week too, as you'll know. I got home at about a quarter past eleven, and most foolishly I didn't bother to put my car away in the garage. Next morning, when I looked out of the window? The drive was completely empty. The car was gone!'

'Metro, wasn't it?' asked Price.

Ullman nodded. 'I've had it for nine years.'

Stockman coughed slightly. 'Was it *worth* pinching, Eric?'

'It was worth a lot to me,' said Ullman simply.

Price grinned. 'Three hundred quid—in part exchange? No more.'

'You didn't *hear* anything?' asked Morse.

'No. And shall I tell you something else? They'd even closed the gates behind them.'

'Probably *pushed* it out of the drive,' suggested Morse. 'Saves any noise. And you're only a couple of hundred yards from the Ring Road . . .'

'I suppose so.'

'Did you ring us? Ring the police?'

'Straightaway. It would probably turn up in three or four days, they said. Out on one of the estates—minus wheels, minus radio, minus anything detachable—panels kicked in—windows smashed . . .'

'Bloody *mind*-less, isn't it!' Price shook his head vehemently. 'I know what I'd give some of these young sods—and it *wouldn't* be a few gentle hours of community service!'

'Just—just a minute.' Ullman raised his right hand, and the others were silent again. 'You see, they *didn't* find it out in East Oxford. Oh no. Three days went by, and then on Monday—last Monday—I was invited out to dinner at The Randolph. And when I got back, about eleven or so, there—there in the drive . . .'

Ullman was telling his little tale well, and three pairs of eyes now betrayed an unexpected interest.

'. . . completely undamaged—in fact looking *very* spick-and-span. And under the windscreen wiper—this!'

From his breast-pocket he took out a letter, a letter written in a small, neat, upright script, with no address, no date, no salutation, no valediction; a letter which each of Ullman's immediate audience now read in turn:

Sorry about the inconvenience—very sorry indeed. I just had to have a car and your's was there. Its had a shampoo and I filled the petrol tank—unleaded, like it says in the handbook. Your little car saved my bacon, that's the truth, and I'm grateful. Please then do me the honour of accepting the enclosed ticket. I know you enjoy opera. I wasn't sure what performance to choose but Wagner is king for me, and in my opinion Die Valkurie is the greatest thing he ever wrote. Enjoy your evening, and thanks again.

Morse was the last to read the letter, his face betraying some slight puzzlement—as Ullman produced a ticket for the following Friday's performance.

£40!

Phew!

'Is it genuine?' queried Stockman.

'"Ring-side" seat, if you see what I mean,' replied Ullman.

Morse smiled gently at the little man's pleasantry as he held the ticket up to the light and pretended to be checking a possible irregularity of watermark.

'Genuine enough, I reckon,' he said, wishing dearly that the ticket was his own.

Beer glasses were empty again now, and Morse decided that it was either him or Stockman for the next round.

Let it be Stockman!

The back bar was a popular venue—ill-designed, intimate, awkward—and was now almost full this mid-lunchtime as Morse excused his premature departure and carefully squeezed his way past the woman to his right. Apparently she had been paying more attention to Ullman than to her crossword puzzle, for as far as Morse could see she had made very little, if any, progress.

And indeed Morse was right. Like most of the other customers there she had been very interested in Ullman's tale; interested in one or two other things as well. Had anyone apart from herself, for example, noticed that Morse (inadvertently?) had forgotten to hand back to Ullman the letter from the car thief? Had anyone apart from herself observed the conspiratorial exchange of glances between the two of them—between the man the others called Morse and Ullman himself? 'Conspiratorial'? No, that was too strong a word for it, perhaps. But something *like* that had been there. She could have sworn it.

Interesting!

There was something else too. After Morse had left, the little man's eyes had caught hers—almost as if she might have been a vague acquaintance. Not that she was: she'd never seen him in her life before. But she thought there'd been something almost . . . sinister about his look. 'Sinister'? Yes, that *wasn't* too strong a word for it. It was as if he knew something about her that she hardly knew herself.

Morse sauntered around Blackwell's for half an hour before walking over to the bus stop in Cornmarket. On the ride back to Kidlington he read the letter twice more, reflecting yet again on the bizarre coincidence that a car thief—a car thief!—should share his own highly idiosyncratic view about the greatest opera ever composed . . . Reflecting also on just those two (forgivable?) lapses in English grammar; and on that one (wholly unforgivable!) lapse which still puzzled Morse sorely as he walked up the incline to Police HQ.

'Nice, er, lunch, sir?' Lewis broke off his typing and looked down at his wrist-watch.

'Shut up and listen! Chap has his car pinched—OK? Few days later it's returned, in better nick than when it was pinched—with a note saying very sorry but I had to have a car and to make up for all the trouble here's an expensive ticket for the opera. You with me?'

Lewis nodded.

'So this chap goes along to the opera and when he gets back home—'

'He finds he's been burgled,' said Lewis flatly.

'You been sleeping in the knife-box?'

'No. Heard of it before, sir. There was a case like that a few weeks ago out in High Wycombe—so one of the lads was saying.'

'Oh!'

'Sorry to disappoint you, sir.'

'You think many other people have heard of it?'

'Doubt it. Not the sort of thing you want broadcasting, is it? I mean, you'd probably get lots of copy-cat crimes. For a start anyway.'

'Mm.'

'Clever though.'

'Bloody clever!'

'Why did you mention it, sir?'

Morse grinned. 'What are you doing on Friday evening?'

'Not sure. The wife's got a Tupperware party, I think, but—'

'Would you be glad to get away?'

It was Lewis's turn to grin. 'What time do you want me?'

It was at one minute past seven, from the front seats of a white Self Hire van, that the pair of them saw the man leave his property and walk briskly away.

'You're a *very* clever bugger to think of this, you know, Millie!'

'Don't count your chickens—not yet.'

'No—plenty o' time.'

'Three and a half hours—Christ!'

'More'n two football matches.'

'You're a philistine, Charlie!'

'What me? Don't be daft. Wagner's me greatest passion in life, didna tell yer?'

It was from their unmarked car that Morse and Lewis observed Ullman leave on foot. With a new alarm system fitted, and with a stout Krooklok fixed between steering-wheel and clutch, the Metro was now safely housed in the bolted garage. Clearly Ullman was taking no further risks; and in any case, buses were fairly fre-

quent down the Banbury Road—down to the City Centre—down
to the Apollo Theatre.

At half-past eight, Lewis ventured his first criticism:

'What time do you say this thing started?'

'Give 'em a *chance*, Lewis! They've got till midnight, near as
dammit.'

'But we've already been here—'

'Ssshhh!' hissed Morse as a strong-bodied woman walked up
the gravel drive to Ullman's front door, looked around with some
interest—before pushing what appeared to be a free newspaper
into the letter-box; then retracing her steps, and closing the gate to
the drive behind her.

'Exciting little incident, wouldn't you say, sir?' asked Lewis
wearily.

But Morse refused to rise to the bait.

At ten minutes past nine, a man opened the drive gate, closed it
behind him, and walked up to the front door, where he looked
over his shoulder for a good many seconds as if almost expecting to
see someone, before extracting the newspaper from the letter-box,
finding a key, and entering the house.

Dr Eric Ullman.

Morse was still shaking his head a quarter of an hour later when
Lewis came back from the bar at the Dew Drop in Summertown
with a pint of Best Bitter, and half a glass of Beamish.

'He might just have got fed up with it, sir? Not everybody's cup
o' tea—Wagner.'

'It's *his* cup o' tea though: that's the whole point. No, there's
something very wrong somewhere, I'm sure of it, Lewis. They
must've *known* he'd come back early . . . They must have got wind
of it somehow.'

'Perhaps Dr Ullman guessed—well, what *you* guessed, sir?'

'Ye-es! Do you know, I think you may be right.' Morse took out the letter yet again. 'You see, whoever wrote this says he's a great Wagner fan, agreed?'

'Like you.'

'Like me, yes. But I don't believe him. Look!' Morse jabbed a forefinger at two words in the letter: 'Die Valkurie'.

Lewis looked appropriately vague. 'All German to me, sir.'

Morse tried to smile. 'Oh no, Lewis! That, if I may say so, is precisely the point. It *isn't* German! If you spend your life with anything—if you read about it—if you think about it—if you play it time and time again—'

'Like you.'

'Like me, yes.'

'I'm still not—'

'He can't even *spell* the bloody word!'

'We all make the occasional spelling mistake—'

'What? Three spelling mistakes in one word? *Three*? Come off it! He spells it with a "V" instead of a "W"; he sticks a spurious "i" in before the "e"; and he misses the umlaut off the "u"—'

'The what, sir?'

Morse peeled the back off a beer-mat and wrote out the correct spelling of the opera: 'Die Walküre'.

'Ullman's a German though, isn't he?' asked Lewis slowly.

'German origin, yes.'

'So why . . . why didn't *he* notice, well—what you noticed?'

'I'm beginning to think he did, Lewis. I'm beginning to think he did.'

'But you still felt pretty certain that Dr Ullman was going to be burgled tonight?'

'If I'd felt all *that* certain, I'd have had a few heavies round the corner in a police van.'

'Well, at least he's still got all that valuable furniture of his— that's one good thing.'

'That's one way of looking at it.'

'You got anything valuable in the furniture line yourself, sir?'

'Me? Oh, just the one piece, that's all. The family heirloom—nest of tables—Chippendale—1756. What about you?'

'Just the big mahogany wardrobe—Utility—1942. We've been trying to give it away this last year but nobody seems to appreciate the quality.'

Lewis drove the two of them back up to North Oxford, where on Morse's instruction they stopped for a brief while outside Ullman's residence once again. And even as they watched, the small portly figure of Eric Ullman passed across the uncurtained window of the lighted front room.

'If he's been burgled tonight, I'm a Dutchman,' volunteered Lewis.

But Lewis was no Dutchman, Morse knew that. 'You get off home, Lewis. I'll walk from here.'

'You sure, sir? It must be all of three hundred yards.'

'Less of the sarcasm, Sergeant!'

'Night, sir.'

Morse had put out his two Co-op semi-skimmed milk tokens, and was pouring himself a touch of the malt—when he suddenly knew that something was terribly wrong. Why hadn't he spotted the short note on the kitchen table immediately?

Sorry about the inconvenience—very sorry indeed. It was the only thing you'd got worth pinching though and I'm hoping I'll get a good price.

That was all.

Morse bounded up the stairs, where on the landing he surveyed the empty square of unhoovered carpet upon which, until so very recently, had stood the one *objet d'art* that had been passed down from one generation of the Morse clan to the next—the family heirloom—the nest of tables—Chippendale—1756.

It was Sergeant Dixon on night duty. 'Thank goodness you've rung, sir. We've been trying to get you but your phone's not been answering—'

'I've been *out*, man! You don't *mind*, do you?'

'Course not. It's just that you've had burglars, I'm afraid—'

'That's exactly what I'm ringing to tell you!'

'No need to worry though, sir. They didn't pinch anything. We've caught 'em—the pair of 'em.'

'You've done *what*?'

'You see this fellow rang us and said there was somebody in your flat, but when our boys got there they'd scarpered. This fellow'd got the number though—white Self Hire van—and we stopped it out on the A40 near Wheatley. Just a few old tables in the back—don't think they could've taken anything of yours, sir. They must have got wind of us somehow, I reckon.'

'Who *was* this fellow?'

'A Dr Ullman, sir—lives quite near you, so he said.'

Morse was shaking his head yet again as he put down the phone. Everything—almost everything—was becoming clear at long last. The same thought must have struck the two of them, both himself and Ullman, in the King's Arms that lunchtime; the same strange thought that far from being a gesture of courtesy and gratitude, the letter and the opera ticket were merely the appropriate stages in a subtle strategy of deception.

Yes!

And Morse's thinking had gone one step further.

And Ullman's thinking had gone *two* steps further.

Morse locked his front door very carefully behind him and walked out into the night.

'A wee drop of the malt, Chief Inspector?'

'Excellent!'

'I was hardly expecting you *tonight*.'

'Did you ever think of joining the police force, Doctor?'

'I'm not tall enough.'

'You were always a move or so ahead of me!'

'Ah! But to be honest with you I *did* have one little advantage over you. I've got a pair of wrens nesting in the front garden, you see, and I was watching them through the field-glasses recently when I noticed a woman, at the bus stop just outside; and I could see that *she* was watching something too—watching the house, the drive, the garage . . . Then two days later I saw her again, and I looked at her *very* closely through the field-glasses and I could see she was copying something down in a red notebook, writing with her left hand—and I noticed that she had a white scar on the nail of her middle finger, as if she'd trapped it in a door. And then I saw her *again*, didn't I . . .?'

Ullman smiled, and as he did so his features momentarily took on an almost sinister appearance.

'And you felt pretty certain that it was *me* who was going to get burgled tonight,' said Morse slowly.

'It seemed logical, yes. After all, if you were watching *my* property, you couldn't be watching your own as well, now could you?'

'You took a huge risk though.'

'You think so?' The little man appeared puzzled.

'Well, if they burgled *you*, while you were round at my place watching *me* . . .'

'Oh no. I've finished taking risks, you see. The private detective I hired to keep a look-out here was the very best in the business, so they told me: black belt at judo, Lord knows what else.'

'He must have been pretty good—we certainly didn't spot him.'

'*Her*, Chief Inspector. She said she'd probably do her "free-newspaper-delivery" routine—'

'Bloody 'ell!' mumbled Morse to himself.

'—and I told her she could pack it in for the night just after I'd rung the police—just before I got back here—about nine o'clock.'

'Ten past nine, to be accurate—that's when we spotted you.'

'Er'—Ullman coughed modestly and drained his malt—'if we're to be accurate, Chief Inspector, shouldn't it be when *we* spotted *you?*'

For the last time that day Morse shook his head. Then draining his own glass and making his farewell, slowly he walked the three hundred yards back home.

A CASE OF
MIS-IDENTITY

His friend and foil, the stolid Watson with whom he shares rooms in Baker Street, attends Holmes throughout most of his adventures.

(*The Oxford Companion to English Literature*)

Long as had been my acquaintance with Sherlock Holmes, I had seldom heard him refer to his early life; and the only knowledge I ever gleaned of his family history sprang from the rare visits of his famous brother, Mycroft. On such occasions, our visitor invariably addressed me with courtesy, but also (let me be honest!) with some little condescension. He was—this much I knew—by some seven years the senior in age to my great friend, and was a founder member of the Diogenes Club, that peculiar institution whose members are ever forbidden to converse with one another. Physically, Mycroft was stouter than his brother (I put the matter in as kindly a manner as possible); but the single most striking feature about him was the piercing intelligence of his eyes —greyish eyes which appeared to see beyond the range of normal mortals. Holmes himself had commented upon this last point: 'My dear Watson, you have recorded—and I am flattered by it—something of my own powers of observation and deduction. Know, however, that Mycroft has a degree of observation somewhat the equal of my own; and as for deduction, he has a brain that is unrivalled—*virtually* unrivalled—in the northern hemisphere. You may be relieved, however, to learn that he is a trifle lazy, and quite decidedly somnolent—and that his executant ability on the violin is immeasurably inferior to my own.'

(Was there, I occasionally wondered, just the hint of competitive envy between those two unprecedented intellects?)

I had just called at 221B Baker Street on a fog-laden November afternoon in 188–, after taking part in some research at St Thomas's Hospital into suppurative tonsilitis (I had earlier acquainted Holmes with the particulars). Mycroft was staying with Holmes for a few days, and as I entered that well-known sitting room I caught the tail-end of the brothers' conversation.

'Possibly, Sherlock—possibly. But it is the *detail*, is it not? Give me all the evidence and it is just possible that I could match your own analyses from my corner armchair. But to be required to rush hither and thither, to find and examine witnesses, to lie along the carpet with a lens held firmly to my failing sight . . . No! It is not my *métier*.'

During this time Holmes himself had been standing before the window, gazing down into the neutral-tinted London street. And looking over his shoulder I could see that on the pavement opposite there stood an attractive young woman draped in a heavy fur coat. She had clearly just arrived, and every few seconds was looking up to Holmes's window in hesitant fashion, her fingers fidgeting with the buttons of her gloves. On a sudden she crossed the street, and Mrs Hudson was soon ushering in our latest client.

After handing her coat to Holmes, the young lady sat nervously on the edge of the nearest armchair, and announced herself as Miss Charlotte van Allen. Mycroft nodded briefly at the newcomer, before reverting to a monograph on polyphonic plainchant; whilst Holmes himself made observation of the lady in that abstracted yet intense manner which was wholly peculiar to him.

'Do you not find,' began Holmes, 'that with your short sight it is a little difficult to engage in so much type-writing?'

Surprise, apprehension, appreciation, showed by turns upon her face, succeeded in all by a winsome smile as she appeared to acknowledge Holmes's quite extraordinary powers.

'Perhaps you will also tell me,' continued he, 'why it is that you came from home in such a great hurry?'

For a few seconds, Miss van Allen sat shaking her head with incredulity; then, as Holmes sat staring towards the ceiling, she began her remarkable narrative.

'Yes, I did bang out of the house, because it made me very angry to see the way my father, Mr Wyndham, took the whole business

—refusing even to countenance the idea of going to the police, and quite certainly ruling out any recourse to yourself, Mr Holmes! He just kept repeating—and I *do* see his point—that no real harm has been done . . . although he can have no idea of the misery I have had to endure.'

'Your father?' queried Holmes quietly. 'Perhaps you refer to your step-father, since the names are different?'

'Yes,' she confessed, 'my step-father. I don't know why I keep referring to him as "father"—especially since he is but five years older than myself.'

'Your mother—she is still living?'

'Oh, yes! Though I will not pretend I was over-pleased when she remarried so soon after my father's death—and then to a man almost seventeen years younger than herself. Father—my real father, that is—had a plumbing business in the Tottenham Court Road, and Mother carried on the company after he died, until she married Mr Wyndham. I think he considered such things a little beneath his new wife, especially with his being in a rather superior position as a traveller in French wines. Whatever the case, though, he made Mother sell out.'

'Did you yourself derive any income from the sale of your father's business?'

'No. But I do have £100 annual income in my own right; as well as the extra I make from my typing. If I may say so, Mr Holmes, you might be surprised how many of the local businesses—including Cook and Marchant—ask me to work for them a few hours each week. You see' (she looked at us with a shy, endearing diffidence) 'I'm quite good at *that* in life, if nothing else.'

'You must then have some profitable government stock—?' began Holmes.

She smiled again. 'New Zealand, at four and a half per cent.'

'Please forgive me, Miss van Allen, but could not a single lady get by very nicely these days on—let us say, fifty pounds per annum?'

'Oh, certainly! And I myself live comfortably on but ten shillings per week, which is only half of that amount. You see, I never touch a single penny of my inheritance. Since I live at home, I cannot bear the thought of being a burden to my parents, and we have reached an arrangement whereby Mr Wyndham himself is empowered to draw my interest each quarter for as long as I remain in that household.'

Holmes nodded. 'Why have you come to see me?' he asked bluntly.

A flush stole over Miss van Allen's face and she plucked nervously at a small handkerchief drawn from her bag as she stated her errand with earnest simplicity. 'I would give everything I have to know what has become of Mr Horatio Darvill. There! Now you have it.'

'Please, could you perhaps begin at the beginning?' encouraged Holmes gently.

'Whilst my father was alive, sir, we always received tickets for the gas-fitters' ball. And after he died, the tickets were sent to my mother. But neither Mother nor I ever thought of going, because it was made plain to us that Mr Wyndham did not approve. He believed that the class of folk invited to such gatherings was inferior; and furthermore he asserted that neither of us—without considerable extra expenditure—had anything fit to wear. But believe me, Mr Holmes, I myself had the purple plush that I had never so much as taken from the drawer!'

It was after a decent interval that Holmes observed quietly: 'But you *did* go to the ball?'

'Yes. In the finish, we both went—Mother and I—when my step-father had been called away to France.'

'And it was there that you met Mr Horatio Darvill?'

'Yes! And—do you know?—he called the very next morning. And several times after that, whilst my step-father was in France, we walked out together.'

'Mr Wyndham must have been annoyed once he learned what had occurred?'

Miss van Allen hung her pretty head. 'Most annoyed, I'm afraid, for it became immediately clear that he did not approve of Mr Darvill.'

'Why do you think that was so?'

'I am fairly sure he thought Mr Darvill was interested only in my inheritance.'

'Did Mr Darvill not attempt to keep seeing you—in spite of these difficulties?'

'Oh yes! I thought, though, it would be wiser for us to stop seeing each other for a while. But he did write—every single day. And always, in the mornings, I used to receive the letters myself so that no one else should know.'

'Were you engaged to this gentleman?'

'Yes! For there was no problem about his supporting me. He was a cashier in a firm in Leadenhall Street—'

'Ah! Which office was that?' I interposed, for that particular area is known to me well, and I hoped that I might perhaps be of some assistance in the current investigation. Yet the look on Holmes's face was one of some annoyance, and I sank further into my chair as the interview progressed.

'I never did know exactly which firm it was,' admitted Miss van Allen.

'But where did he live?' persisted Holmes.

'He told me that he usually slept in a flat on the firm's premises.'

'You must yourself have written to this man, to whom you had agreed to become engaged?'

She nodded. 'To the Leadenhall Street Post Office, where I left my letters *poste restante*. Horatio—Mr Darvill—said that if I wrote to him at his work address, he'd never get to see my envelopes first, and the young clerks there would be sure to tease him about things.'

It was at this point that I was suddenly conscious of certain stertorous noises from Mycroft's corner—a wholly reprehensible lapse into poor manners, as it appeared to me.

'What else can you tell me about Mr Darvill?' asked Holmes quickly.

'He was very shy. He always preferred to walk out with me in the evening than in the daylight. "Retiring", perhaps, is the best word to describe him—even his voice. He'd had the quinsy as a young man, and was still having treatment for it. But the disability had left him with a weak larynx, and a sort of whispering fashion of speaking. His eyesight, too, was rather feeble—just as mine is— and he always wore tinted spectacles to protect his eyes against the glare of any bright light.'

Holmes nodded his understanding; and I began to sense a note of suppressed excitement in his voice.

'What next?'

'He called at the house the very evening on which Mr Wyndham next departed for France, and he proposed that we should marry before my step-father returned. He was convinced that this would be our only chance; and he was so dreadfully in earnest that he made me swear, with my hand upon both Testaments, that whatever happened I would always be true and faithful to him.'

'Your mother was aware of what was taking place?'

'Oh, *yes*. And she approved so much. In a strange way, she was even fonder of my fiancé than I was myself, and she agreed that our only chance was to arrange a secret marriage.'

'The wedding was to be in church?'

'Last Friday, at St Saviour's, near King's Cross; and we were to go on to a wedding-breakfast afterwards at the St Pancras Hotel. Horatio called a hansom for us, and put Mother and me into it before stepping himself into a four-wheeler which happened to be in the street. Mother and I got to St Saviour's first—it was only a few minutes' distance away. But when the four-wheeler drove up and we waited for him to step out—he never did, Mr Holmes! And when the cabman got down from the box and looked inside the carriage—*it was empty*.'

'You have neither seen nor heard of Mr Darvill since?'

'Nothing,' she whispered.

'You had planned a honeymoon, I suppose?'

'We had planned,' said Miss van Allen, biting her lip and scarce managing her reply, 'a fortnight's stay at the Royal Gleneagles in

Inverness, and we were to have caught the lunchtime express from King's Cross.'

'It seems to me,' said Holmes, with some feeling, 'that you have been most shamefully treated, dear lady.'

But Miss van Allen would hear nothing against her loved one, and protested spiritedly: 'Oh, no, sir! He was far too good and kind to treat me so.'

'Your own opinion, then,' said Holmes, 'is that some unforeseen accident or catastrophe has occurred?'

She nodded her agreement. 'And I think he must have had some premonition that very morning of possible danger, because he begged me then, once again, to remain true to him—whatever happened.'

'You have no idea what that danger may have been?'

'None.'

'How did your mother take this sudden disappearance?'

'She was naturally awfully worried at first. But then she became more and more angry; and she made me promise never to speak to her of the matter again.'

'And your step-father?'

'He seemed—it was strange, really—rather more sympathetic than Mother. At least he was willing to discuss it.'

'And what was his opinion?'

'He agreed that some accident must have happened. As he said, Mr Darvill could have no possible interest in bringing me to the very doors of St Saviour's—and then in deserting me there. If he had borrowed money—or if some of my money had already been settled on him—then there might have been some reason behind such a cruel action. But he was absolutely independent about money, and he would never even look at a sixpence of mine if we went on a visit. Oh, Mr Holmes! It is driving me half-mad to think of—' But the rest of the sentence was lost as the young lady sobbed quietly into her handkerchief.

When she had recovered her composure, Holmes rose from his chair, promising that he would consider the baffling facts she had put before him. 'But if I could offer you one piece of advice,' he added, as he held the lady's coat for her, 'it is that you allow Mr Horatio Darvill to vanish as completely from your memory as he vanished from his wedding-carriage.'

'Then you think that I shall not see him again?'

'I fear not. But please leave things in my hands. Now! I wish you to send me a most accurate physical description of Mr Darvill, as well as any of his letters which you feel you can spare.'

'We can at least expedite things a little in those two respects,' replied she in business-like fashion, 'for I advertised for him in last Monday's *Chronicle*.' And promptly reaching into her hand-bag, she produced a newspaper cutting which she gave to Holmes, together with some other sheets. 'And here, too, are four of his letters which I happen to have with me. Will they be sufficient?'

Holmes looked quickly at the letters, and nodded. 'You say you never had Mr Darvill's address?'

'Never.'

'Your step-father's place of business, please?'

'He travels for Cook and Marchant, the great Burgundy importers, of Fenchurch Street.'

'Thank you.'

After she had left Holmes sat brooding for several minutes, his fingertips still pressed together. 'An interesting case,' he observed finally. 'Did you not find it so, Watson?'

'You appeared to read a good deal which was quite invisible to me,' I confessed.

'Not invisible, Watson. Rather, let us say—unnoticed. And that in spite of my repeated attempts to impress upon you the importance of sleeves, of thumb-nails, of boot-laces, and the rest. Now, tell me, what did you immediately gather from the young woman's appearance? Describe it to me.'

Conscious of Mycroft's presence, I sought to recall my closest impressions of our recent visitor.

'Well, she had, beneath her fur, a dress of rich brown, somewhat darker than the coffee colour, with a little black plush at the neck and at the sleeves—you mentioned sleeves, Holmes? Her gloves were dove-grey in colour, and were worn through at the right forefinger. Her black boots, I was not able, from where I sat, to observe in any detail, yet I would suggest that she takes either the size four-and-a-half or five. She wore small pendant earrings, almost certainly of imitation gold, and the small handkerchief into which the poor lady sobbed so charmingly had a neat darn in the monogrammed corner. In general, she had the air of a reasonably well-to-do young woman who has not quite escaped from the slightly vulgar inheritance of a father who was—let us be honest about it, Holmes!—a plumber.'

A snort from the chair beside which Holmes had so casually thrown Miss van Allen's fur coat served to remind us that the recumbent Mycroft had now reawakened, and that perhaps my own description had, in some respect, occasioned his disapproval. But he made no spoken comment, and soon resumed his former posture.

''Pon my word, Watson,' said Holmes, 'you are coming along splendidly—is he not, Mycroft? It is true, of course, that your description misses almost everything of real importance. But the method! You have hit upon the *method*, Watson. Let us take, for example, the plush you mention on the sleeves. Now, plush is a most wonderfully helpful material for showing traces; and the double line above the wrist, where the type-writist presses against the table, was beautifully defined. As for the short-sightedness, that was mere child's play. The dent-marks of a *pince-nez* at either side of the lady's nostrils—you did not observe it? Elementary, my dear Watson! And then the boots. You really *must* practise the art of being positioned where all the evidence is clearly visible. If you wish to observe nothing at all, like brother Mycroft, then you will seek out the furthest corner of a room where even the vaguest examination of the client will be obscured by the furniture, by a fur coat, by whatever. But reverting to the lady's boots, I observed that although they were very like each other in colour and style, they were in fact *odd* boots; the one on the right foot having a slightly decorated toe-cap, and the one on the left being of a comparatively plain design. Furthermore, the right one was fastened only at the three lower buttons out of the five; the left one only at the first, third, and fifth. Now the deduction we may reasonably draw from such evidence is that the young lady left home in an unconscionable hurry. You agree?'

'Amazing, Holmes!'

'As for the glove worn at the forefinger—'

'You would be better advised,' suddenly interposed the deeper voice of Mycroft, 'to concentrate upon the missing person.'

May it have been a flash of annoyance that showed itself in Holmes's eyes? If so, it was gone immediately. 'You are quite right, Mycroft! Come now, Watson, read to us the paragraph from *The Chronicle*.'

I held the printed slip to the light and began: 'Missing on the 14th November 188–. A gentleman named Mr Horatio Darvill: about 5 feet 8 inches in height; fairly firmly built; sallow complexion; black hair, just a little bald in the centre; bushy black side-whiskers and moustache; tinted spectacles; slight infirmity of speech. When last seen, was dressed in—'

'But I think,' interrupted Holmes, 'he may by now have changed his wedding vestments, Watson?'

'Oh, certainly, Holmes.'

There being nothing, it seemed, of further value in the newspaper description, Holmes turned his attention to the letters, passing them to me after studying them himself with minute concentration.

'Well?' he asked.

Apart from the fact that the letters had been typed, I could find in them nothing of interest, and I laid them down on the coffee-table in front of the somnolent Mycroft.

'Well?' persisted Holmes.

'I assume you refer to the fact that the letters are type-written.'

'Already you are neglecting your newly acquired knowledge of the *method*, Watson. Quite apart from the one you mention, there are three further points of immediate interest and importance. First, the letters are very short; second, apart from the vague "Leadenhall Street" superscription, there is no precise address stated at any point; third, it is not only the body of the letter which has been typed, but the signature, too. Observe here, Watson—and here!—that neat little "Horatio Darvill" typed at the bottom of each of our four exhibits. And it will not have escaped you, I think, how conclusive that last point might be?'

'Conclusive, Holmes? In what way?'

'My dear fellow, is it possible for you not to see how strongly it bears upon our present investigations?'

'*Homo circumbendibus*—that's what you are, Sherlock!' (It was Mycroft once more.) 'Do you not appreciate that your client would prefer some positive action to any further proofs of your cerebral superiority?'

It is pleasing to report here that this attempt of Mycroft to provoke the most distinguished criminologist of the century proved largely ineffectual, and Holmes permitted himself a fraternal smile as his brother slowly bestirred his frame.

'You are right, Mycroft,' he rejoined lightly. 'And I shall immediately compose two letters: one to Messrs Cook and Marchant; the other to Mr Wyndham, asking that gentleman to meet us here at six o'clock tomorrow evening.'

Already I was aware of the easy and confident demeanour with which Holmes was tackling the singular mystery which confronted us all. But for the moment my attention was diverted by a small but most curious incident.

'It is just as well, Sherlock,' said Mycroft (who appeared now to be almost fully awakened), 'that you do not propose to write three letters.'

Seldom (let me admit it) have I seen my friend so perplexed: 'A *third* letter?'

'Indeed. But such a letter could have no certain destination, since it apparently slipped your memory to ask the young lady her present address, and the letters she entrusted to you appear, as I survey them, to be lacking their outer envelopes.'

Momentarily Holmes looked less than amused by this light-hearted intervention. 'You are more observant today than I thought, Mycroft, for the evidence of eye and ear had led me to entertain the suspicion that you were sleeping soundly during my recent conversation with Miss van Allen. But as regards her address, you are right.' And even as he spoke I noted the twinkle of mischievous intelligence in his eyes. 'Yet it would not be too difficult perhaps to *deduce* the young lady's address, Mycroft? On such a foul day as this it is dangerous and ill-advised for a lady to travel the streets if she has a perfectly acceptable and comfortable alternative such as the Underground; and since it was precisely 3.14 p.m. when Miss van Allen first appeared beneath my window, I would hazard the guess that she had caught the Metropolitan-line train which passes through Baker Street at 3.12 p.m. on its journey to Hammersmith. We may consider two further clues, also. The lady's boots, ill-assorted as they were, bore little evidence of the mud and mire of our London streets; and we may infer from this that her own home is perhaps as adjacent to an Underground station as is our own. More significant, however, is the fact, as we all observed, that Miss van Allen wore a dress of linen—a fabric which, though it is long-lasting and pleasing to wear, is one which has the disadvantage of creasing most easily. Now the skirt of the dress had been most recently ironed, and the slight creases in it must have resulted from her journey—to see me. And—I put this forward as conjecture, Mycroft—probably no more than three or four stops on the Underground had been involved. If we remember, too, the "few minutes" her wedding-carriage took from her home to St Saviour's, I think, perhaps . . . perhaps . . .' Holmes drew a street-map towards him, and surveyed his chosen area with his magnification-glass.

'I shall plump,' he said directly, 'for Cowcross Street myself—that shabbily genteel little thoroughfare which links Farringdon Road with St John Street.'

'Very impressive!' said Mycroft, anticipating my own admiration. 'And would you place her on the north or the south side of that thoroughfare, Sherlock?'

But before Holmes could reply to this small pleasantry, Mrs Hudson entered with a slip of paper which she handed to Holmes. 'The young lady says she forgot to give you her address, sir, and she's written it down for you.'

Holmes glanced quickly at the address and a glint of pride gleamed in his eyes. 'The answer to your question, Mycroft, is the south side—for it is an even-numbered house, and if I remember correctly the numbering of houses in that part of London invariably begins at the east end of the street with the odd numbers on the right-hand side walking westwards.'

'And the number is perhaps in the middle or late thirties?' suggested Mycroft. 'Thirty-six, perhaps? Or more likely thirty-eight?'

Holmes himself handed over the paper to us and we read:

Miss Charlotte van Allen
38, Cowcross Street

I was daily accustomed to exhibitions of the most extraordinary deductive logic employed by Sherlock Holmes, but I had begun at this point to suspect, in his brother Mycroft, the existence of some quite paranormal mental processes. It was only some half an hour later, when Holmes himself had strolled out for tobacco, that Mycroft, observing my continued astonishment, spoke quietly in my ear.

'If you keep your lips sealed, Dr Watson, I will tell you a small secret—albeit a very simple one. The good lady's coat was thrown rather carelessly, as you noticed, over the back of a chair; and on the inside of the lining was sewn a tape with her name and address clearly printed on it. Alas, however, my eyes are now not so keen as they were in my youth, and sixes and eights, as you know, are readily susceptible of confusion.'

I have never been accused, I trust, of undue levity, but I could not help laughing heartily at this coup on Mycroft's part, and I assured him that his brother should never hear the truth of it from me.

'Sherlock?' said Mycroft, raising his mighty eyebrows. 'He saw through my little joke immediately.'

It was not until past six o'clock the following evening that I returned to Baker Street after (it is not an irrelevant matter) a day of deep interest at St Thomas's Hospital.

'Well, have you solved the mystery yet?' I asked, as I entered the sitting room.

Holmes I found curled up in his armchair, smoking his oily clay pipe, and discussing medieval madrigals with Mycroft.

'Yes, Watson, I believe—'

But hardly were the words from his mouth when we heard a heavy footfall in the passage and a sharp rap on the door.

'This will be the girl's step-father,' said Holmes. 'He has written to say he would be here at a quarter after six. Come in!'

The man who entered was a sturdy, middle-sized fellow, about thirty years of age, clean-shaven, sallow-skinned, with a pair of most penetrating eyes. He placed his shiny top-hat on the sideboard, and with an insinuating bow sidled down into the nearest chair.

'I am assuming,' said Holmes, 'that you are Mr James Wynd-ham and' (holding up a type-written sheet) 'that this is the letter you wrote to me?'

'I am that person, sir, and the letter is mine. It was against my expressed wish, as you may know, that Miss van Allen contacted you in this matter. But she is an excitable young lady, and my wife and I will be happy to forgive her for such an impulsive action. Yet I must ask you to have nothing more to do with what is, unfortunately, a not uncommon misfortune. It is clear what took place, and I think it highly unlikely, sir, that even you will find so much as a single trace of Mr Darvill.'

'On the contrary,' replied Holmes quietly, 'I have reason to believe that I have already discovered the whereabouts of that gentleman.'

Mr Wyndham gave a violent start, and dropped his gloves. 'I am delighted to hear it,' he said in a strained voice.

'It is a most curious fact,' continued Holmes, 'that a type-writer has just as much individuality as does handwriting. Even when completely new, no two machines are exactly alike; and as they get older, some characters wear on this side and some on that. Now in this letter of yours, Mr Wyndham, you will note that in every instance there is some slight slurring in the eye of the "e"; and a most easily detectable defect in the tail of the "t".'

'All our office correspondence,' interrupted our visitor, 'is typed on the same machine, and I can fully understand why it has become a little worn.'

'But I have four other letters here,' resumed Holmes, in a slow and menacing tone, 'which purport to come from Mr Horatio Darvill. And in each of these, also, the "e"s are slurred, and the "t"s un-tailed.'

Mr Wyndham was out of his chair instantly and had snatched up his hat. 'I can waste no more of my valuable time with such trivialities, Mr Holmes. If you can catch the man who so shamefully treated Miss van Allen, then catch him! I wish you well— and ask you to let me know the outcome. But I have no interest whatsoever in your fantastical notions.'

Already, however, Holmes had stepped across the room and turned the key in the door. 'Certainly I will tell you how I caught Mr Darvill, if you will but resume your chair.'

'What?' shouted Wyndham, his face white, his small eyes dart-
ing about him like those of a rat in a trap. Yet finally he sat down
and glared aggressively around, as Holmes continued his analysis.

'It was as selfish and as heartless a trick as ever I encountered.
The man married a woman much older than himself, largely for
her money. In addition, he enjoyed the interest on the not incon-
siderable sum of the step-daughter's money, for as long as that
daughter lived with them. The loss of such extra monies would
have made a significant difference to the lifestyle adopted by the
newly married pair. Now the daughter herself was an amiable,
warm-hearted girl, and was possessed of considerable physical
attractions; and with the added advantage of a personal income, it
became clear that under normal circumstances she would not
remain single for very long. So he—the man of whom I speak—
decided to deny her the company and friendship of her contempo-
raries by keeping her at home. But she—and who shall blame her?
—grew restive under such an unnatural regimen, and firmly
announced her intention to attend a local ball. So what did her
step-father do? With the connivance of his wife, he conceived a
cowardly plan. He disguised himself cleverly: he covered those
sharp eyes with dully tinted spectacles; he masked that clean-
shaven face with bushy side-whiskers; he sank that clear voice of
his into the strained whisper of one suffering from the quinsy. And
then, feeling himself doubly secure because of the young lady's
short sight, he appeared *himself* at the ball, in the guise of one Horatio Darvill, and there he wooed the fair Miss van Allen for his
own—thereafter taking the further precaution of always arrang-
ing his assignations by candlelight.'

(I heard a deep groan which at the time I assumed to have come
from our visitor, but which, upon reflection, I am inclined to think
originated from Mycroft's corner.)

'Miss van Allen had fallen for her new beau; and no suspicion of
deception ever entered her pretty head. She was flattered by the
attention she was receiving, and the effect was heightened by the

admiration of her mother for the man. An "engagement" was agreed, and the deception perpetuated. But the pretended journeys abroad were becoming more difficult to sustain, and things had to be brought to a head quickly, although in such a *dramatic* way as to leave a permanent impression upon the young girl's mind. Hence the vows of fidelity sworn on the Testaments; hence the dark hints repeated on the very morning of the proposed marriage that something sinister might be afoot. James Wyndham, you see, wished his step-daughter to be so morally bound to her fictitious suitor that for a decade, at least, she would sit and wilt in Cowcross Street, and continue paying her regular interest directly into the account of her guardian: the same blackguard of a guardian who had brought her to the doors of St Saviour's and then, himself, conveniently disappeared by the age-old ruse of stepping in at one side of a four-wheeler—and out at the other.'

Rising to his feet, Wyndham fought hard to control his outrage. 'I wish you to know that it is you, sir, who is violating the law of this land—and not me! As long as you keep that door locked, and thereby hold me in this room against my will, you lay yourself open—'

'The law,' interrupted Holmes, suddenly unlocking and throwing open the door, 'may not for the moment be empowered to touch you. Yet never, surely, was there a man who deserved punishment more. In fact . . . since my hunting-crop is close at hand—' Holmes took two swift strides across the room; but it was too late. We heard a wild clatter of steps down the stairs as Wyndham departed, and then had the satisfaction of watching him flee pellmell down Baker Street.

'That cold-blooded scoundrel will end on the gallows, mark my words!' growled Holmes.

'Even now, though, I cannot follow all the steps in your reasoning, Holmes,' I remarked.

'It is this way,' replied Holmes. 'The only person who profited financially from the vanishing-trick—was the step-father. Then, the fact that the two men, Wyndham and Darvill, were never actually seen *together*, was most suggestive. As were the tinted spectacles, the husky voice, the bushy whiskers—all of these latter, Watson, hinting strongly at disguise. Again, the type-written signature betokened one thing only—that the man's handwriting was so familiar to Miss van Allen that she might easily recognize even a small sample of it. Isolated facts? Yes! But all of them leading to the same inevitable conclusion—as even my slumbering sibling might agree?'

But there was no sound from the Mycroft corner.

'You were able to verify your conclusion?' I asked.

Holmes nodded briskly. 'We know the firm for which Wyndham worked, and we had a full description of Darvill. I therefore eliminated from that description everything which could be the result of deliberate disguise—'

'Which means that you have *not* verified your conclusion!' Mycroft's sudden interjection caused us both to turn sharply towards him.

'There will always,' rejoined Holmes, 'be a need and a place for informed conjecture—'

'*Inspired* conjecture, Holmes,' I interposed.

'Phooey!' snorted Mycroft. 'You are talking of nothing but wild *guesswork*, Sherlock. And it is my opinion that in this case your guesswork is grotesquely askew.'

I can only report that never have I seen Holmes so taken aback; and he sat in silence as Mycroft raised his bulk from the chair and now stood beside the fireplace.

'Your deductive logic needs no plaudits from me, Sherlock, and like Dr Watson I admire your desperate hypothesis. But unless there is some firm evidence which you have thus far concealed from us . . . ?'

Holmes did not break his silence.

'Well,' stated Mycroft, 'I will indulge in a little guesswork of my own, and tell you that the gentleman who just stormed out of this room is as innocent as Watson here!'

'He certainly did not *act* like an innocent man,' I protested, looking in vain to Holmes for some support, as Mycroft continued.

'The reasons you adduce for your suspicions are perfectly sound in most respects, and yet—I must speak with honesty, Sherlock!— I found myself sorely disappointed with your reading—or rather complete misreading—of the case. You are, I believe, wholly correct in your central thesis that there is no such person as Horatio Darvill.' (How the blood was tingling in my veins as Mycroft spoke these words!) 'But when the unfortunate Mr Wyndham, who has just rushed one way up Baker Street, rushes back down it the other with a writ for defamation of character—as I fear he will!—then you will be compelled to think, to analyse, and to act, with a little more care and circumspection.'

Holmes leaned forward, the sensitive nostrils of that aquiline nose a little distended. But still he made no comment.

'For example, Sherlock, two specific pieces of information vouchsafed to us by the attractive Miss van Allen herself have been strongly discounted, if not wholly ignored, in your analysis.' (I noticed Holmes's eyebrows rising quizzically.) 'First, the fact that Mr Wyndham was older than Miss van Allen *only by some five years*. Second, the fact that Miss van Allen is so competent and speedy a performer on the type-writer that she works, on a free-lance basis, for several firms in the vicinity of her home, including Messrs Cook and Marchant. Furthermore, you make the astonishing claim that Miss van Allen was totally deceived by the disguise of Mr Darvill. Indeed, you would have her not only blind, but semi-senile into the bargain! Now it is perfectly true that the lady's eyesight is far from perfect—*glaucopia Athenica*, would you not diagnose, Dr Watson?—but it is quite ludicrous to believe that she would fail to recognize the person with whom she was living. And it is wholly dishonest of you to assert that the assignations were always held by candlelight, since on at least two occasions, the morning after the first meeting—the *morning*, Sherlock!—and the morning of the planned wedding ceremony, Miss van Allen had ample opportunity of studying the physical features of Darvill in the broadest of daylight.'

'You seem to me to be taking an unconscionably long time in putting forward your own hypothesis,' snapped Holmes, somewhat testily.

'You are right,' admitted the other. 'Let me beat about the bush no longer! You have never felt emotion akin to love for any woman, Sherlock—not even for the Adler woman—and you are therefore deprived of the advantages of those who like myself are able to understand both the workings of the male and also the female mind. Five years her superior in age—her step-father; *only five years*. Now one of the sadnesses of womankind is their tendency to age more quickly and less gracefully than men; and one of the truths about mankind in general is that if you put one of each sex, of roughly similar age, in reasonable proximity . . . And if one of them is the fair Miss van Allen—then you are inviting a packet of trouble. Yet such is what took place in the Wyndham ménage. Mrs Wyndham was seventeen years older than her young husband; and perhaps as time went by some signs and tokens of this disproportionate difference in their ages began to manifest themselves. At the same time, it may be assumed that Wyndham himself could not help being attracted—however much at first he sought to resist the temptation—by the very winsome and vivacious young girl who was his step-daughter. It would almost certainly have been Wyndham himself who introduced Miss van Allen to the part-time duties she undertook for Cook and Marchant—where the two of them were frequently thrown together, away from the restraints of wife and home, and with a result which it is not at all difficult to guess. Certain it is, in my own view, that Wyndham sought to transfer his affections from the mother to the daughter; and in due course it was the daughter who decided that whatever her own affections might be in the matter she must in all honour leave her mother and step-father. Hence the great anxiety to get out to dances and parties and the

like—activities which Wyndham objected to for the obvious reason that he wished to have Miss van Allen as close by himself for as
long as he possibly could. Now you, Sherlock, assume that this
objection arose as a result of the interest accruing from the New
Zealand securities—and you are *guessing*, are you not? Is it not just
possible that Wyndham has money of his own—find out, brother!
—and that what he craves for is not some petty addition to his
wealth, but the love of a young woman with whom he has fallen
rather hopelessly in love? You see, she took *him* in, just as she took
you in, Sherlock—for you swallowed everything that calculating
little soul reported.'

'Really, this is outrageous!' I objected—but Holmes held up his
hand, and bid me hear his brother out.

'What is clear, is that at some point when Wyndham was in
France—and why did you not verify those dates spent abroad? I am
sure Cook and Marchant would have provided them just as quickly
as it furnished the wretched man's description. But as I was saying,
with Wyndham in France, mother and daughter found themselves
in a little *tête-à-tête* one evening, during the course of which a whole
basketful of dirty linen was laid bare, with the daughter bitterly disil-
lusioned about the behaviour of her step-father, and the mother hurt
and angry about her husband's infidelity. So, together, the pair of
them devised a plan. Now, we both agree on one thing at least, Sherlock! There appears to be no evidence whatsoever for the independent existence of Horatio Darvill except for what we have heard
from Miss van Allen's lips. Rightly, you drew our attention to the fact
that the two men were never seen together. But, alas, having appreciated the *importance* of that clue, you completely misconceived its *sig-
nificance*. *You* decided that there is no Darvill—because he is
Wyndham. *I* have to tell you that there is no Darvill—*because he is
the pure fabrication of the minds of Mrs Wyndham and her daughter.*'

Holmes was staring with some consternation at a pattern in the
carpet, as Mycroft rounded off his extravagant and completely
baseless conjectures.

'Letters were written—and incidentally I myself would have been far more cautious about those "e"s and "t"s: twin faults, as it happens, of my very own machine! But, as I say, letters were written —*but by Miss van Allen herself*; a wedding was arranged; a story concocted of a non-existent carriage into which there climbed a non-existent groom—and that was the end of the charade. Now, it was you, Sherlock, who rightly asked the key question: *cui bono*? And you concluded that the real beneficiary was Wyndham. But exactly the contrary is the case! It was the mother and daughter who intended to be the beneficiaries, for they hoped to rid themselves of the rather wearisome Mr Wyndham—but not before he had been compelled, by moral and social pressures, to make some handsome money-settlement upon the pair of them—especially perhaps upon the young girl who, as Dr Watson here points out, could well have done with some decent earrings and a new handkerchief. And the *social* pressure I mention, Sherlock, was designed—carefully and cleverly designed—to come from *you*. A cock-and-bull story is told to you by some wide-eyed young thing, a story so bestrewn with clues at almost every point that even Lestrade—given a week or two!—would probably have come up with a diagnosis identical with your own. And why do you think she came to you, and not to Lestrade, say? Because "Mr Sherlock Holmes is the greatest investigator the world has ever known"—and his judgements are second only to the Almighty's in their infallibility. For if you, Sherlock, believed Wyndham to be guilty—then Wyndham *was* guilty in the eyes of the whole world—the whole world except for one, that is.'

'Except for two,' I added quietly.

Mycroft Holmes turned his full attention towards me for the first time, as though I had virtually been excluded from his previous audience. But I allowed him no opportunity of seeking the meaning of my words, as I addressed him forthwith.

'I asked Holmes a question when he presented his own analysis, sir. I will ask you the same: have you in any way verified your hypothesis? And if so, how?'

'The answer, Dr Watson, to the first part of your question is, in large measure, "yes". Mr Wyndham, in fact, has quite enough money to be in no way embarrassed by the withdrawal of Miss van Allen's comparatively minor contribution. As for the second part ...' Mycroft hesitated awhile. 'I am not sure what my brother has told you of the various offices I hold under the British Crown—'

It was Holmes who intervened—and impatiently so. 'Yes, yes, Mycroft! Let us all concede immediately that the, shall we say, "unofficial" sources to which you are privy have completely invalidated my own reconstruction of the case. So be it! Yet I would wish, if you allow, to make one or two observations upon your own rather fanciful interpretation of events? It is, of course, with full justice that you accuse me of having no first-hand knowledge of what are called "the matters of the heart". Furthermore, you rightly draw attention to the difficulties Mr Wyndham would have experienced in deceiving his step-daughter. Yet how you under-rate the power of disguise! And how, incidentally, you *over-rate* the intelligence of Lestrade! Even Dr Watson, I would suggest, has a brain considerably superior—'

For not a second longer could I restrain myself. 'Gentlemen!' I cried. 'You are both—*both* of you!—most tragically wrong.'

The two brothers stared at me as though I had taken leave of my senses.

'I think you should seek to explain yourself, Watson,' said Holmes sharply.

'A man,' I began, 'was proposing to go to Scotland for a fortnight with his newly married wife, and he had drawn out one hundred pounds in cash—no less!—from the Oxford Street branch of the Royal National Bank on the eve of his wedding. The man, however, was abducted after entering a four-wheeler on the very morning of his wedding-day, was brutally assaulted, and then robbed of all his money and personal effects—thereafter being dumped, virtually for dead, in a deserted alley in Stepney. Quite by chance he was discovered later that same evening, and taken to the

Whitechapel Hospital. But it was only after several days that the man slowly began to recover his senses, and some patches of his memory—and also, gentlemen, his *voice*. For, you see, it was partly because the man was suffering so badly from what we medical men term "suppurative tonsilitis"—the quinsy, as it is commonly known—that he was transferred to St Thomas's where, as you know, Holmes, I am at present engaged in some research on that very subject, and where my own professional opinion was sought only this morning. Whilst reading through the man's hospital notes, I could see that the only clue to his identity was a tag on an item of his underclothing carrying the initials "H. D." You can imagine my excitement—'

'Humphry Davey, perhaps,' muttered Mycroft flippantly.

'Oh no!' I replied, with a smile. 'I persisted patiently with the poor man, and finally he was able to communicate to me the name of his bank. After that, if I may say so, Holmes, it was almost child's play to verify *my* hypothesis. I visited the bank, where I learned about the withdrawal of money for the honeymoon, and the manager himself accompanied me back to St Thomas's where he was able to view the patient and to provide quite unequivocal proof as to his identity. I have to inform you, therefore, that not only does Mr Horatio Darvill exist, gentlemen, he is at this precise moment lying in a private ward on the second floor of St Thomas's Hospital!'

For some little while a silence fell upon the room. Then I saw Holmes, who these last few minutes had been standing by the window, give a little start. 'Oh, no!' he groaned. And looking over his shoulder I saw, dimly beneath the fog-beshrouded lamplight, an animated Mr Wyndham talking to a legal-looking gentleman who stood beside him.

Snatching up his cape, Holmes made hurriedly for the door. 'Please tell Mr Wyndham, if you will, Watson, that I have already written a letter to him containing a complete recantation of my earlier charges, and offering him my profound apologies. For the present, I am leaving—by the back door.'

He was gone. And when, a minute later, Mrs Hudson announced that two angry-looking gentlemen had called asking to see Mr Holmes, I noticed Mycroft seemingly asleep once more in his corner armchair, a monograph on polyphonic plainchant open on his knee, and a smile of vague amusement on his large, intelligent face.

'Show the gentlemen in, please, Mrs Hudson!' I said—in such peremptory fashion that for a moment or two that good lady stared at me, almost as if she had mistaken my voice for that of Sherlock Holmes himself.

THE
INSIDE STORY

PART ONE

Dido attempted to raise her heavy eyes again,
but failed; and the deep wound gurgled in her breast.

(Virgil, *Aeneid* IV, 688–9)

'Get a *move* on!'

'I'll get there as fast as I can, sir—I always do.'

'And what's *that* supposed to mean?'

Lewis turned left at Carfax, down into the High, and then over Magdalen Bridge, car siren wailing, before driving past the Asian grocers' shops and the Indian restaurants in the Cowley Road.

'I mean,' replied Lewis finally, 'that here we are with another murder, and *you*'ll get there, won't you? You always do.'

'Nearly always,' conceded Morse.

'And *I* won't. I've got a second-class mind—'

'Don't underrate yourself, Lewis! Let others do it for you.'

Lewis grunted humourlessly. 'I'm like a second-class stamp, and well you know it.'

'But second-class stamps usually get there in the end.'

'Exactly. Just take a dickens of a lot longer—'

'Slow down!'

Morse had been consulting an Oxford street plan, and now jabbed a finger to his right.

'That's it, Lewis: Jowett Place. What number did you say?'

'Probably where those two police cars are parked, sir.'

Morse grinned weakly. 'Maintain that level of deductive brilliance, Lewis, and we'll be through this case before the pubs are open.'

It was 8.50 on the dull, intermittently drizzly morning of Monday, 15 February 1993.

The Oxford City Police had contacted Kidlington CID an hour or so earlier after receiving a 999 call from one Paul Bayley, first-floor tenant of the narrow, two-storey property that stood at 14 Jowett Place. Bayley, an erstwhile History graduate from Magdalen College, Oxford, had found himself out of milk that morning—had walked downstairs—knocked on the door of the woman tenant directly below him, Ms Sheila Poster—had found the door unlocked—and there . . .

Or so he said.

Morse looked down at the fully dressed woman lying just inside the ground-floor living room, the left arm extended, the pleasingly manicured fingernails straining, it appeared, to reach the door. Beneath and in front of the body was a distressingly copious pool of dully matted blood; and although the weapon had been removed it was possible even for such a non-medical man as Morse to unjumble the simple truth that the woman had most probably been stabbed through the heart. Longish dark curls framed the pale face—from which the large brown eyes now stared, for ever fixedly, at a threadbare square of the lime-green carpet.

'Lovely looking girl,' said Lewis quietly.

Morse averted his eyes from the terrible sight, glanced across to the curtained window, then stepped outside the room into the narrow hallway, where Dr Laura Hobson, the police pathologist, stood in subdued conference with a scene-of-crime officer.

'She's all yours,' said Morse, in a tone suggesting that the abdication of responsibility for the body was something of a relief. As indeed it was, for Morse had always recoiled from the sight of violent death.

❧

'Funny name—"Poster"!' volunteered Lewis as the two detectives stepped up the narrow stairs of number 14.

'Is it?' asked Morse, his voice betraying no real interest in the matter.

Bayley was sitting beside a police constable in his untidy living room—a large-buttocked, lank-haired, yet handsome sort of fellow, in his late twenties perhaps; unshaven, pony-tailed, with a small earring in his left ear. To whom, predictably, Morse took an instant and intense dislike.

He had been out drinking (Bayley claimed) throughout most of the previous evening, not leaving the King's Arms in Broad Street until closing time. After which he'd gone back to a friend's flat to continue the celebrations, and in fact had slept there—before returning to Jowett Place at about a quarter past seven that morning. The rest he'd already told the police, OK?

As he gave his evidence, Bayley's hands were nervously opening and closing the Penguin translation of Virgil's *Aeneid*, and Morse noted (again with distaste) the lines of ingrained dirt beneath the fingernails.

'You slept with a woman last night?'

Bayley nodded, eyes downcast.

'We shall have to know her name—my sergeant here will have to check with her. You understand that?'

Again Bayley nodded. 'I suppose so, yes.'

'You didn't leave her at all?'

'Went to the loo coupla times.'

'You in the habit of sleeping around?'

'I wouldn't put it like that, no.'

'Ever sleep with—with the woman downstairs?'

'Sheila? No, never.'

'Ever ask her?'

'Once.'

'And?'

'She said if we were going to have a relationship it would have to be cerebral—not conjugal.'

'Quite a way with words she had, then?'

'You could say that.'

'When did you last speak to her?'

'Week or so ago? We were talking—*she* was talking—about epic poetry. She . . . lent me this . . . this book. I was going to give it back to her . . . today.'

Lewis looked away in some embarrassment as a curtain of tears now covered Bayley's eyes; but for a while longer Morse himself continued to stare cynically at the young man seated opposite him.

Downstairs, in the second of the two rooms which (along with the kitchen) were offered for rent at 14 Jowett Place, Morse contemplated the double bed in which, presumably, the murdered tenant had usually slumbered overnight. Two fluffy pillows concealed a full-length, bottle-green nightdress, which Morse now fingered lightly before turning back the William-Morris-patterned duvet and examining the undersheet.

'No sign of any recent nocturnal emissions, sir.'

'You have a genteel way of putting things,' said Morse.

The room was sparsely furnished, sparely ornamented—with a large mahogany wardrobe taking up most of the space left by the bed. On the bedside table stood a lamp; an alarm clock; a box containing half a dozen items of cheap jewellery; and a single book: *Reflections on Inspiration and Creativity*, by Diogenes Small (Macmillan, £14.99).

Picking up the latter, Morse opened its pages at the point where a blue leather bookmarker ('Greetings from Erzincan') had been placed—and then with no obvious enthusiasm read aloud the few sentences which had been highlighted in the text with a yellow felt-tipped pen:

Obviously our writer will draw upon character and incident taken from personal experience. Inevitably so. Laudibly so. Yet always it is those *fictional* addenda which will effect the true alchemy; which will elevate our earth-bound artist, and send him forth high-floating on the wings of freedom and creativity.

'Bloody 'ell!'

'Pardon, sir?'

'Can't even spell,' muttered Morse, as Lewis picked up the bookmarker.

'Where's Erzincan?'

'Dunno. When I was at school we had to do one of the three "G"s: Greek, German, or Geography.'

'And you didn't do Geography . . .'

But a silent Morse was standing now at the window (curtains drawn back) which looked out onto a patch of leaf-carpeted lawn at the rear of the house. Strangely, something had stirred deep down in his mind, like the opening chords of *Das Rheingold*; chords that for the moment, though, remained below his audial range.

Lewis opened the wardrobe doors, exposing a modest collection of dresses and coats hanging from the rail; and half a dozen pairs of cheap shoes stowed neatly along the bottom.

Overhead they heard the creaking of floorboards as someone— must be Bayley?—paced continuously to and fro. And Morse's eyes rose slowly to the ceiling.

But he said nothing.

Neither the bedroom nor the kitchen had yielded anything of significant interest; and Morse was anxious to hear Dr Hobson's verdict, however tentative, when half an hour later she emerged from the murder-room.

'Sharp knife by the look of things—second attempt—probably entering from above. Bled an awful lot—as you saw . . . still, most of us would—with the knife-blade through the heart. Shouldn't be too difficult to be fairly precise about the time—I'll be having a closer look, of course—but I'd guess, say, eight to ten hours ago? No longer, I don't think. Eleven o'clock, twelve o'clock last night?'

'After the pubs had closed.'

'*She* hadn't been drinking, Inspector.'

'Oh!'

Morse placed his hand lightly on the young pathologist's shoulder and thanked her. Her eyes looked interesting—and interested. Sometimes Morse thought he could fall in love with Laura Hobson; and sometimes he thought he couldn't.

It was almost midday before Morse gave the order for the body to be removed. The scene-of-crime personnel had finished their work, and a thick, transparent sheeting had now been laid across the carpet. Lewis, with two DCs, had long since been despatched to cover the preliminary tasks: to check Bayley's alibi, to question the neighbours, and to discover whatever they could of Sheila Poster's past. And Morse himself now stood alone, and gazed around the room in which Sheila Poster had been murdered.

Almost immediately, however, it was apparent that little was likely to be found. The eight drawers of the modern desk which stood against the inside wall were completely empty; with the almost inevitable conclusion to be drawn that the murderer had systematically emptied the contents of each, as well as whatever had stood on the desk-top, into ... well, into something—black plastic bag, say? And then disappeared into the night; in gloves, like as not, for Morse had learned that no extraneous prints had been discovered—only those left almost everywhere by the murdered tenant. The surfaces of the desk, the shelving, the furniture, the window—all had been dutifully daubed and dusted with fingerprint powder; but it seemed highly improbable that such a methodical murderer had left behind any easily legible signature.

No handbag, either; no documents of any sort; nothing.

Or was there?

Above the desk, hanging by a cord from the picture-rail, was a plywood board, some thirty inches square, on which ten items were fixed by multicoloured drawing-pins: five Medici reproductions of well-known paintings (including two Pre-Raphaelites); a manuscript facsimile of Keats's 'Ode to a Nightingale'; a postcard showing the death-mask of Tutankhamun; a photograph of a kingfisher, a large fish balanced in its mouth, perched on a 'No Fishing' sign; a printed invitation to a St Hilda's Old Girls' evening in March 1993; and a leaflet announcing a crime short-story competition organized by Oxfordshire County Libraries: 'First prize £1,000—Judges Julian Symons and H. R. F. Keating—Final date 10 April 1993'.

Huh! Still seven weeks to go. But there'd now be no entry from Sheila Poster, would there, Morse?

He methodically unpinned each of the cards and turned them over. Four were blank—obviously purchased for decorative purposes. But two had brief messages written on them. On the Egyptian card, in what Morse took to be a masculine hand, were the words: 'Cairo's bloody hot but wish you were here—B.' And on the back of Collins's 'Convent Thoughts', in what Morse took to be a feminine hand: 'On a weekend retreat! I knew I wouldn't miss men. But I do!! Susan.'

On each side of the boarded-up fireplace were five bookshelves, their contents systematically stacked in order: Austen novels, top left, Wordsworth poems, bottom right. Housman's *Collected Poems* suddenly caught Morse's eye, and he extracted his old hero, the book falling open immediately at 'Last Poems' XXVI, where a postcard (another one) had been inserted: the front showing a photograph of streets in San Jose (so it said) and, on the back, a couplet written out in black Biro:

> And wide apart lie we, my love,
> And seas between the twain.

>   (7.v.92)

Morse smiled to himself, for the poem from which the lines were taken had been part of his own mental furniture for many moons.

Yet so very soon the smile had become a frown. He'd seen that same handwriting only a few seconds since, surely? He unpinned the postcard from Cairo again; and, yes, the handwriting was more than a reasonable match.

So what?

So what, Morse? Yet for many seconds his eyes were as still as the eyes that stared from the mask of Tutankhamun.

Lewis came briskly into the room twenty minutes later, promptly reading from his note-book:

'Sheila Emily Poster; second-class honours degree in English from St Hilda's 1990; aged twenty-five—comes from Bristol; Dad died in 'eighty-four—Hodgkin's disease; Mum in a special home there—Alzheimer's; only child; worked for a while with the University Geology Department in the reference section; here in this property almost ten months—£490 a month; £207 in the Building Society; £69.40 in her current account at Lloyds.'

'You can get interest on current accounts these days, did you know that, Lewis?'

'Useful thing for you to know, sir.'

'You've been quick.'

'Easy! Bursar of St Hilda's, DSS, Lloyds Bank—no problems. Murder does help sometimes, doesn't it?'

A sudden splash of rain hatched the front window and Morse stared out at the melancholy day:

> 'I know not if it rains, my love,
>   In the land where you do lie . . .'

'Pardon, sir?'

But Morse seemed not to hear. 'There's all this stuff here, Lewis

. . .' Morse pointed vaguely to the piles of magazines lying around. 'You'd better have a look through.'

'Can't we get somebody else—'

'No!' thundered Morse. 'I need help—*your* help, Lewis. For Chrissake get on with it!'

Far from any annoyance, Lewis felt a secret contentment. In only one respect was he unequivocally in a class of his own as a police officer, he knew that: for there was only one person with whom the curmudgeonly Morse could ever work with any kind of equanimity—and that was himself, Lewis.

He now settled therefore with his accustomed measure of commitment to the fourth-grade clerical chore of sorting through the piles of women's magazines, fashion journals, brochures, circulars, and the like, that were stacked on the floor-space in the two alcoves of the living room.

He was still working when just over an hour later Morse returned from his lunchtime ration of calories, taken entirely in liquid form.

'Found anything?'

Lewis shook his head. 'One or two amusing bits, though.'

'Well? Let's share the joke. Life's grim enough.'

Lewis looked back into one of the piles, found a copy of the *Oxford Gazette* (May 1992), and read from the back page:

CLEANER REQUIRED

Three mornings per week
Hourly rate negotiable
Graduate preferred

Morse was unimpressed. 'We're all of us overqualified in Oxford.'

'Not *all* of us.'

'How long will you be?'

'Another half-hour or so.'

'I'll leave you then.'

'What'll you be doing, sir?'

'I'll still be thinking. See you back at HQ.'

Morse walked out again, down Cowley Road to the Plain; over Magdalen Bridge, along the High, and then up Catte Street to the Broad; and was standing, undecided for a few seconds, in front of Blackwell's book shop and the narrow frontage of the adjoining White Horse ('Open All Day')—when the idea suddenly struck him.

He caught a taxi from St Giles' out to Kidlington. Not to Police HQ though, but to 45 Blenheim Close, the address given on the leaflet advertising the Oxfordshire short-story competition.

'You're a bit premature, really,' suggested Rex De Lincto, the short, fat, balding, slightly deaf Chairman of the Oxford Book Association. 'There's still about a couple of months to go and we'll only receive most of the entries in the last week or so.'

'You've had *some* already, though?'

'Nine.'

De Lincto walked over to a cabinet, took out a handwritten list of names, and passed it across.

1	IAN BRADLEY
2	EMMA SKIPPER
3	VALERIE WARD
4	JIM MORWOOD
5	CHRISTINA COLLINS
6	UNA BROSHOLA
7	ELISSA THORPE
8	RICHARD ELVES
9	MARY ANN COTTON

Morse scanned the list, his attention soon focusing on the last name.

'Odd,' he mumbled.

'Pardon?'

'Mary Ann Cotton. Same name as that of a woman hanged in Durham jail in the 1880s.'

'So?'

'And look at *her*!' Morse's finger pointed to number five, Christina Collins. 'She got herself murdered up on the canal in Staffordshire somewhere. Surely!'

'I'm not quite with you, Inspector.'

'Do you get phoney names sometimes?'

'Well, you can't tell, really, can you? I mean, if you say you're Donald Duck—'

Morse nodded. 'You *are* Donald Duck.'

'You'd perhaps use a *nom de plume* if you were an established author . . .'

'But this competition's only for first-timers, isn't it?'

'You've been reading the small print, Inspector.'

'But how do you know who they are if they've won?'

'We don't sometimes. Not for a start. But every entrant sends an address.'

'I see.'

Morse looked again at the list, and suddenly the blood was running cold in his veins. The clues, or some of them, were beginning to lock together in his mind: the short-story leaflet; the advice of Diogenes Small, that guru of creative writing; the book that young Bayley had borrowed . . . the translation of Virgil's *Aeneid*, in which Dido, the queen of Carthage, had fallen in love with Aeneas and then stabbed herself in her despair . . . Dido . . . known also by an alternative name—Elissa!

Morse took out a pencil and lightly made twelve oblique strokes through each letter of ELISSA THORPE, in what seemed to De Lincto a wholly random order; but an order which in Morse's

mind spelled out in sequence the letters of the name SHEILA
POSTER.

Morse rose to his feet and looked across at the cabinet. 'You'd
better let me have story number seven, if you will, sir.'

'Of course. And if I may say so, you've made a very good choice,
Inspector.'

Only one message was awaiting Morse when he returned to his
office at HQ: Dr Hobson had called to say that Sheila Poster was
about twelve weeks pregnant. But Morse paid scant attention to
this new information, for there was something he had to do immediately.

He therefore sat back comfortably in the old black-leather
armchair.

And read a story.

PART TWO

Yet always it is those *fictional* addenda which will effect the true alchemy.

(Diogenes Small, *Reflections on Inspiration and Creativity*)

The story (printed verbatim here) which Morse now began to read was cleanly typed and carefully presented.

I'd seen the advert in the Gazette.
She was going to be a woman who walked silent and unsmiling through any door held open for her; a woman who would speak in a loud voice over the counter at a bank; a woman conscious of her congenital superiority over her fellow beings.
In short she was going to be a North Oxford lady.
And she was—a double-barrelled one.

I was gratified though surprised that my carefully worded application had been considered and I caught the bus in good time.
At 10.30 a.m. to the minute I walked along the flagged path that bisected the weedless front lawn and knocked at the door of The Grange in Squitchey Lane.
A quarter of an hour later, after a last mouthful of some bitter-tasting coffee, I'd landed the job.
How?
I wasn't sure, not then. But when she asked me if I'd enjoyed the coffee, I said I preferred a cup of instant, and she'd smiled thinly.
'That's what my husband says.'

I hoped my voice showed an appropriate interest.

'Your husband?'

'He's abroad. The Americans are picking his brains.'

She stood up.

'Do you know why I've offered you the job?'

It was a bit risky but I said it: 'No one else applied?'

'I'm not surprised you have a degree. You're quite bright really.'

'Thank you.'

'You need the money, I suppose?'

I lowered my eyes to the deep Wilton and nodded.

'Goodbye,' she said.

I left her standing momentarily there at the front door—slim, elegantly dressed, and young—well, comparatively young.

And, yes, I ought to admit it, uncommonly attractive.

The tasks allotted to me could only just be squeezed into the nine hours a week I spent at The Grange.

But £36 was £36.

And that was a bonus.

Can you guess what I'm saying? Not yet?

You will.

Two parts of the house I was forbidden to enter: the master bedroom (remember that bedroom!) and the master's study—the latter by the look of it a large converted bedroom on the upstairs floor whose door was firmly closed.

Firmly locked, as I soon discovered.

There was no such embargo on the mistress's study—a fairly recent addition at the rear of the house in the form of a semi-conservatory, its shelves surfaces and floor all crammed with books and littered with loose papers and typescripts. And dozens of house-plants fighting for a little Lebensraum.

I was invariably fascinated with the place as I carefully (too carefully) watered the plants, replaced the books in alphabetical order, shuffled untidy piles into tidy piles, and carefully (too carefully) hoovered the carpeted floor and dusted around.

I love charging around with a duster. It's one of the only jobs I do where I can actually see a result.

And I like seeing a result . . .

There was only one thing wrong with that room.

The cat.

I hate all cats but especially <u>this</u> cat, which occasionally looked at me in a mysterious knowing aristocratic potentially ferocious manner.

Like his mistress.

A small two-way cat-flap had been cut into the door leading from the conservatory to the rear garden through which the frequently filthy-pawed 'Boswell' (huh!) would make his exits and his entrances.

Ah, but bless you, Boswell!

I felt confident that Mrs Spencer-Gilbey could not have taken up my single reference since from the beginning she called me 'Virginia' without the slightest hint of suspicion.

For my part, I called her 'ma'am', to rhyme with 'jam'. It was five syllables shorter than any more formal address, and I think the royal connotation was somewhat pleasing to her.

Early on the Wednesday morning of my third week the amateurish tack-tack-tack of the typewriter in the conservatory stopped and my employer came through into the downstairs lounge to inform me she had to go out for two hours.

It was at that point I made my first bold move.

I took a leather-bound volume from the bookshelf beside me and blew a miniature dust-storm along the golden channel at the top of its pages.

'Would you like me to give the books a wipe with a duster?'

For a few seconds I thought I saw in those cold grey eyes of hers something very close to hatred.

'If you can put them all back exactly as you found them.'

'I'll try, ma'am.'

'Don't try. <u>Do</u> it!'

It was going to be a big job.

Bookshelves lined three whole sides of the room, and at mid-morning I had a coffee-break in the kitchen.

Outside by the garden shed I saw the steatopygous odd-job man who appeared intermittently—usually when I was leaving—to fix a few things as I supposed.

I held my coffee-cup up to the window and my eyes asked him if he'd care to join me.

His eyes replied yes and I saw he was younger than I had thought.

More handsome too.

I asked him how well he knew her ladyship but he merely shrugged.

'She's writing a book, did you know?' I asked.

'Really?'

He took a swallow of his coffee and I saw that his hands though grubby enough were not those of a manual labourer.

'On Sir Thomas Wyatt,' I continued. 'I had a look when I was hoovering.'

'Really?'

If his vocabulary seemed rather limited, his eyes ranged over me more widely, and he smiled in a curiously fascinating way.

'I don't suppose you know much about Sir Thomas Wyatt?'

He shrugged again. 'Not much. But if you're going to tell me he died in 1542, you'll be wasting your time, won't you?'

Jesus!

He smiled again, this time at my discomfiture; then leaned forward and kissed me fully on the lips.

'Are you on the pill?'

'It's all right. You see, I'm pregnant,' I replied.

❖

Afterwards we dared to have a cigarette together. It was the first I'd smoked for six months and it tasted foul.

Stupid!

His lighter was out of fuel and I used one of the extra-long Bryant & May matches kept in the kitchen for various purposes.

For various purposes . . .

I'd almost finished the second wall of bookshelves when milady came back.

Just after I had turned round to acknowledge her presence a single sheet of paper fluttered to the floor.

Quickly I bent down to pick it up but she was immediately beside me, snatching it from my hand.

It was only a brief note and its contents could be read almost at a glance:

> Darling J
> Please do try to keep these few lines
> somewhere as a memento of my love?

The message had been typed on cheap thin paper with the signatory's name written in light-blue Biro —'Marie', the 'i' completed in girlish fashion with a largish ring instead of the usual dot.

But Mrs S-G said nothing, and half an hour later I was on my way home—unobtrusively as ever.

I had advertised to no one the fact that I was working as a part-time charwoman and I took care to be seen by as few people as possible.

There were reasons for this. You will see.

The following Monday I asked Mrs S-G if I could vary my time slightly and start half an hour earlier.

'Do you <u>have</u> to?' Her voice was contemptuous of the request.

'It's just that if I caught the earlier bus—'

'Oh, don't <u>explain</u>, for heaven's sake! Do you <u>have</u> to?—that's all I asked.'

I said I did, and it was agreed that I should henceforth begin at 8.30 a.m.

On Friday of that same week the postman called at 8.50 a.m., and three letters seemed to slither through the front door: a communication from British Telecom; a letter addressed to Mrs S-G, marked 'Strictly Private'; and a letter for Mr S-G, the name and address written in light-blue Biro, the 'i' of 'Squitchey' completed in girlish fashion with a largish ring instead of the usual dot.

Even as I picked up the letters I knew that my employer was just behind me.

'Thank you. I'll take them.'

Her manner was offensively brusque. But I made no demur and continued wiping the skirting boards around the entrance hall.

'I'm sorry,' I said (it was the following Wednesday), 'but I shan't be able to come on Friday.'

'Oh?'

'You see I've got to go to the ante-natal clinic . . .'

'Don't <u>explain</u>, for heaven's sake. I thought I'd told you that before.'

'You did, yes.'

She said no more.

Nor did I.

The phone was seldom used at The Grange but that morning I heard her ring up someone from the conservatory.

I stood close to the door and tried hard to listen but the only part of the proceedings I caught was 'Saturday night . . .'

⚜

My appointment at the hospital was for 10.30 a.m.
but an emergency put the morning's programme back by
about an hour.

During the wait I read a few articles from various
magazines, including an interview with an old gar-
dener now aged one hundred who claimed that for getting rid of dandelions there was nothing quite so
effective as arsenic, a small quantity of which he
always kept in his garden shed.

Was it at this point I began to think of getting
rid of Mrs S-G? Along with the dandelions?

I suppose I'd already pondered the problems likely
to face unmarried mums. Problems so often caused by
married dads.

What really irks me more than anything, though, is
all that sickening spiel they come up with. You
know, about not wanting anyone to get hurt. Above
all not wanting the little <u>wife</u> to get hurt.

Hypocrites!

It was my turn for receiving letters on the Thursday of the following week. Two of them.

The first was from the hospital. I was fine. The
baby was fine. I felt almost happy.

The second was from the father of my child, with
the postmark 'Los Angeles'.

Here's the bit I want you to read:

Haven't you heard of women's equal rights and
responsibilities, you stupid girl? Yes, of
course there's such a thing as a condom. OK! And
there's also such a thing as the pill! What did
you think you were playing at? But that's all
water under the bridge. Abortion's the only
answer. I'll foot the bill on condition there's

a complete break between us. Things can't go on like this. I land at Heathrow at lunchtime on Saturday 13th, so we can meet next Sunday. Let's say the usual—twelve noon in the back room of the Bird and Baby. Please be there—for both our sakes.

How nice and cosy that would be!

And I would be there, perhaps.

Yes, there was a chance that I would be there.

The following day, Friday, was to be my last in employment as a cleaning lady, and that morning I put the finishing touches to my plan.

Originally I had intended to kill only Mrs S-G. But my terms of reference had now widened.

That same afternoon I acted in an uncharacteristically careless way. I wrote a letter to my former employer:

Dear Mrs S-G

I was grateful to you for employing me but I shall not be coming to work for you again.

My circumstances have changed significantly in the past few days.

I am sure you will not have any difficulty in finding a replacement.

Yours

Virginia

It would have been tit-for-tat in the resignation-dismissal stakes. But I didn't post the letter that day.

Nor the next.

Mrs S-G however had clearly been better stocked with first-class stamps and her letter lay on the hall-mat the following morning, Saturday 13th, with mine still propped up against the Kellogg's packet on the kitchen table.

❧

Dear Marie Lawson,

Oh yes I do know your real name and I made no
attempt to take up your bogus reference. At
first I thought you were quite bright and I told
you so. But in truth you must be as stupid as
you obviously consider me to be. I was curious
about why you'd applied and it amused me to
offer you the job. So I watched you. And all the
time you thought you were watching me! You see
my husband told me all about your affair
although I didn't know you were pregnant. Nor,
as it happens, do I believe you are. The cha-
rades with the note and the letter were prettily
performed yet really quite unnecessary. I
steamed open the letter as no doubt you wished
me to in what (I have to assume) was your futile
plan for bringing matters out into the open. I
made a photocopy of the letter and forwarded
your pathetic plea to America. I think the real
reason for my writing—apart from giving you the
sack—is to thank you for those two pieces of
evidence you provided. I am informed by my
lawyer that they will significantly expedite the
divorce proceedings I shall be bringing against
my husband. After that I expect my own life to
turn into happier paths, and I trust that if I
later re-marry I shall be more fortunate with my
second husband than I was with the man who
amused himself with a whole host of harlots
besides yourself.
V. Spencer-Gilbey (Mrs)

Stupid.
Both of them had called me stupid.

On that same Saturday night—or rather in the early
hours of the Sunday morning—I waited with great
patience for the light to be switched off in the
master bedroom. (You remember it?)

If they were not in the same bed at least they were in the same bedroom, since I had seen the two figures silhouetted several times behind the curtains.

I further waited one whole hour, to the minute, before moving soundlessly along the side of the house and then into the rear garden where I stooped down beside the conservatory door.

Good old Boswell! (Remember him?) I almost hoped he'd decided to sleep out in the open that night.

I struck one of the extra-large Bryant & May matches. (Remember them?) And shielding the flame I pushed my hand slowly through the cat-flap.

Behind the glass-panelled door I could see the loose sheets of paper (so carefully stacked) catching light almost immediately.

No more than ten seconds later I felt rather than heard the sudden 'whoosh' of some powerful updraught as a tongue of flame licked viciously at the items (so carefully stacked) beside the conservatory door.

The colour of the blaze reminded me so very much of Boswell's eyes.

I departed swiftly via the front path before turning round fifty or so yards down the road.

The window of the master bedroom was still in darkness. But at the rear of the house I had the impression that although it was still only 2.15 a.m. the rosy-fingered dawn was beginning to break already.

It was big news.

Headlined in Monday's edition of <u>The Oxford Mail</u>, for example, I read:

TWO DIE IN NORTH OXFORD INFERNO

It seems unlikely that the burned-out shell of the listed thatch-and-timber property in Squitchey Lane (picture p. 2) will provide too many clues to the cause of the fire. The blaze spread with such rapid intensity that . . .

My eyes skipped on to the next paragraph:

> The remains of two bodies, charred beyond all
> chance of recognition, have been recovered from
> a first-floor bedroom and it is feared that
> these are the bodies of Mr J. Spencer-Gilbey and
> of his wife Valerie. Mr Spencer-Gilbey had just
> returned from America where . . .

But I wasn't really interested about where.

So I turned to look at the picture on page two.

It hadn't after all seemed worthwhile to turn up
at the Bird and Baby the previous day. So I hadn't
gone.

You can see why.

The fire was still big (bigger) news in the Tuesday evening's edition of The Oxford Mail:

BLAZE MYSTERY DEEPENS

The Oxford City Police were amazed to receive
a call late yesterday evening from Heathrow. The
caller was Mr John Spencer-Gilbey who, it had
been assumed, had perished with his wife in the
fire which completely destroyed their home in
Squitchey Lane, Oxford, in the early hours of
Sunday morning.

Mr Spencer-Gilbey had been expected back in
England on Saturday from a lecture tour in America. However it now appears that industrial
action by air-traffic controllers on the western
seaboard of America had effected the cancella-
tion of the original flight, and Mr Spencer-
Gilbey told the police that he had earlier rung
his wife to inform her of the rescheduling of
his return to England.

A police spokesman told our reporter that several aspects of the situation were quite extraordinarily puzzling and that further enquiries
were being pursued. The police appeal to anyone
who might have been in or near Squitchey Lane in

the late evening of Saturday 13th or the early morning of Sunday 14th to come forward to try to assist in these enquiries. Please ring (0865) 266000.

'. . . he had earlier rung his wife . . .'
Yes.
And he had also rung me.
For a start I was tempted to 'come forward' myself —over the phone and anonymously—with a tentative (hah!) suggestion about the identity of that second fire-victim.

God rot his lecherous soul!

But I shan't make that call.

One call I shall quite certainly make though. Once the dust, once the ashes have started to settle.

You see, I think that a meeting between the two of us could possibly be of some value after all. Don't you?

And even as I write I almost hear the words that I shall use:

'John? Sunday? The usual? Twelve noon in the back room of the Bird and Baby? Please be there!'

Yes, John, please be there—for both our sakes . . .

PART THREE

They flee from me, that sometime did me seek
With naked foot, stalking in my chamber.

(Sir Thomas Wyatt, *Remembrance*)

Lewis came into Morse's office just before four o'clock that afternoon.

'Not much to report, sir. There's a card on the noticeboard there —looks as if it might be from a boyfriend.'

'I saw it.'

'And there's this—I reckon it's probably in the same handwriting.'

Lewis handed over a postcard showing a caparisoned camel standing in front of a Tashkent mosque. On the back Morse read the brief message: 'Travelling C 250 K E.'

'What's that all about, do you think, sir?'

Morse shook his head: 'Dunno. Probably the number of the aeroplane or the flight number or . . . something. Where did you find it, anyway?'

'There was an atlas there and I was looking up that place—you know, Erzincan. The postcard was stuck in there. You know, like a sort of marker.'

'Oh.'

'Don't you want to know where Erzincan is?'

'No. I looked it up when I got back here.'

'Oh.'

With a glint of triumph in his eyes, Morse now picked up the pink folder containing the Sheila Poster story and quickly explained its provenance.

'I want you to read this.'

'What, *now*, sir?'

'Did you think I meant on your summer holidays?'

'I'm a slow reader, you know that.'

'So am I.'

'You want me to read it *here?*'

'No. I've got things to be getting on with here. Go and have a sandwich. And take your time. Enough clues there to fill a cross-word puzzle.'

After Lewis had gone, Morse looked at his watch and started on *The Times* crossword.

When, eleven minutes later, he filled in the four blanks left, in –E–S–I–, he knew he should have been quicker in solving that final clue: 'Gerry-built semi is beginning to collapse in such an upheaval' (7).

Not bad, though.

A further hour passed before Lewis returned from the canteen and sat down opposite his chief.

'Lot's o' clues, you're right, sir. Probably made everything up, though, didn't she?'

'Not *everything*, not by a long chalk—not according to Diogenes Small.'

'According to who, sir?'

'To *whom*, Lewis—please!'

'Sorry, sir. I'm getting better about spelling, though. She made *one* mistake herself, didn't she?'

'Don't *you* start making things up!' Morse passed a handwritten list across the desk. 'You just rope in Dixon and Palmer—and, well, we can get through this little lot in no time at all.'

Lewis nodded: 'Have the case sewn up before the pubs close.'

For the first time that day there appeared a genuine smile on Morse's face. 'And these are only the obvious clues. You'll probably yourself have noticed a good many clues that've escaped *my* notice.'

'*Temporarily* escaped,' muttered Lewis, as he looked down at Morse's notes:

— Names (road, house, people): all phoney, like as not?

— Gazette: same ad you found? check

— Mr X (potential father): an academic surely? lecture tour of USA?

— Boswell: owners of this strange orange-eyed breed? check with the Cat Society

— Publishers (OUP etc): any recent work known/commissioned on Sir T W?

— Ante-natal clinics: check—esp. JR2

— Bird and Baby: check, with photograph

'We should come up with *something*, I agree, sir. But it's going to take quite a while.'

'You think so?'

'Well, I mean, for a start, *is* there such a thing as the Cat Society?'

'That's what you're going to check *up* on, Lewis!'

'Seven lots of things to check up on, though.'

'Six!' Morse rose from his armchair, smiling happily once again. 'I'll check up on that last bit myself.'

'But where are you going to get a photo from?'

'Good point,' conceded Morse, allowing, in his mind, that occasionally it was perfectly acceptable to end a sentence with a preposition.

At 10.15 p.m. Lewis rang Morse's home number, but received no reply. Was the great man still immersed in his self-imposed assignment—with or without a photograph?

In fact Morse was at that moment still sitting in the murder-room at 14 Jowett Place.

His mind had earlier informed him that he had *missed* something there; and at 8.15 p.m. he had re-entered the property, assuring the PC guarding the front door that he wouldn't be all that long.

But nothing had clicked in that sad room. And the overbeered Morse had sat in the sole armchair there and fallen asleep—finally awakening half an hour after midnight, and feeling as rough (as they say) as a bear's backside.

The following morning Lewis reported on his failures, Dixon's failures, Palmer's failures; and Morse reported on his own failures.

'You know this *house* business?' volunteered a rather subdued Lewis. 'She's very specific about it, isn't she? Listed building, thatched, timbered, conservatory at the back—couldn't we try the Council, some of the up-market estate-agents . . .'

'Waste o' time, I reckon.'

'So? What do we do next?'

'Perhaps we ought to look at things from the, er, the motivation angle.'

'Doesn't sound much like *you*, sir.'

No, it wasn't much like him—Morse knew that. He loved to have some juicy facts in front of him; and he'd never cared to peer too deeply down into the abyss of human consciousness. Yet there now seemed no alternative but to erect *some* sort of psychological scaffolding around Sheila Poster's hopes and fears, her motives and mistakes . . . And only then to look in turn once more through each of the windows; once more to ask what the murdered woman was trying to tell everyone—trying to tell *herself*—in the story she had written.

Morse sought to put his inchoate thoughts into words whilst Sergeant Lewis sat opposite and listened. Dubiously.

'Let's assume she's had a fairly permanent job in the past—well, we know she has—but she's been made redundant—she's got hardly any money—everything she owns is just that bit cheap— she meets some fellow—falls for him—he's married—but he promises to take her where the lemon trees bloom—she believes him—she carelessly gets herself pregnant—by chance she finds an advert his *wife* has put in the local rag—she goes to work there—she's curious about the wife—jealous about her—she wants the whole situation out in the open—things turn sour though—lover-boy has second thoughts—he jilts her—the wife gives her the sack into the bargain—and our girl is soon nourishing a hatred for *both* of them—she wants to *destroy* both of them—but she can't really bring herself to destroy the father of her child—so in her story she changes things a bit—and sticks the wife in bed with a lover of her own—because then her *own* lover, Sheila's lover, will still be around, still alive —so there'll always be the chance of her winning him back—but he's bored with her—there's some academic prefer-ment in the offing perhaps—he wants to get rid of her for good—he's prepared to play the faithful husband again—but Sheila won't play ball—she threatens to expose him—and when he goes to see her she becomes hysterical—he sees red—he sees all the colours of the rainbow—including orange, Lewis—because he knows she *can* ruin everything—*will* ruin everything—and then he knifes her . . .'

'*Who* knifes her?' asked Lewis quietly.

Morse shook his head. 'I haven't the faintest idea. I know what, though. I know I'm *missing* something!'

For a few moments the look on Morse's face was potentially bel-ligerent—like that of Boswell in the story; and Lewis felt diffident about asking the favour.

Yet his wife had insisted that he did.

'I hope you won't mind, sir, but if I could take a couple of hours off this lunchtime? The wife—'

Morse's eyebrows rose. 'Doesn't she know you're in the middle of a murder enquiry? What's she want you to do? Take her a bag of spuds home?'

Lewis hesitated: 'It's just that, well, there's this great big crack that's appeared overnight in the kitchen wall and the wife's wor-ried stiff that if we don't—'

'Bit of subsidence, you reckon?' (The pedantic Morse gave the stress to the first of the three syllables.)

'More like an earthquake, sir.'

For several seconds Morse sat utterly immobile in his chair, as if petrified before the sight of the Gorgon. And for the same several seconds Lewis wondered if his chief had suffered some facial paralysis.

Then Morse's lips slowly parted in a beatific smile. 'Lewis, my old friend, you've done it again! You've-gone-and-done-it-once-again! I think I see it. Yes, I think I see *all* of it!'

The happily bewildered Lewis sat back to learn the nature of his latest involuntary feat; but any enlightenment would have to wait awhile—that much was clear.

'Don't you let that missus of yours down!' beamed Morse. 'She's one in a million, remember that! Get off and sort things out with the surveyor or something—'

'Or the demolition squad.'

'—and get back here' (Morse looked at his watch) 'two o'clock, say?'

'You're sure—?'

'Absolutely. I've got a few important things to do here. And, er, just ask Dixon to come in, will you? *And* Palmer, if he's there?'

Lewis's euphoria was dissipating rapidly; but he had no opportunity to remonstrate, for Morse had already dialled a number and was asking if he was through to the Atlas Department of the Oxford University Press.

Sergeant Lewis returned to Kidlington HQ just before 2 p.m., almost three hours later, having finally received some reasonable reassurance that the Lewis residence was in minimal danger of imminent collapse. And at least *Mrs* Lewis was now somewhat happier in her mind.

❖

It soon became apparent to Lewis that during his absence someone —the doughnut-addicted Dixon? the pea-brained Palmer?—had been back out to Jowett Place; and Morse himself (what *else* had he been up to?) now sat purring like some cream-crammed orange-eyed long-hair as he surveyed the evidence before him on his desk —ready, it appeared, to lead the way along the path of true enlightenment.

'Clue Number One.' Morse opened the magnum opus of Dio-genes Small and lovingly contemplated the bookmark: 'Greetings from Erzincan'. 'All right, Lewis?'

'Clue Number Two.' He held up the postcard from Tashkent, turned it over, and read out its brief message once more: ' "Travel-ling C 250 K E". Not too bright, were we? It means exactly what it says: Travelling about two hundred and fifty kilometres east, east of Tashkent, where we find, Lewis—the Susamyr Valley in Kirgyzstan.

'Clue Number Three. Dear old Toot-and-come-in—another postcard, another message, pretty certainly in the same handwrit-ing: "Cairo's bloody hot but wish you were here." Remember? Signed "B".

'Clue Number Four.' Morse picked up the couplet from 'Last Poems'. 'Lines from a love poem, Lewis—with the seas between the pair of them—written from Los Angeles—the place to which the letter was re-addressed by Mrs S-G in the story. Remember? And we know *why* he went to all these places, don't we?'

Lewis didn't. But he nodded.

Why not?

'Then there was Clue Number Five—that walloping great clue *you* found straightaway: the fact that Sheila Poster had worked in the *Geology* Department here. Huh! I was blind.

'Then there was Clue Number Six . . . from *The Times* cross-word yesterday . . . Well, no, perhaps that was just a coincidence.

'And to cap it all you tell me about those almighty cracks in your bedroom wall . . .'

'*Crack*—only *one* crack, sir—in the *kitchen*, actually.'

Morse waved his right hand as if dismissing such trivial inaccuracies as of minor moment.

'*And*, Lewis, the dates all match—*all* of 'em. In each case they fall about ten days or a fortnight after the events—I've checked 'em with a lovely girl called Eunice Gill in the OUP cartographical section.'

(What *hadn't* Morse done, Lewis was beginning to wonder.)

'And she faxed me this,' continued Morse.

Lewis took the sheet and read a newspaper paragraph, dated 28.xi.92:

EARTHQUAKE SUMMIT

Following the major earth tremors which recently shook central Los Angeles, seismologists from all over the world, including the UK, will be assembling in Sacramento early in the new year to discuss improvements in the forecasting of potential disasters. No conference of similar scale has previously been held, and its anticipated 6-week duration reflects the urgency which is attached to this cosmic problem.

It had all taken Lewis far too long, of course; but now he let the information sink in. And finally he spoke:

'So what we need is a list of the delegates at the conference. Shouldn't take—'

But he got no further, for Morse handed him a sheet on which the members of the UK delegation were listed.

'Good man—Sergeant Dixon—you know,' said Morse.

Lewis ignored the tribute. 'None of 'em with the initial "B", though.'

'Why not try "R"?' asked Morse quietly.

So an embarrassed Lewis tried 'R', and looked again at the middle name of the five: Robert Grainger, D.Phil., MA.

'So all we need is to find out his address—'

'Cumnor Hill, Lewis. Not far off, is it? Palmer traced him. Good man—Palmer—you know.'

PART FOUR

White on a throne or guarded in a cave
   There lives a prophet who can understand
Why men were born . . .

   (James Elroy Flecker, *The Golden Journey to Samarkand*)

'Why do you think he did it?' asked Lewis as they drove along the Botley Road.

'Grainger's possible motives, you mean? Well, he was hot favourite for the chair in Geology—you've just discovered that for yourself. Great honour, you know, having a professorial chair at Oxford. Biggest prize of the lot. For some people.'

Lewis nodded, for he half understood now, and himself took up the thread: 'And Sheila Poster was going to ruin it all. Just as he's going to claim his birthright, he's suddenly faced with the prospect of scandal and failure and divorce . . . and the nightmare of some squawking infant into the bargain.'

Morse was unusually slow in his reply as they started to climb Cumnor Hill. 'I wouldn't know about those last two things, Lewis.'

They walked along the flagged path that bisected the well-tended lawn, weedless even in winter, and knocked on a front door which was immediately opened by a prematurely grey-haired man, slimly built, in his late forties or so, his eyes looking at them over half-lensed spectacles.

'You're the police, I suppose?'

Morse showed his warranty. 'Dr Grainger?'

For a few seconds the man hesitated. Then stood back and ushered his visitors into a well-appointed lounge, three of its walls completely lined with books.

'Yes. I suppose we'd better get it over with.'

He spoke quite slowly, and without emotion—at least to begin with. Yes, he knew that Sheila Poster had been murdered. He'd read it in the *Oxford Mail*. Yes, he'd had an affair with her; she'd been putting pressure on him to leave his wife and go to live with her; she'd told him she was pregnant—though he'd doubted the claim. His wife now knew most of the truth, but had only become directly involved because Sheila had contrived somehow to get a job as a cleaning-woman in the house there, and then had sought to poison the marital relationship—what little there was left of it . . .

It was at this point that the belittled Lewis (seemingly to Morse's mild amusement?) decided to assert himself.

'It'll be up to *Mrs* Grainger to give us details about her side of things, sir. You yourself weren't here, were you, when Miss Poster was working for your wife?'

Grainger, who hitherto had been speaking directly to Morse, now turned his eyes upon Lewis.

'You mean you're not prepared to take *my* word about what my wife has told me?'

'We're not here to answer questions, Dr Grainger—we're here to ask them,' snapped Lewis.

Irritatedly, Grainger turned back to Morse. 'Is it necessary for us to have this man with us, Inspector? I am *not* used to being spoken to in this way and I find it wholly and unnecessarily offensive!'

'This is a *murder* enquiry, sir,' began Morse rather lamely. 'You must understand—'

'But I *do* understand. And I'm telling you you're wasting your time if you think you'll find any murderer in *this* house.'

'Where were you on Sunday night?' asked Morse quietly.

'Huh! I'll tell you. I was in America—that's where I was.'

'And you can prove that?'

Grainger stood up, and followed by Lewis walked over to a bureau on which, beside a framed wedding-photograph, lay an envelope (as it proved) of travel documents. He handed it to Morse.

'As you'll see, I arrived back only yesterday afternoon—Monday. The plane, believe it or not, landed punctually at 4.15 p.m. I caught the Heathrow bus just after five o'clock, and I got to Oxford about quarter to seven.'

'It'll certainly be pretty easy to check up, then,' said Lewis, smiling serenely; and it was Morse who now looked round at his sergeant, more in admiration than in anger. Yet he himself sat silent and listened only, as Grainger snarled at Lewis once more, the antagonism between the two men now almost physically tangible.

'Oh yes. It'll hardly require a man of your calibre to check up on *that*. And it'll be pretty easy to check up on my wife as well. But let me tell you something, Sergeant! It won't be *you* who sees her. Is that clear? She's extremely upset—and you can understand why, can't you? Sheila was here *working* for her until a fortnight or so ago. All right? Now *you* might get a bit blasé about murders, Sergeant—but other people *don't*. My wife is under sedation and she's not going to see *anyone*—not today she isn't. And she won't see *you*, in any case! Your inspector here sounds a reasonably humane and civilized sort of fellow—and perhaps there are still a few others like him in the Force. So any of *them* can see my wife. All right? But it won't be *you*, Sergeant. Why? *Because I say so!*'

Phew!

Morse now intervened between the warring parties: 'That'll be fine, sir. Have no fears! I'll be interviewing your wife myself. But ... but it would help us, sir, if you *do* happen to know where Mrs Grainger was on Sunday night?'

'She went to some gala do in London with one of her friends—lady-friends. As I understand it, the pair of them missed the 11.20

from Paddington and had to catch the 12.20—the "milk-float", I think they call it—landing up here at about 2 a.m. They got a taxi home from the station. That's all I know.'

'Have you got this friend's telephone number?'

'You won't need it. She lives next door.'

Grainger pointed vaguely to the right; and Morse nodded his unspoken instruction to Lewis.

And Lewis left.

Morse was already seated in the Jaguar when Lewis rejoined him ten minutes later.

'He's right, sir. They got back here to Cumnor about half-past two in the early hours of Monday morning.'

Morse showed no emotion, for he'd fully expected confirmation of Mrs Grainger's alibi.

And he began to explain.

'You see, Lewis, it's not the *who*-dunnit aspect of this particular case that's really important—but the *why*-dunnit. *Why* was Sheila Poster murdered? She must surely have posed a threat to someone, either a man or a woman. And more likely a man, I'm thinking. She must have stood in the way of some man's hopes and calculated advancement. So *much* of a threat that when she refused to compromise, at some show-down between them, she was murdered precisely for that refusal of hers. So we'd no option but to work backwards—agreed? And we knew *her* side of things, to some extent, from the story she wrote. Now *some* things in that story reflected actuality fairly closely, didn't they? The Graingers' house —"The Grange", huh!—her job there—her affair with the husband—her overwhelming wish to force the issue with the wife—'

'Don't forget the baby, sir!'

'No, I won't forget the baby. But Grainger didn't seem to think she was telling the truth about that, did he?'

'She *was* pregnant, though.'

'Yes, she was telling the truth about being pregnant. In fact, she was telling a whole lot more of the truth perhaps than she was prepared to admit—even to herself. Let's make a hypothetical case. What, say, if she really wanted to murder *not* the married couple she was telling herself she hated? What if—in her story—she wanted to murder the very people she *did* in fact murder: the lady-of-the-house and *that lady's lover*? What if the pair of *them* had fallen deeply in love? What if—again as in the story—the lady-of-the-house had been only too glad to learn of her husband's infidelity? Because then she could divorce him, and marry her new lover ... the man who stood by the flower-beds and tended the lawns there ...'

'The man who came in for a cup of coffee, sir.'

'Perhaps so. But don't forget she wasn't just telling us a string of *facts* in the story—she was making a whole lot of it up as she went along.'

'Really, sir?'

Lewis, as Morse could just about make out in the gloaming, was smiling quietly to himself.

'What the hell's got *into* you, Lewis? You antagonize one of our leading witnesses; you go off and find an unshakeable alibi for his missus; and now you sit there grinning like a Cheshire—'

'By the way, sir, they do have a cat—I asked next door. "Johnson", its name is.'

'You've nothing *else* to tell me, have you?' asked Morse, looking curiously at his sergeant.

'Actually, there is, sir—yes.'

'Out with it, man!'

'Yesterday, sir, when we interviewed Paul Bayley, he said he'd been with his girlfriend all night.'

'You told me that. You told me you'd checked.'

'I did check. Bayley told me she was in the middle of moving flats that very day—seemed she'd been a little bit too generous with her favours for the landlord's liking; and—just temporarily, mind—she was registered as of no fixed address. But Bayley said she'd almost certainly be in the City Centre Westgate Library—where she went most mornings—in the Local History Section—'

'Where she was!'

Lewis nodded. 'Doing some research on Nuneham Courtenay and the Deserted Village. So she told me.'

'Well?'

'Well . . . that's about it.'

'Is it?'

'She's a very beautiful woman, sir.'

'More beautiful than Sheila Poster?'

'I'd say so. More to my taste, anyway.'

'And most men would fancy her?'

'If they had the chance.'

'And Bayley *did* have the chance.'

'I'm pretty sure he did. He's been in Jowett Place for about four months or so now. Unemployed for a start; but then *in* work—so his landlord says.'

'His landlord? When did you see *him*?'

'He called in yesterday lunchtime, when you were in the pub. And from what he said—'

'You didn't mention this before.'

'Thought I'd just do a bit of investigation off my own bat, sir. You didn't mind?'

'See if *you* could solve the case, you mean?'

'Try to, yes. And the landlord said it was Sheila Poster who'd told Bayley about the vacancy in the flat upstairs and who'd put in a good word for him, you know—gave him a good-behaviour reference. Not only that, though. I reckon she was the one who told Bayley about the odd-job vacancy going up at the Graingers' place.'

'Phew!' Morse whistled quietly. 'You're saying *Bayley* was the odd-job man?'

'I'm saying exactly that, sir!'

'You're *sure* of this?'

'Not yet,' replied Lewis, beaming happily.

'Let me get this clear. You're suggesting that Bayley goes to work for Mrs Sylvia Grainger—she falls for *him*—he falls for *her*—she knows her husband's having an affair with the *charwoman*—she's proof of it. Then' (Morse paused slightly for dramatic effect) 'just when things are looking hunkydory, this charwoman claims she's pregnant. Not by Grainger, though . . .'

'. . . but by *Bayley*. Yes, sir.'

'And Bayley goes down on Sunday night—has it out with her—she refuses to play ball—and she gets herself murdered. Is that the idea?'

'Exactly!'

'But Bayley's got an alibi! This local history woman of yours—she says she was with him all night.'

'From about nine p.m. to seven a.m. the following morning. Correct. Slept on the floor together in a friend's house in Cowley somewhere—she refuses to say exactly where.'

'She's probably trying to protect her friends or something.'

'Or something,' repeated Lewis.

'Just you bear in mind all the adverse publicity we're getting about "confessions under duress", OK? We've got to tread carefully, you know that.'

It was still only four o'clock, yet already the afternoon had darkened into early dusk.

'Can you guess, sir, why Dr Grainger was so worried about *me* interviewing his wife?'

'He probably thought you were a bit crude, Lewis—preferred a sensitive soul like me. And by the way, don't forget that there are few in the Force more competent at that sort of thing than me.'

'You can't think of any other reason?'

'*You* obviously can.'

Lewis savoured his moment of triumph. 'Did you see the wedding-photo just now—the one Dr Grainger had on the bureau?'

'Well, yes—at a distance.'

'Beautiful woman, Mrs Grainger—*very* beautiful.'

'Taken quite a few years ago, that photo—she's probably changed since then.'

'No! You're wrong about that, sir.'

'How do *you* know?'

'Because I met her very recently. Met her yesterday morning, in fact. In the Westgate Library. She told me her name was Wendy Allsworth. But it isn't, sir. It's *Sylvia Grainger*.'

'Extraordinary!' said Morse, his voice strangely flat.

'You don't sound all that surprised.'

'Just tell me one thing. When you took the statement from—from Mrs Grainger, do you think she knew about the murder?'

'No, I don't.'

'*You* didn't tell her?'

'No. So unless they planned things—'

'Very doubtful!' interposed Morse.

'—Bayley must have rung her up early that morning.'

'Do you think *he* told her?'

'I don't think so. If she'd known it was a murder enquiry . . . No, I don't think he told her.'

'I agree. She was prepared to go a long way—*did* go a long way. Not that far, though.'

Lewis hesitated. 'You'll excuse me for saying so, but as I said you don't sound very *surprised* about all this.'

'What? Of course I am. From where I sat I couldn't have recognized the *Queen* if she'd been in that photo. The old eyes are not as sharp as they were.'

'You *knew*, though, didn't you?' asked Lewis quietly.

'Not *all* of it, no,' lied Morse.

Yet Lewis's silence was saddeningly eloquent, and Morse finally nodded. Then sighed deeply.

'I've always *told* you, Lewis, haven't I? The person who finds the body is going to be your prime suspect. That's always been my philosophy. It's *compulsive* with these murderers—they want their victim *found*. It'd send 'em crackers if the body lay undiscovered somewhere for any length of time.'

'So?' asked Lewis dejectedly.

'So! So I had Bayley brought in this morning —this lunchtime.'

'While I was with the builder.'

'Yes. And Bayley continues to be detained at Her Majesty's Pleasure.'

'You interviewed him yourself?'

'Yes. As I just told you, there's no one in the Force so firmly and fairly competent as me—not in that line of business.'

Lewis was smiling wryly now—first nodding, then shaking his head. He might well have known . . .

He nodded towards the Graingers' home: 'Shall we go and take *her* in as well?'

'Actually she's, er, she's already helping with our enquiries.'

Lewis almost exploded. 'But you *can't*—you *can't* mean . . .'

'I do, yes. I had Bayley tailed and he went out to meet Sylvia Grainger—in the bar at The Randolph—about a quarter to twelve, that was. She'd told her husband she was going to her sister's for a few hours. That's what she said. So! So there's really not much point in us sitting here freezing any longer, is there?'

Lewis turned the key in the ignition, the Jaguar spurted into life, and the two detectives now sat silently side by side for several minutes as they drove back down into Oxford.

It was Lewis who spoke first: 'You know, it really is nonsense what you say, sir—about the first person finding the body. I just don't know where the *evidence* is for that. And then you say it's "compulsive"—didn't you say that?—for murderers to want the body found. But some of 'em take enormous time and trouble for the body *never* to be found.'

'You're right, I agree. I was exaggerating a bit.'

'So what *did* make you think it was Bayley? There must have been *something*.'

'It's all these wretched crosswords I do. You meet some odd

words, you know. The first time I saw Bayley in his room I thought what a great big fat-arsed sod he was. And then, this morning, I read Sheila Poster's story again—and well, things went sort of "click". You remember that long word Sheila Poster used— about the odd-job man? Mind you, she *was* an English graduate.'

Lewis did remember, but only vaguely; he'd look it up once they got back to HQ.

'It was always going to be a straightforward case,' continued Morse. 'We'd have been sure to find out where Bayley had been working, sooner or later.'

'"Sooner or later",' repeated Lewis. 'And for once I thought it was me who was sooner. It's just like I said: I've got a second-class mind—I'm just like a second-class—'

'Ah! That reminds me. Just pull in here a minute, will you?'

Lewis turned into a slip-road alongside a row of brightly lit shops just before the Thames Valley Police HQ buildings.

'Where exactly—?'

'Here! Here's fine.'

Morse jabbed a finger to the left, and Lewis braked outside a sub post-office.

'Just nip in and get me a book of stamps, please.'

'First- or second-class?' For some reason Lewis was feeling reasonably happy again.

'No need to go wild, is there? I'll have one book of second-class, all right? These days they get there almost as quickly as first, you know that.'

Morse had been pushing his hands one after the other into the pockets of overcoat, jacket, trousers—seemingly without success.

'You'll never believe it, Lewis, but . . .'

'I think I will, sir. Remember what that fellow Diogenes Small wrote about people's flights of imagination?'

'You've been soaring up there yourself, you mean?'

'Not quite, no. All I'm saying is it wouldn't take a detective to see what you're trying to tell me.'

'Which is?'

'You haven't got any money.'

'Ah!'

Morse looked down silently at the car-mat; and Lewis, now smiling happily, opened the driving-seat door of the Jaguar, and was soon to be seen walking towards the premises of the sub post-office in Kidlington, Oxon.

MONTY'S REVOLVER

Women sometimes forgive those who force an opportunity, never those who miss it.

(Talleyrand)

It wasn't often that Professor Rawlins bothered her with his personal letters. Occasionally, though—like this afternoon; and like yesterday afternoon, come to think of it. But he always insisted on putting his own stamps on such letters, never allowing them through the Department's franking-machine. Bit too obviously self-righteous, she thought. She glanced at the tiny gold watch (a wedding present) on her left wrist: almost a quarter to five. TGFF. Thank God For Friday!

Rawlins took off his half-glasses, pinched the top of his nose, turned over a page of his desk diary, lit another cigarette, and looked across at Carol Summerson.

'Professor Smithson's coming on Monday morning. Will you nip out first thing and get me a bottle of Glenfiddich?'

Carol made a note, closed her shorthand book, uncrossed her elegant legs, and smiled as she looked at him. And he, half smiling himself, looked back across at her; and she felt pleasingly surprised. (Or was it surprisingly pleased?) There had been so few moments of real communication between them during the three months she'd been working for him—the man she'd more than once heard described as 'the cleverest fellow in Oxford'.

She was glad to get out of his office, though. He would never open the window and the smell in the room was invariably horrid. How she wished he'd stop smoking! (John never smoked, thank goodness.) How old was he? Sixty? Overweight, and with a chest that sounded like a loose-strung harp, he was just the sort to die before his time from heart trouble or lung cancer or chronic bronchitis or emphysema—or like as not the whole lot of them listed on his death certificate. Why didn't his *wife* do something about him, for Christ's sake?

'Good night, sir,' she heard herself say; and for a moment she fancied that she'd almost like to look after him herself.

John was waiting for her, sitting on his wife's swivel-chair and turning over the papers that lay on her desk. (He always picked Carol up on Fridays.) While she was out in the cloakroom, he looked through a few more recent carbons, each neatly stapled to its originating letter. One carbon in particular caught his eye:

> Dear Jack,
>
> Glad you still remember me and—yes!—I still keep the old collection going. But anything that belonged to Monty is sure to spark off some keen bidding—all a bit too high for me. As you say, though, the reserve price seems fair enough.
>
> How long is it since we met? Seven—eight years? Marion died six years ago—malignant tumour. Not unexpected, but all desperately sad and very upsetting for the boys. I remarried two years later, and since then I've had another son!—and another!!—and another!!! Do you know the odds against a penny coming down *six* times on the trot?
>
> If you're ever near Oxford, let me know. I promise not to show you round the Department.
>
> Sincerely yours,

Carol looked at her husband as she re-entered her office. At twenty-two, he was a year younger than herself; yet in many ways since their marriage two years previously, he'd shown himself the more mature, the more dependable, of the two. There had been a few patches of squabbling—mostly her fault; and the one continuing sadness . . . But she was glad she'd married him.

That, at least, is what Carol Summerson was telling herself that December afternoon.

'You reading my boss's correspondence again?'

He nodded.

'Interesting?'

'Not really.'

As she unhooked her coat from the wall-cupboard, John glanced quickly at the originating letter, stapled behind the carbon he had just been reading. A letterhead announced a 'J. Wingate, Gunsmith', with an address in Guildford, the letter itself reporting the forthcoming auction of a revolver that had belonged to Field Marshal Bernard Montgomery—reserve price £3,000.

'I didn't know he was interested in revolvers,' said John, unlocking the nearside door to the Metro.

'I've told you *before*. You shouldn't read—'

'Didn't mind, did you?'

'Course not!' She brushed her full lips against his cheek as she fastened her safety-belt.

'His big hobby. One of the girls went to his house once when he'd got bronchitis or something and she said he'd got all these revolvers like in cases sort of thing hanging round the walls. Not very nice really, is it? You'd think that with all those young children—'

She stopped suddenly and a silence fell between them.

At 5.20 p.m. Rawlins locked the door of his office and left the Department. Florence (at thirty-two, exactly half his age) would have the fish all ready. TGFF. Thank God For Florence!

That night, for no immediately apparent reason, Frank Rawlins dreamed of Carol Summerson.

It was just before 11 a.m. the following Monday that Smithson arrived. Carol was not introduced to him, but from her adjacent room she could hear his voice; could hear, too, the occasional gurgle of Glenfiddich and the clink of the office glasses. Just over an hour later, after the pair of them had walked past her window, she entered Rawlins' office, took the two glasses, washed them out in the ladies' loo, and bent down to put them back in the cupboard beside the bottle—now empty.

'Hello!'

She hadn't heard him come back in, and she felt slightly confused as he steered her by the elbow into her own office.

'Don't you think it's about time I treated my confidential secretary to lunch?'

He looked—and sounded—surprisingly sober; and she felt flattered. Soon he was holding her coat ready, and she was slipping her arms into the sleeves.

Easily.

He was interesting—no doubt about that. He told her of the time he and Smithson had worked together in a VD clinic in Vienna; and as he reminisced of this and other experiences Carol felt herself enriched, and newly important.

'Another?'

'I've had enough, thank you.'

'Nonsense!' He picked up her glass and made his slightly unsteady way to the bar once more.

Her third gin-and-tonic tasted strong. Nice, though! Was it a double? His own drink looked very much like the orange juice he'd promised himself; and after he'd left her to visit the gents' she took a sip of it: it tasted even more strongly of gin than hers.

'We'd better be getting back, sir.'

'Yes.'

'Thanks for a lovely lunch.'

'Carol! I've had a lot to drink—you know that. But I just want you to know how ver' much I'd like to go to bed with you this afternoon.'

Carol's heart sank.

'Don't be silly! Come on, let's get back!'

He was hurt, she knew that; a bit ashamed, too. And as they walked back he tried so very hard to sound his usual sober self.

That night Carol Summerson dreamed of Frank Rawlins. Erotically.

Carol's raise came through in mid-January, and she was thrilled.

'I'm ever so grateful, sir.'

'You deserve it.'

'Will you come out one day and have lunch with *me*?'

'When?'

'Whenever you're free.'

'Today?'

'Today!'

She saw to it that he drank almost all the wine, and she insisted on buying him a glass of brandy after their meal. They were sitting close together now, and gently she moved her right leg against the rough tweed of his trousers. And, just as gently, he responded, saying nothing, yet saying everything.

'Another brandy?' she ventured.

Rawlins looked down at his empty glass, and smiled a little sadly.

'Have you ever thought how wonderful it would be to have a quiet, civilized little place all to yourself where—'

He stopped, and there was a long silence between them before Carol spoke softly in his ear.

'But I've *got* a nice little place out at Wheatley. You see, John's away for a few days . . .'

Seven weeks later, Carol's GP told her that she was quite definitely pregnant.

On the Friday evening of that same week, John Summerson

called as usual to collect his wife. It was quarter to five—exactly so—when he walked through into Rawlins' office and sat down in the chair that his wife had just vacated.

Over his glasses, Rawlins' eyes registered puzzlement: it was as though a new boy had just strolled into the Masters' Common Room.

'Can I help you? John—isn't it?'

'You had sex with my wife.' Summerson spoke quietly, firmly—defying all denial.

'Where on earth did you get such—?'

'You're lying!'

'Look here! You can't be serious—'

'She's pregnant!'

'But you can't—'

'I *watched* you!' hissed Summerson.

'But you—'

'Shut up! I'm not the father. I can *never* be a father. You do understand what I'm saying, don't you?'

'Yes,' answered Rawlins softly.

'Did you *enjoy* it?' The young man's eyes were blazing with a terrible anguish.

'I just—'

'*Shut up!*'

Rawlins sank back in his chair, his shoulders sagging.

'I'm redundant now,' continued Summerson. 'They gave me £3,000 for the five years I worked there. There's not *much* you can do with £3,000, is there, Professor?'

Rawlins closed his eyes and thought of his sons and thought of Florence and thought of himself, too: he knew exactly what £3,000 might possibly have bought.

When he opened his eyes he saw the revolver in Summerson's right hand—a British Enfield .380, Number 2, Mark 1, the wooden stock a dirty nicotine-brown, the gunmetal of the fluted barrel as clean and gleaming as a polished stone. Summerson swivelled the revolver round until it pointed straight at Rawlins' heart, and his finger squeezed the trigger until the hammer lifted to the limit of the catch.

'Pretty accurate, they tell me, at such close range as this, Professor!'

Rawlins said nothing, his eyes seemingly mesmerized as he stared at the cylinder-chamber. But now the revolver was no longer pointing at him; for with slow deliberation Summerson turned it round upon himself and brought the tip of the shining barrel up against his own right temple, where the index finger of his right hand finally exacted that minimal extra pressure on the double-action trigger, and the hammer drove against the cylinder-chamber.

The children had eaten half an hour previously, and Florence Rawlins looked down sadly at the juiceless fillet that lay beneath the low-burning grill. Why couldn't Frank be more thoughtful?

Six o'clock.

Ten past.

Twenty past.

At half-past six she rang his private office number, but there was no reply.

'Fine! Fine!' The young gynaecologist had repeated. 'No problems. Now you'll promise not to smoke, won't you?' 'I promise.' Of course she wouldn't smoke! Her thoughts drifted back happily to Rawlins ... With a father like Rawlins, it would surely be a *boy*—and pretty certainly a *clever* little boy, at that! She'd longed to be a mother ever since she'd been a young girl, when she'd played incessantly, obsessively almost, with her dollies—dressing them, combing their lank locks, bending their stiff joints before propping them up against the backs of chairs ...

Six weeks after that first ante-natal clinic, an oblong parcel was delivered to the Rawlins' residence, where later in the day the Professor of Forensic Medicine inspected its contents with enthusiasm. The new case would naturally take pride of place, perhaps just inside the front entrance, he thought. He fitted the revolver carefully inside the specially constructed case, closed the glass cover, and held the exhibit up against some imaginary hook on the facing wall. Not a bad reward, really, for being trapped into exercising his dubiously enviable knack of procreating male offspring with even the most perfunctory ejaculation. And even that extraordinary afternoon when young Summerson had pointed the revolver at his heart hadn't been all that traumatic an experience really, because long before the final, cosmically anticlimactic 'click' he had known (as any expert in the field would have known) that there were no bullets in the open chambers of the revolver—not a single one. For all that though, it had been a great relief when the revolver had at last been lowered, and a genuine surprise when Summerson had presented it to him across the desk—reward for services rendered, so to speak. And he really *had* needed those two large whiskeys, although he'd afterwards agreed with a worried, tearful Florence that he should have told her he'd be late.

On September 29 of that same year, a baby was delivered on the third floor of the Maternity Hospital up at Headington, and the young father had the name all ready. The gunsmith from Guildford may not have bothered to work out any mathematical odds, but John Summerson had calculated the chances of a penny coming down heads for a *seventh* time; and at 128:1, they'd seemed to him wildly improbable.

They called the lovely little girl 'Francesca'.

THE CARPET-BAGGER

He who is conceived in a cage
Yearns for the cage.

(Yevtushenko, *Monologue of a Blue Fox on an Alaska Animal Farm*)

1

There were longish periods now when the A34 was quiet, almost completely free of the swishing traffic. Only up there along the lay-by, two 'Long Vehicle' lorries ahead, was there still any continuum of activity—where at the side of a converted white caravan a single electric light bulb illuminated MACS SNAX—Open 24 Hour's.

Though with little formal education behind him, Danny had still felt the itch to transpose that single apostrophe from the last word to the first when, three-quarters of an hour earlier, he'd walked along to the serving-hatch and ordered a cup of tea and a Melton Mowbray pork-pie. Two other drivers had stood there then, chatting in desultory fashion and intermittently stamping their feet, their white plastic cups of piping-hot tea steaming brightly in the cold air of that late-January night. But apart from swopping first names, the three of them had said little to each other.

Now, back in the cab of the furniture van, Danny began to realize how very cold he was. Yet he told himself that 'cold' was only a relative concept and was trying to convince himself that he was only *relatively* cold. As with many things in life, it was all a question of mind over matter. His feet *felt* bloody frozen—Christ, they did. But they weren't *really* frozen, were they, Danny boy? What if he were standing barefoot on the far North Pole? He'd always believed there was just that one square yard of ice and snow comprising yer actual North Pole, and no one yet had managed to persuade him otherwise.

There were two newspapers in the cab: the *Daily Telegraph*

(oddly?) and a late edition of the *Oxford Mail*. And newspapers were super for insulation, everyone knew that. Just stick a few sheets all the way round between your shirt and your jumper . . .

He looked at his wrist-watch: half-past midnight, just gone.

It had been most unlike him to make one mistake—let alone two—on such an important day. How stupid, in the first place, to have left his faithful old army greatcoat behind! And absolutely bloody stupid to have drunk more than a little too much that lunchtime, because more than a little had amounted to more than a lot and he had spent far more than he could really afford of his meagre savings.

At a service station just north of Oxford he had stopped to buy two litre bottles of Spring Water—as well as the *Oxford Mail*—prior to pulling into the next lay-by, just before the M40 interchange. It was a bit naïve, he knew, but he'd always believed that considerable quantities of water must significantly, and soon, serve to dilute and thereby to diminish the alcoholic level in the human bloodstream. And so it was that, an hour earlier, he'd forced himself to swallow all that flat and tasteless fluid to the final drop.

How come he'd been so careless?

Nervousness partly; and partly the exhilaration of the chase—of the fox keeping a few furlongs ahead of the yapping hounds. Perhaps the fox wasn't really exhilarated at all though—just frightened. Like he was, if he were honest with himself.

Just a bit.

Yet as he now sat behind the steering-wheel in the darkened cab, he couldn't really believe he'd find himself in much trouble with the police that night. He wasn't sure whether they *could* nick him for being over the limit in charge of a stationary vehicle. But they'd still need *some* reason for breathalysing him, wouldn't they? They'd have one if they spotted the number-plate, of course. But that was a pretty unlikely possibility, he reckoned. He hadn't read much of the *Oxford Mail*, but he'd seen one of its front-page headlines—OXON POLICE 'UNABLE TO COPE' WITH CRIME—and at least that was a nugget of encouragement in a naughty old world. A vehicle, so it seemed, was stolen every something seconds in the Thames Valley region and that was very good news indeed—considerably lengthening the odds against him being caught.

No. There was something else that was worrying him much more: the wretched 'tachometer' just to the left of the steering-wheel—a device (as he was now learning) that showed details of speeds and times, of stoppings and startings. He just couldn't *understand* the thing, that was the trouble. Nor the pile of paper discs, looking like so many CDs, that stood beside it—discs marked 'Freightchart', with lines and spaces and boxes for Name and Base and Destination and Cargo and Date and Mileage and God knows what else. Confusing. Unfamiliar. He could gauge all the other risks all right; but not this one. Perhaps the police couldn't give him a random breath-test. But could they give him a random tacho-test?

He switched on the dimmish light in the roof of the cab and picked up one of the white discs, noting that two lines had already been completed, presumably in the cheap blue Biro that lay beside the pile: SMITH, JOHN; Southampton.

Danny shook his head; and turned to the *Oxford Mail* again.

The main editorial picked up the page-one article on car-related crime, and Danny smiled to himself as he read the last few sentences:

> The truth is that some of us, especially in the present cold snap, find it difficult enough to start our cars anyway—in spite of the considerable advantage of possessing our own car-keys. So how is it that even some comparatively incompetent car thief can enter our vehicles in a matter of seconds, twist a couple of wires together (so we're told), and be seen two minutes later outpacing a pursuing police car along the nearest motorway? Come on, you manufacturers! Let's have a bit more resource and ingenuity in a fully committed nationwide crusade against this growing social evil.

Danny inclined his head slightly to the right and wondered what exactly the manufacturers *could* do—given the nature of electric current. And already it was considerably more difficult than the editor was suggesting. Four minutes it had taken him with this particular van at Southampton—a ramshackle heap that'd have about as much chance with a police car as a moped would with Nigel Mansell.

Brrr . . . was it cold, though! And getting colder.

He could have turned on the engine for a quarter of an hour or so, but he was reluctant to waste any diesel. There was a long journey north ahead of him; and while he reckoned he'd be safe enough on the busy daytime motorways, he didn't really want to stop again. At the same time he daren't drive any further, either—not until he'd had a few hours' rest; or kip, if he were lucky. Twice, only an hour or so since, he'd almost fallen asleep at the wheel, his eyes slowly drooping downwards . . . and further downwards, until his head followed them, only—suddenly!—to jerk upright in panic as consciousness reasserted itself.

Death had never figured prominently among his deepest fears, but he'd hardly had much of an innings as yet. And with all that cargo sitting there just behind him, well, it would have been criminal—*extra* criminal—to take any needless risks.

Thinking of all that cargo, though . . .

Why'd it taken him so long to think of it?

Earlier he'd leafed through the bundle of inventories and invoices, and counted at least—what, eighty?—eighty or more oriental rugs and carpets from Turkey, from Persia, from the Caucasus, from places sounding like Something-stan, with prices ranging from £4,500 (several such from Isfahan) to the cheapest (huh!) at only a thousand or so apiece. Danny's skill at scoring for his local darts team had once been legendary and his mind dwelt lovingly now on those accumulated spondulicks.

But the carpets weren't just precious, were they? They'd be *warm* too. Climb into the back, lie down under a couple of those beautifully embroidered beauties and—like his mum used to say —he'd soon be as snug as a bug in a rug.

A Persian rug.

There was no key to be found for the rear doors, but opening locks was Danny's hobby; his specialism. Some few people, he knew, could finish a fiendish crossword puzzle in a matter of minutes; a few others could spot a master-move to some complex chess problem in hardly any time at all. And he was like that with opening locks.

Only quicker.

And immediately disappointed.

Inside, no neatly laid-out pile of carpets presented itself for him to lie on, like the princess on the mattresses. Instead, facing him, from floor to ceiling, lying lengthways along the sides of the van, stood a honeycomb of tightly packaged carpets rolled up in their thick cardboard cylindrical wrappings. Jes-*us*! Even with an outsize Stanley knife it'd probably take him half an hour to liberate only *one* of them. And he couldn't just slide one out and carve it up in the middle of the lay-by, now could he?

Aagh! Forget it.

He walked back, clambered up the two metal foot-holds, and sat once more in the front cab, now grown even chillier. One bit of luck, though. The *Daily Telegraph* proved to be a pretty substantial broadsheet, and he was dividing the multipaged wodge in half when he spotted the headline, in the Home News section, and was soon reading the article beneath it:

TRUSTY ABSCONDS

Wiltshire Police report the escape of Daniel Smithson from Winchester Gaol, where most recently he was serving a four-year sentence for robbery.

For the last three months it appears that Smithson had been privileged to enjoy the maximum range of freedom within the prison régime, and indeed during the past week had been working

in a garden adjacent to the prison with a brick wall only some four
feet high separating him from the outside world.

Although prison authorities are unwilling to give specific
details, it is understood that the ex-soldier Smithson, who for the
last twelve years has seen little except the inside of a cell in one of
HM prisons, was due for release shortly.

Aged forty-three, he is five feet seven inches in height, of slim-
to-medium build, and has shortish brown hair. Lightly tattooed on
the back of the lower knuckles of the left hand are the letters I—L
—Y—K, supposed by fellow prisoners to commemorate a former
girlfriend: 'I Love You Kate'.

The escapee has no record of any criminal violence, and it is the
view of the prison officers at Winchester that he poses no threat
whatsoever to the public at large. An early re-arrest is expected.

Characteristically, Danny tilted his head to the right, and
glanced through the article again. Then nodded to himself. There
were people who couldn't cope with life outside the Rules and Reg-
ulations of an institution—just as there were people (hadn't he just
read it?) who couldn't quite cope with all this crime. And it was
easy to read between the lines of that last couple of sentences, wasn't
it? 'No need to clap the darbies round the poor sod's wrists. Nah!
He'll probably soon be knocking on the gates o' the nearest nick
hisself.'

Funny old business, life. Full o' pitfalls—full of opportunities,
too. Just watch out for the first—and make sure you grab hold o'
the second. Common sense, innit? That's what his dad had told
him.

Danny clasped his hands, left over right, and rubbed them vigorously together against the numbing cold. And even as he did so,
he found himself looking down at the lower knuckles of his upper
hand.

2

'I coulda scored the bloody thing in me carpet slippers, honest I could.'

'You reckon?'

'And if Oxford hadn't buggered up that last-minute penalty—'

'You'da won a fortune.'

'Third divi on the treble-chance.'

'About sixpence.'

'We've gone decimal, Sarge—remember?'

PC Watson accelerated up the slip-road into the A34 (N) from the Pear Tree roundabout, noting as he did so the miraculously civilized deceleration of a couple of cars behind him.

'Better take a gander somewhere, I s'pose,' suggested Sergeant Hodges a couple of miles further on, pointing to one of the several lay-bys on the twin-track road that led up to the M40 interchange.

No snack bar here. Just the black hulks of two juggernauts; and tucked in behind them an old man in an old car studying an old map.

'Need any help, sir?'

'No!'

Sod you then, thought Watson, as he moved forward past the two container-lorries.

At the far end of the lay-by—not spotted earlier—was a Jaguar of indeterminate colour: 'indeterminate' partly because during the hours of darkness light reflected oddly from the metallic sheen of some cars; and partly because Watson was in any case wholly colour-blind between the reds and the blues.

But he made no further advance as he saw the grey head of the driver jerk round and the dusky-headed young maiden beside him hasten to fasten up the buttons on her blouse.

'Any joy?' asked Hodges.

Watson shook his head as he got back into the car. 'Well, 'cept for the fellow up front there in the Jag, perhaps.'

Half a mile or so further along, Hodges nodded again to his left, and this time the Vauxhall Senator pulled in behind a furniture van.

'Coffee for me, Barry. Not too much milk, and two sugars, please.'

But Watson was no more than a few seconds into his mission before he stopped and stared. When (only an hour since) he'd glanced through the briefing-files and the traffic telexes back in Kidlington Police HQ, the last three letters of one particular stolen vehicle had caught his notice. How otherwise? For those last three letters were the initials of his own name, Barry Robert Watson; and here, on the van in front of him, was the registration number C 674 BRW.

There was always an awful lot of luck needed in apprehending villains, Watson had already learnt that—unless you were looking for a ginger-bearded giant, with a wooden leg, and a dinosaur tattooed on his balding head. And this *was* a bit of luck. Surely so.

Back in the police car, Hodges rang through to the Control Room at HQ, where within only a few seconds an operator read from his Police National Computer screen that the said vehicle, reg. C 674 BRW, had been stolen earlier that evening in Southampton. The number had appeared in the Thames Valley briefing-files only because there seemed to be some suggestion that the vehicle might be heading north. Along the A34. Up into Oxfordshire.

His head cushioned on his arms, the driver appeared to be deeply asleep, since only after a series of staccato raps on the cab window did he raise his head above the steering-wheel.

'This your vehicle?' bawled Watson.

'Wha'?'

'Police!'

The driver slowly wound down his window. 'Wha's the trouble, mate?'

'This your vehicle?'

'Wha', this? I wouldn't have it if you gev it me!'

'Let's see your licence, please.'

'What licence?'

'Not your bloody *dog* licence, is it!'

'You got so many days on producin' yer licence, you know that.'

'Haven't got one—is that what you're saying?'

'Not on me, no.'

'What's your name?' (It was Hodges who took over now.)

'John Smith.'

'Sorry, yeah. Shoulda known.'

'Anything else I can help you with?'

'You'd better get down and come along with us.'

'Have I got any option, mate?'

'Not much.'

'Hold on a tick, then. I'd better just fill in the old tacho thing here. Got to keep yer records up to date, you know—'specially if you get delayed a bit.'

'Yeah, well, let's say you look like getting delayed a bit.'

Beckoning Watson to the other side of the van, and with one foot now on the lower foot-hold, Hodges raised himself to look into the cab, where he saw the driver filling in a white tachometer disc—writing slowly and innocently enough with a cheap blue Biro.

The driver of the lorry in front walked back to the van.

'Everything OK, Officer?'

Hodges nodded and stepped down. 'No problems.'

'Everything OK, Danny?' continued the other, as the cab-door now opened.

'Fine, yeah! Just forgot me licence, din I?'

'"Danny", eh?' remarked Sergeant Hodges as he steered the man into the near-side rear seat of the Vauxhall, conscious that the slimly built, quietly spoken man beside him hardly fitted the stock profile of any tearaway joyrider.

'Yeah! What do we call you?' added PC Watson over his shoulder.

'"Mr Smith"?' suggested Danny quietly.

3

If the Custody Suite at Bicester Police Station is not a match for the British Airways Club Class lounge at Heathrow, it is at least a well-lit, well-ventilated room—separated from the cell-area, and affording its present occupant a comfortable enough introit into his temporary detention.

In the presence of the arrested person himself (in the presence too of PC Watson) Sergeant Russell, the Custody Officer, standing in shirt-sleeves at a tall desk, has recited the statutory 'Notice to Accused Persons', and is now completing the Custody Record, as the law requires of him. Russell is an older man, a stickler for procedure, and he fills in the lengthy sections with scrupulous care. He has already made the decision to authorize the continued custody of the prisoner.

'Let me just put it to you once more, lad. What's your real name?'

'Told you, din I? How many more times I got to tell you?'

Russell sighs wearily. There is little he can do if the man persists in such manifest falsehoods.

Yet Danny does so persist; has been so persisting for the past half-hour—ever since he'd slid a letter addressed to him beneath the driver's seat in the front of the cab; ever since he'd jumped down into the strong arms of the law. Literally so.

'Still no news of your address?'

'No fixed abode, innit? Told you, din I? I'm a new-age traveller.'

'Occupation, then—"Traveller". OK?'

'Yeah.'

'And you travelled down here in a vehicle stolen from a depot in Southampton at approximately 9.35 p.m. yesterday evening, right?'

'Who told you that?'

'Relax! I've got to put *summat* down here, that's all—in the "Grounds for Detention" bit. Don't you understand that?'

Russell collects together his sheets of white A4, and prepares to call it a day. Or a night. 'I just hope the Southampton boys've got as much patience as I have, that's all.'

'Do we fingerprint him?' asks Watson.

'We do not! We follow the rule-book; and the rule-book says he's got the right to a nice hot cuppa, if he wants one.'

Danny very much wants one, for his mouth is dry. But he is suddenly frightened and in danger of losing his self-control.

'You can't bloody keep me 'ere!' The voice has grown harsh, the muscles are tightened in the neck. There is, for the first time since the arrest, a strong hint of a tightly coiled spring within the prisoner's sinewy frame. His head moves forward over the desk which separates him from his interlocutor.

'Constable!' Russell is fully prepared; he experiences no fear, as he steps towards the door at the back of the room which leads to his office. 'Put the cuffs on him, will you? I shan't be more'n a minute or two—'

'No!'

As suddenly as it has appeared, the tension has now gone. The voice is quiet once more; the muscles once more relaxed. The man breathes out a long, deep sigh, then holds up his hands in a gesture of mock surrender.

And Russell steps back to the desk, lays down the Custody Record, and takes out his pen again.

'OK. Let's be having things, lad.'

Ten minutes later, from his own office, Sergeant Russell has introduced himself, and is speaking on the telephone to a Senior Prison Officer at Winchester.

'You've got somebody there who's just scarpered, I think?

Rather you *haven't* got somebody there, if you see what I mean. Name o' Smithson.'

'Oh God, no!'

'Pardon?'

'Just keep him, will you?'

'We *are* keeping him. He's here—at Bicester—locked in his cell.'

'Excellent! As I say, just keep him there.'

'What's *that* supposed to mean?'

'It means we don't want him back here, that's what.'

'I'm not with you.'

'Either keep him, or lose him, that's what I'm saying. Yes . . . Not a bad idea that, Sergeant. Why don't you just *lose* him, and do us all a bloody favour?'

There is a chuckle at the Winchester end of the line before the voice continues, in a more serious vein, to explain these strange rejoinders.

Daniel Smithson had joined the army at the age of sixteen, as a boy-soldier; become a mercenary in Africa at the age of twenty-two; served in the SAS for six years after that; and then . . . and then served somewhere else—in prison, for virtually the whole of the past twelve years, his offences ranging from petty theft to hefty larceny. *And* (and this was the real point) the magistrates and the judges and the prison authorities were all becoming increasingly undecided about how to deal with the fellow. What he'd do was this. He'd keep his nose immaculately clean, cause no trouble to anybody, and end up by getting a 'trusty' job. Then, well, he'd bugger off a day or two before he was due for release. Huh! Once outside, he'd pinch as much as his pockets could accommodate, nick a car, live it up for a few days; then (inevitably) get re-arrested, and return to his old haunts and his old mates, with the Prison Governor treating him like the Prodigal Son. The simple truth was that Smithson just couldn't settle down outside the prison walls: he needed—enjoyed!—the stable routine of a familiar nick. Though not a big fellow, he was a strong and wiry one, and his SAS history had reached the prison well ahead of him. No one buggered about (if that was the right word) with Mr Danny Smithson.

'Oh no, Sergeant. No one.'

One thing has been troubling Russell during the recital of the Winchester prisoner's CV: the fact that his man hardly looks the part of some ex-SAS paratrooper, or whatever; and Russell puts his thoughts into words.

'You sure we've got the right fellow—the fellow you're talking about?'

'Put him on the line, if you like. I'll soon tell you.'

'No, I don't think I can allow that.'

'Easy enough to tell, anyway. He's got some letters tattooed on the back of one of his hands—left hand, I think it is. They mentioned it in the papers. Hold on! Shan't be a tick.'

In fact four minutes drag by before the Prison Officer reads from a folder; and Russell listens carefully.

'I'll go and check straightaway. Shan't be a tick.'

Danny is not asleep. He sits on the side of the bed, staring at the floor—and looking up with no apparent interest as Russell unlocks the door.

'Just lift up your hands, will you, Danny Boy.'

The prisoner lifts up his hands as if, once again, he is surrendering to the foe.

'Good. Now turn your hands round, please.'

So Danny turns his hands round; and on the lower joints of the fingers on his left hand Russell reads the letters I–L–Y–K.

This time it is the Winchester end which has waited through four long minutes.

'Well?'

'Yep—it's him, all right. When'll you be coming to fetch him?'

'Not before breakfast, I'll tell you that! We'll let you know.'

'OK.'

'By the way, what exactly are you holding him on?'

'Theft of vehicle; theft of goods in transit; driving without a licence; driving without—'

'Same old stuff.'

'Same old sentence, like as not.'

'Unless some judge suddenly decides to show a bit o' sense and refuses to lock the silly sod away again.'

Russell is not prepared to enter any penological discussion, and prepares to sign off.

'Thanks anyway. Will you be coming yourself?'

'Me? God, no. I'll be seeing him soon enough.'

'And no handcuffs, you say.'

'That's it. No need. Let him have a stroll round Bicester after breakfast by all means—no problem. No cuffs, though. He's one of those who can't stand any physical contact with people. Know what I mean?'

'Doesn't sound as if he'll give us any trouble, anyway.'

'I wouldn't go quite so far as that.'

'What do you mean?'

'Nothing really. Just don't be surprised if he—well, if he strings you along a bit. Know what I mean? He's a bit of a joker is our Danny. Always was. Probably ask you for a bottle of champers for breakfast—say it's doctor's orders.'

'We do a nice little line in tea-bags down here in Bicester.'

'Cheers then.'

'Cheers.'

⚜

PC Watson has finished his report, and now looks in for the last time at his prisoner.

'Anything you want?'

Danny shakes his head. 'Unless you'd like to gimme me Biro back.'

Returning to the Custody Suite, Watson passes on the request; and Sergeant Russell looks down, first at the cash envelope, then at the property bag—from the latter finally taking out the cheap blue pen with which Danny had written on the tacho-disc.

'No harm, I suppose. He probably wants to write a poem on the loo-paper.'

4

At 8.20 a.m. the minibus from Winchester arrived in the front yard of Bicester Police Station, where one of the two prison personnel immediately alighted and reported to the Information Desk.

Everything was ready.

Driven now into the yard behind the main building ('Police Vehicles Only'), the minibus was backed up alongside the wall, its rear window coming to a halt only a few feet from the single external door of the Custody Suite.

The prisoner had not after all ordered champers for breakfast; instead he had done splendid justice to the sausages and beans brought to him an hour earlier. Yet he did make one request when the cell door was again unlocked for his departure, just after 8.30 a.m. Two spare blankets were folded beside the bed, and he'd asked if he could have one to put round him on the journey. He had no overcoat; it was a cold morning.

Not very much to ask at all really, was it?

It had all happened so very suddenly that no one afterwards had any particularly clear picture of the events. But it went something like this . . .

As he was walking through the exit door from the Custody Suite, the blanket which the prisoner was holding about his head and shoulders was dramatically whisked away and equally dramatically whipped over the head and shoulders of the tall, bearded officer who was about to unlock the near-side door of the minibus. Then, dodging lightly past him, the prisoner sprinted the thirty or so yards to the tall beech-hedge which enclosed the rear yard. The hedge was strengthened by a six-foot meshed-wire fence—the fence, in turn, supported every six or seven yards by concrete posts. These posts were some five feet in height, finishing a foot or so below the top of the hedge. One of the posts—and only one—was itself strengthened by a concrete strut which formed an angle of 45 degrees to the ground and which joined the post roughly halfway up, looking rather like a lambda in the Greek alphabet.

At full speed the prisoner leapt at this structure, his left foot landing firm on the top of the strut, his right foot equally firm on the top of the post; and then, propelled by such twin leverage, he had cleared the beech-hedge by several inches, landing neatly on the grass of a school playing-field beyond. Someone later said it was a bit like watching a Russian gymnast clearing a vaulting-horse at the Olympics.

The prisoner was gone.

Neither of the heavy Winchester men could hope to match such a nimble-footed feat of levitation; and it was ten minutes before a wailing police car, forced to take the long way round the front of the station, was criss-crossing the maze of streets in the King's End estate behind, where (it was believed) the prisoner was last sighted.

But not sighted again.

5

The loo-paper in the cells at Bicester may by no means be described as 'Savoy Soft', stiffly reluctant as it is to accommodate itself to the contours of the average human backside. Yet (as Sergeant Russell had earlier intimated) it makes unexpectedly fine writing-paper; and it was two sheets of this paper which one of the cleaners found just before lunchtime that same day—between the folds of the remaining blanket in the cell which had housed the escaped prisoner.

The escape had caused no little embarrassment to the officers concerned, and (worse still) would almost certainly hit the national headlines the following day. Thus it was that Chief Inspector Page of Thames Valley CID (no less) had little compunction in summoning the now off-duty officers Russell, Hodges, and Watson, to his office in Kidlington at 11 a.m. to review the matter—and the cleaner's discovery.

The spelling and punctuation were both a bit shaky, but the import of the letter could hardly have given a clearer answer to what had hitherto seemed the increasingly bewildering question of the escaped man's identity:

The Torygraph did it, very useful paper and a lot of criminals vote tory. It was Smithson give me the idea because we got the same name see. If he got nicked he gets good treatment but if I got nicked no, so what about him and me changing places for a little wile and no harm done is it? Besides, probably gives me a best chance of scarpering—lots of that now days, perhaps its the resession to blame like for every thing else. There was just that one problem, that tatoo I read about and when you coppers thought I was filling in the old tacko with the blue byro I was just writing out them four letters on the old nuckles see, easy! Then I done a pretty good job really with all that stuff about me name, dont you think so? Well well Danny Smithson boy, I wonder where you are, have you desided to keep out this time, why not?

I'll leave this letter in the bottom blanket because I've got ideas with the top one. If I get away what a big laugh for me when you find it, and if I dont its your turn for the big laugh
Samuel (Danny) Lambert
PS you can give me old comb and spare hanky to Oxfam or the Sally army, its up to you

Newly recruited to the Force, PC Watson was glad to have someone to chat with—even a subdued-looking Sergeant Russell —as they stood in the lunch queue in the HQ canteen.

'Rotten bit o' luck, Sarge . . .' he began.

'You make your own luck, lad. I shoulda been far more careful checking out that tattoo.'

'I was thinking more about both of 'em being named "Danny".'

'*Nick*named, you mean—one of 'em.'

'Yeah. I mean, there's your "Pongo" Warings . . .'

'And your "Nobby" Clarks . . .'

'How come your "Danny" Lamberts, though?'

'Dunno.'

The queue moved a couple of feet, and the plain-clothes man in front of them turned round to proffer a suggestion:

'Might be someone from Stamford? Stamford in Lincolnshire? Lamberts there often get called "Danny", after Daniel Lambert— fellow who weighed fifty-two stone odd—still in the *Guinness Book of Records*.'

'Who's *he* when he's at home?' asked Watson, after they'd been served.

'You don't know?'

Watson shook his head.

'That, my lad, was Chief Inspector Morse.'

Watson frowned slightly. He'd never heard of the man; yet for a fleeting second he'd thought he'd almost recognized the profile as that grey head had turned towards them in the queue . . .

❧

Next morning, the Governor of HM Prison Winchester received a full report on the case, now becoming widely known as the 'Cock-up at Bicester Corral', including a photocopy of the letter found in the escapee's cell. He immediately summoned the Senior Prison Officer from D Wing, where Smithson had spent so many comparatively contented months and years.

'You'll be interested in this.' The Governor handed over the file.

Price, a thick-set Irishman, sat down and began reading.

'No news of our Danny?' interrupted the Governor.

Price shook his head. Then, halfway through the letter, his eyes suddenly widened with a new and startling notion.

'You don't think, sorr ...?' he began slowly, pointing to the letter.

The Governor groaned, permitting himself also, albeit briefly, to contemplate the unimaginable.

'Don't tell me *that*! Please! Don't tell me it's *Smithson's* writing?'

Price studied the writing of the letter again. 'Yes, sorr. I'm sorry. But I'm pretty sure it is.'

And for a few moments the two men sat there in silence, each of them visualizing their erstwhile prisoner perched aloft in the cabin of a stolen van, and carefully over-tracing his own tattoos with a cheap blue Biro pen ...

LAST CALL

Wives invariably flourish when deserted; it is the deserting male who often ends in disaster.

(William McFee)

Not too carefully—not carefully at all really—Morse looked down at the man lying supine on the double bed, dressed only in an unbuttoned white shirt, Oxford-blue pants, and black socks. The paleness of the man's skin precluded the probability of any recent holiday on the Greek islands—with only the dullish-red V below the throat suggesting the possibility of any life outside the executive-suited higher echelons of British management.

Late forties, by the look of him; a firmly built man, with a pleasantly featured, clean-shaven face, and frizzy, grey-flecked hair. The jacket of a subfusc herring-bone suit was hanging inside the open-doored wardrobe, a maroon tie over it; and neatly aligned at the near side of the bed was a pair of soft black leather shoes.

A methodical, successful businessman, thought Morse.

A quiet knock on the door of Room 231 of The Randolph Hotel heralded the arrivals of Sergeant Lewis and Dr Laura Hobson—the latter immediately stepping forward to peer down at the dead man's face. Blood was still seeping slowly from a deep gash that slanted over the closed right eye like some monstrous acute accent. But there was no other sign of red in the face, for the lips were a palish shade of purple.

'Probably had a heart attack,' volunteered the pathologist.

Lewis looked down at the Corby trouser-press, standing to the left of the bathroom door, on which a pair of subfusc herring-bone trousers were draped over the opened leaf.

'Probably bashed his head on that?' suggested Lewis.

And Morse nodded.

The cream paint of the left-hand door-jamb was splashed with elongated flecks of scarlet, and two feet inside the bathroom itself, on the blue-and-white-tiled floor, was a patch of darkly dried blood.

'If he'd tripped it could have brought on a heart attack, don't you think, sir?'

Again Morse nodded. 'And if he'd had a heart attack he could have tripped and cracked his head, yes.'

Turning her head momentarily towards them, Dr Hobson put the situation rather more simply: 'Which came first—the chicken or the egg?'

'The chicken?' said Morse.

But the blonde pathologist was clearly in favour of an each-way bet. 'Like as not it happened contemporaneously.'

Lewis's eyebrows shot up. 'Big word, that.'

Dr Hobson smiled at him, attractively. 'I've finished with it for now, Sergeant. It's all yours if you'd like to have it.'

On the dressing table to the right of the bathroom door, beside the phone, lay two items which had been recovered from the bathroom floor: a calibrated syringe, its orange hood still in place over the needle; and the glass fragments of what had been a small phial, some three inches long, which had contained (as indicated by its label) 'Human Actrapid Insulin'—the colourless liquid having almost completely seeped away into a layer of white tissue-paper.

For a minute or so longer, Chief Inspector Morse stood exactly where he was, visualizing much—visualizing almost everything, perhaps—of what had happened there on the threshold of the bathroom, his eyes finally concentrating on the telephone, its receiver cradled firmly on its base.

Then he announced his strategy: 'I think we'll just nip down to the bar, Lewis—while Doctor Hobson finishes off here.' He looked at his wrist-watch. 'That's two nights running I've missed *The Archers*. For nothing, too—there's been no murder here.'

But before leaving Room 231, he dipped a hand gently into the inside breast-pocket of the dead man's jacket, withdrawing a wallet of pigskin leather.

'Do we know who found him—and how?' asked Lewis, as the two detectives walked down the grandly wide staircase to the reception area of The Randolph.

'That's exactly what I hope you're going to find out for me.'

Three-quarters of an hour later Sergeant Lewis had discovered all there was to be known. Not much, but enough. And he reported to Morse.

Sherwood had reserved the double-bedded, en suite, five-star room by phone only the previous evening—with no opportunity thus afforded for any written confirmation. He had booked in, on his own, at about 5.40 p.m. But the form, duly completed at reception, was comparatively uninformative: **Name(s)**—'Sherwood'; **Home Address**—'53 Leominster Drive, Shrewsbury'; **Signature**—'Peter Sherwood'. The two boxes beside the questions **Are you here on business? On Leisure?** remained unticked, and the space for **Car Registration** was completed with a dismissive dash. That was all, except for a tick in the **Cash** box alongside **How do you intend to settle your account?**

The Guest Registration Card thus negotiated, £140 (in twenties) had been paid; and no further details were disclosed by Sherwood or demanded by the chicly uniformed receptionist. Any wake-up call in the morning? 'No.' Any newspaper? 'Yes—the *Telegraph*.' Sherwood had taken the key, politely declined the offer of help with his two suitcases, and that was that.

No woman on the scene—no one remembered a woman at all.

Sherwood was scheduled to attend a two-day conference on Computer Technology being held at Rewley House—very close by, just up at the top of St John Street, almost immediately opposite The Randolph.

Now clearly of importance had been two telephone calls. The first, probably an outside call, asking to be put through to Mr Sherwood; the second, presumably made from inside the hotel, reporting to the operator that medical assistance was urgently required in Room 231. The Senior Concierge, Roy Harden, had immediately gone up to the room, where he'd found the door slightly ajar —and Sherwood lying across the threshold of the bathroom. Already dead by the look of him. From the room itself Harden had promptly telephoned the house-doctor; and then the manager, with whose assistance two minutes later he'd carried Sherwood's body over to the bed. A room-maid had cleared up the broken glass from the bathroom—for there seemed to be no suspicious circumstances at the time. It was only because of the house-doctor's marginal unease over the head wound that the manager had deemed it prudent to call in the police. Just to be on the safe side.

'What do you think so far?' asked Morse.

'Same as you, sir. *Cherchez la belle femme*. He's off to another conference—he invites his mistress—they know how to work things—he has a heart attack—she's scared out of her wits—rings for the doc—and then gets pretty smartish out of it.'

'Ye-es . . .' Morse picked up the dead man's wallet. 'No railway tickets in here, Lewis.'

'So?'

'They don't very often *collect* railway tickets from passengers these days, do they?'

Lewis followed the drift of Morse's thinking. 'They probably came by car, you mean?'

'*Her* car, like as not. He tells his wife he's going to the railway station, and his lady-love picks him up there. Then when she gets him here, she just nips off and parks her car somewhere nearby— and there's no need for anyone to know her registration number or anything. Very neat. Very easy.'

Lewis nodded agreement. 'It's getting easier all the time to commit adultery.'

Morse looked up sharply. 'Let's be slightly more accurate about things, Lewis. What you mean is that the preconditions for adultery are easier to handle: fewer eyebrows raised; fewer questions asked; fewer details to be filled in; just fork out your fee for the room ... But whether it's really become emotionally easier, psychologically easier ... *physically* easier—well, I just wouldn't know, would I?'

Saving Lewis the possible embarrassment of any reply, the young pathologist now appeared beside them in the Chapters Bar.

Morse beamed happily, and pushed forward his emptied glass. 'Ah, Doctor Hobson! What'll you have to drink? Lewis here is in the chair.'

But Dr Hobson shook her pretty head. 'I can't stay, I'm afraid.'

'Pity!'

'You're feeling all right, Chief Inspector?'

'Pardon?'

'They told me the only thing you ever wanted from any pathologist was an estimated time of death.'

'Oh, I know that already,' replied Morse. 'Six o'clock—to the minute, I'd say.'

Laura Hobson smiled, refusing to rise to the bait. 'About six o'clock, yes. I hope you don't expect me to be *quite* so precise as you, though? I'm just a humble medical scientist myself. No foul-play, though. I'm fairly sure of that.'

'*Fairly* sure?'

'As I say, I'm just a scientist. Good night.'

'He was a neat and tidy enough man,' resumed Lewis. 'The bag he'd packed for himself—well, it was all laid out with sort of military precision. You know, socks, hankies, spare pants, washing kit —all in their proper compartments.'

'Condoms?'

'Yes, sir, in a little compartment at the front.'

'It's all very sad, isn't it?'

'More sad for the wife, if you ask me.'

'It was the wife I was thinking of,' replied Morse quietly.

Lewis thought it wise to change tack. 'You seem very sure about the time?'

'There's a Diabetic Card here in the wallet, giving details and times of daily injections: 7 a.m.; 6 p.m.; 10.30 p.m. "Military precision", did you say? I think you're right.'

'We'd know it was just before or just after six anyway, wouldn't we? From the telephone calls, I mean.'

'Ye-es.'

'Who do you think made the first call, sir?'

'Same woman who made the second. She rang from a phone-box outside—said she'd parked OK—asked him for the room number—told him to leave the door slightly ajar—promised she'd be with him in just a few minutes . . .'

'. . . saw him lying there—realized he was dead—and rang for help.'

'Where did she ring from, though?' asked Morse slowly.

'Bedroom, I should think?'

'I wonder . . . She'd have to stand just over him when she rang, wouldn't she?'

'Not everybody's quite so put off by dead bodies as you, sir.'

The Senior Concierge, now re-summoned, briskly confirmed his earlier evidence, and Morse had only one additional question.

'Was the telephone off the hook when you went into the room?'

'Yes, sir. Dangling on the cord.'

'And you replaced it?'

'I replaced it.'

'I see.'

'Should I have left it?'

'No, no!' For some reason Morse seemed almost relieved, and the concierge left.

'I wish all our witnesses were as bright and unequivocal as Mr Harden, Lewis!'

'Important, is it, this phone business?'

'No. I don't think so. Not now.'

Lewis looked at his watch. 'We shall have to do something about his wife, sir.'

'You know the routine better than I do.'

Yes, Lewis did.

'Tell 'em to be gentle with her. Just to say her husband's had a fatal heart attack. We can arrange transport—well, *they* can—if she wants to come to Oxford tomorrow. Not tonight, though. Get her local GP in. Well—you know the ropes.'

Morse drained his beer and his eyes reflected the curious sadness he clearly felt for the woman left alone that night in Shrewsbury.

'Another pint?' suggested Lewis.

But Morse shook his head and stood up to go, the pigskin wallet held tightly in his right hand.

Three-quarters of an hour later, a police car drew up outside the double-garaged property that stood at 53 Leominster Drive, Shrewsbury. Accompanying the police sergeant was a young smartly attractive WPC, who did the talking:

'Mrs Sherwood?'

'Yes?'

'I'm afraid we've got some bad news for you.'

Sometimes the police had the lousiest job in the whole world.

Mid-morning the following day Morse had received Dr Hobson's preliminary report:

Heart attack—death following almost immediately. Little or no chance of survival, even if any more sophisticated treatment had been available earlier. Massive h.a. Subject a heavily dependent insulin diabetic, with (probably) high blood-pressure. Often a risky —sometimes fatal—combination. Every indication that onset of h.a. precipitated subject's imbalance and collapse, with head injury incurred only subsequently. Blood sugar at time of death: 26.8. <u>Very</u> high.

Doing one or two other little tests. Will keep you informed.

L.H.

And now Lewis read through the findings.

'Things seem to have happened, er, contemporaneously, sir.'

'Clears it up, certainly, as far as I'm concerned.'

'Mrs Sherwood's coming down this morning. Identify the body and . . .'

Morse nodded. 'Keep her out of The Randolph, if you can. No need for her to know anything about the room or . . . or anything.'

'I suppose not.'

'Look! Nobody's going to profit from parading any dirty linen, agreed?'

'Least of all Mrs Sherwood.'

'*And* her family.'

'OK.'

'Have we discovered much about her?'

Lewis consulted his note-book.

'Aged forty-five; son and daughter—both early twenties; she works part-time; bags o' money; everybody seemed to think the marriage was fine.'

Morse nodded sombrely. 'Death's bad enough, but . . . Remember that Greek Archbishop, Lewis? Had a heart attack in his local knocking-shop at Athens? Poor sod!'

'At least he hadn't got a wife.'

'How do *you* know?'

'Perhaps *Mrs* Sherwood was having a bit on the side, too.'

But Morse appeared not to be listening. He took from the dead man's wallet a passport-sized colour photograph of a duskily tressed and deeply tanned young beauty, wearing thinly rimmed schoolma'amish spectacles, and looking half-seriously into the camera—yet with lips beginning to curl in a sensuous smile.

'Lovely!' said Morse. 'Lovely!'

'And that's . . . ?'

'That's *Mr* Sherwood's "bit on the side", as you so elegantly phrase things.'

Then Morse, after glancing briefly at the back of the photo, slowly tore it into smaller and smaller pieces.

'Destroying evidence, that is. Could be valuable in the case—'

'*What* case?'

Lewis shrugged. 'You're in charge, sir.'

Morse was now on his feet. 'Just nip me down to Oxford, will you? Railway station for a couple of minutes—then on to St Aldates. What time's Mrs Sherwood due here?'

'Eleven-thirty. Driving down—dunno if it's the Rolls or the BMW, though!'

Morse shot off at an odd angle: 'Do you believe in any after-life, Lewis?'

'Not sure, really. What about you?'

'No, not me. I think death's just a process of chemical disintegration.'

'Perhaps *she* could tell us—Mrs Sherwood. She took a Chemistry degree at Cambridge.'

'How on earth did you find that out?'

Lewis too now rose. 'I'm a detective, sir, remember?'

'She must have been a clever lass at school.'

'But you still don't want to see her?'

'No.'

As he'd promised, Morse spent only a brief while inside Oxford railway station; and five minutes later Lewis was driving down St Aldates, when Morse peremptorily announced a slight change of plan. It was just after 11 a.m.

'Drop me anywhere here! I'll just nip in to see how the landlord is.'

He gestured vaguely to the Bulldog, and Lewis brought the
police car to a stop opposite Christ Church.

'Just give this to Mrs Sherwood, will you?'

Lewis took the proffered wallet. 'No more photos in it?'

'Only one of the four of 'em: mum and dad and the two kids.
Everything's all right now.'

Lewis had arrived back at Kidlington HQ at 2 p.m. to find that the
chief had not yet returned—from wherever.

Mrs Sherwood had been a quarter of an hour late (in the
BMW), and Lewis had looked quickly through the contents of
her late husband's wallet as he'd waited in a small ante-room in
the Pathology Institute. The usual plastic cards were there, relat-
ing to monies and memberships; £110 in banknotes; the family
photograph that Morse had mentioned (but no others); and something else, yes—two green-and-orange British Rail tickets, one
'Out' and one 'Return', between Shrewsbury and Oxford. Neither
had received the attention of any ticket-collector's clip. Yet they
looked genuine enough. *Were* genuine enough, except for the fact
that the date printed on each of them was not yesterday's—but
today's.

Lewis smiled wryly to himself.

Mrs Pamela Sherwood had turned out to be a slim, well-
groomed, delicately featured woman—distressed, yes, but well in
control. Lewis himself never really knew what to do or what to say
in times of bereavement; but that was exactly why (as Morse well
knew) he performed the job so successfully, since it was not
unusual on such sad occasions for roles to be reversed and for the
bereaved themselves to feel an instinctively reciprocal sympathy
with the good sergeant.

As now.

Over coffee, and after identifying her husband's body, Mrs Sherwood herself had looked quickly through the contents of the wallet, her eyes intent as she took out one item after another, including the tickets.

One item after another ... except of course for the photograph of the dusky siren whose features for a little while had recently held the Chief Inspector mesmerized.

But it was the message on Morse's Ansaphone which displaced any thoughts of Mrs Sherwood; a message left by the manager of The Randolph; a message which Lewis, now for the third time, replayed as he waited for Morse to return.

Bamber Goodall here, Chief Inspector. I had a personal call this morning just before twelve. A woman, youngish woman by the sound of her, said she'd got to speak to me and I accepted the call. She said she was feeling guilty because she was the woman who was going to stay with Mr Sherwood. She said she'd driven him down in her own car. She'd kept out of the way when he'd booked in, and when he'd gone up to the room with their luggage. Then he'd come down again, given her the room-key, and said he'd expect her in about ten or fifteen minutes, after she'd parked the car—which she had done, up in Norham Gardens. It seems they'd both been worried about leaving the car in the hotel garage. Then when she got back and walked up to their room she'd opened the door to find him lying there, and she'd just 'panicked'—her word—and grabbed her case—still unopened—and got the hell out of things. She drove out to the Cotswolds, and then back home this morning. She was still feeling awful about it, she said. Somehow she'd known he was dead—though she didn't say *how* she knew. Well, that's it really. When I said she ought to talk to the police she said she couldn't. I tried to keep her talking but it was no good. She just kept saying that if only Mrs Sherwood could be kept out of it all—you know—kept in the dark about things, about *her*, well, she'd be extremely grateful. So that's it, really. I'll be in the hotel here till about eight-thirty this evening ... if you want me.

During the replay of this message, Lewis had been conscious that Morse was standing beside him, listening (it seemed) intently; and as Goodall signed off, Lewis noted that Morse's eyes were shining with excitement; and impatience, too—like a camel sniffing the coolness of the air and eager to ride forth at evening from the wells . . .

Although Lewis himself would not have made that particular simile.

Morse's verdict, whispered and intense, was barely audible in the now silent office:

'She did it! She murdered him!'

For a few moments Lewis looked across the desk with mouth agape, like a young lad bidden to display his tonsils to the doctor. He would have asked about that unspecified 'She', but already Morse had picked up the phone, asking to be put through to the Path lab—urgently. And as he covered the speaker with the palm of his left hand, he gave his instructions:

'Go and take a full statement from the manager, Lewis. I want to know *exactly* what she told him. *Verbatim*, as far as—

'Ah, Doctor Hobson?'

'*You* can drive back,' Morse had said the following morning when just after 10 a.m. he himself took the wheel of the maroon-coloured Jaguar and began the drive up to Shrewsbury, via Motorways 40, 42, 6, and 54. One hundred and ten miles. No Services. An hour and a half. Lewis, whose only indulgence in life (apart from eggs and chips) was speedy driving, would have cut fifteen minutes off the time.

Did cut fifteen minutes off, on the return journey.

'Difficult to know why anyone'd ever want to go from Shrewsbury to Oxford by British Rail,' declared Lewis, as Morse pulled up outside the elegantly appointed, detached house that stood at 53 Leominster Drive.

✤

'Mrs Sherwood,' began Morse, 'we have some difficult things to tell you. When your husband went off to Oxford, we have every reason to believe, I'm afraid, that he'd arranged to spend two nights with a woman-friend—with a mistress—in The Randolph Hotel. She'd driven him down to Oxford in her own car—'

Mrs Sherwood shook her head and closed her eyes, like a young girl refusing to believe that Santa Claus was just a dream.

'You've got it all wrong! He went to Oxford by *train*—I took him to the station myself. He knew he'd be having quite a lot to drink at the conference—'

'He went to Oxford by *car*,' countered Morse. 'His mistress drove him there.'

'But that's *nonsense*! I've got the rail tickets—'

'Show me!'

From her handbag, Mrs Sherwood took out her husband's wallet; and from the wallet, the two tickets—which she handed to him.

'*We* decided to buy these for you, Mrs Sherwood, because we wanted to spare you some of the anguish and the pain of all this trouble. And if you'd been more observant, you'd have spotted the wrong date on them. Until yesterday, you see, we'd no suspicion at all that your husband's death was due to anything but natural causes.'

Her eyes flicked up sharply. 'And now you're saying . . . ?'

Morse made no direct answer, but looked away from those compelling eyes, and slowly tore the rail tickets into smaller and smaller pieces, just as earlier he'd torn the photograph.

'Did you know your husband's mistress?'

For a while it seemed that Mrs Sherwood would challenge the premiss of Morse's brutal question. But she didn't.

'I know her.'

'We did find a photograph,' continued Morse, 'but foolishly I tore it up, because, as I say, we wanted to—'

'She was hardly the first, Chief Inspector.'

'Please tell me who she is and where we can find her.'

But Mrs Sherwood shook her head as she stared into some middle distance. 'I felt jealous about his other women—of course I did. But I *envied* this one. I'd found out a few things about her and I think she was everything to Peter that I'd never been. You see, I'm so very careful and tight about life—about emotions, money, everything. And she's open and vivacious, and wonderful in bed, for all I know . . .'

'And very young,' added Morse cruelly.

'About half Peter's age, yes. Perhaps that's what hurt more than anything.'

'But who *is* she, Mrs Sherwood?'

Morse had lifted his fiercely blue eyes to challenge hers. Yet to no avail; and it was Lewis who pursued the questioning.

'We're interested in two telephone calls, Mrs Sherwood, made about the time your husband died: one just before six o'clock; and one five or ten minutes later. At first we believed both calls were made by the same person. Yesterday, though, a woman rang and admitted making the second call—the one asking for a doctor—but she claimed quite certainly that she hadn't made any earlier call—a call, we thought, possibly asking for your husband's room-number, or whatever it was she needed to know. She said she already *knew* the room-number: he'd gone upstairs with the luggage after checking in, and then come down and actually *given* her the key—before she drove off to park the car somewhere. So what reason could she have had for ringing him?'

Mrs Sherwood shrugged her thin shoulders. 'Doesn't seem much point, does there?'

'Do you think it was one of his other lady-loves?'

'Could have been—'

'*You*, perhaps?' broke in Morse, very quietly.

Rising from her armchair, Mrs Sherwood walked over to the french window and stood gazing out across the wide lawn.

'Is a wife not allowed to ring her husband? At least he almost always told me *where* he was staying, if not who he was staying with.'

'What time did you make the call?' continued Morse.

'Six—sixish? As you say.'

'Before or after?'

'Does it matter?'

'You said you're—what was it?—a bit tight and careful about things like money.'

She nodded. 'Silly really. We'd plenty of money—two salaries coming in.'

'You work in a pharmaceutical lab, I think?'

'Part-time, yes.'

'And you're a Chemistry graduate.'

'Huh! You know all about me. But all you really want to know is about *her*. Am I right?'

'I'd like to know *more* about you, though. For example, the phone-rate gets cheaper after six o'clock, doesn't it? So why didn't you wait till *after* six o'clock—it was only a matter of a few minutes.'

'I didn't think.'

'Come on, Mrs Sherwood! You can do better than that.'

'No, I can't.'

'You'll have to, if you want us to find out who murdered your husband.'

She turned from the window, and in the pale face the eyes were now ablaze.

'Murdered?'

'Yes, murdered.'

'But you're wrong! He died of a heart attack. That's what they told me—the medical people—in Oxford.'

'We've had a further report from the police pathologist, Mrs Sherwood. Sergeant!'

Lewis now read out the relevant extract from Dr Hobson's second report:

The glass capsule had shattered into small pieces, and the liquid contents had been almost entirely spilled. Our analysis however shows that the original insulin within the capsule had been injected with Sodium Fluoroacetate, a substance readily soluble in water; and extremely poisonous even in the smallest quantity, interfering fatally and almost immediately as it does with the Krebs cycle of metabolism. For obvious reasons this substance is never openly available to the general public.

'But would be available,' added Morse slowly, 'to someone working in a pharmaceutical lab.'

'My husband died of a heart attack! I was told so. Are you now saying he didn't?'

'No.'

'So please tell me what you *are* saying! What's all this about murder?'

'*You* wished to murder your husband, Mrs Sherwood. *You* poisoned the insulin capsule. That's what I'm saying.'

She turned to stare out of the window again.

'And if I did?' she asked finally.

'I don't know,' replied Morse simply. 'But I believe you *intended* to poison your husband. You'd lived with him for twenty-odd years and you knew him to be an extremely meticulous and methodical man. You knew perfectly well that in Oxford, just as here at home, he'd almost certainly be taking his insulin at six o'clock that evening. And the reason you rang him up just *before* six o'clock was to make sure he *didn't* inject himself from the capsule you'd poisoned. Please tell me if I'm wrong, Mrs Sherwood! But I think that in spite of all that had happened, in spite of all his infidelities, you didn't hate him *quite* enough to go through with your plan. In the last analysis, you wanted him to stay alive. Perhaps you even hoped he'd come to love you once again.'

She nodded weakly, and spoke in a sing-song voice as if the events she now described were distanced and unreal.

'Five to six, it was when I rang. The line was engaged at first and I began to panic. But then I *did* get through. It was just like when I was a girl; when I used to play little games with myself. I just asked him if he was going to sleep with her that night . . . I wanted to shock him, you see . . . And if he said "no", I was going to tell him about the insulin.'

She stopped.

'And if he said "yes"?'

'It never got that far. I just—I just heard a great crash.'

'Don't you think you may have murdered him just as surely as if you'd poisoned him yourself?'

She shook her head, more in bewilderment, it seemed, than in denial. 'What will happen to me?'

'I just don't know,' said Morse.

At the front door, she laid a hand lightly on his arm, and lowered her eyes.

'It was very kind of you—what you did.'

'But you won't tell me who this other woman is?'

'No.'

Once the Jaguar had disappeared from view, Mrs Sherwood moved back inside the house, a semi-smile upon her lips.

Too clever for his own good, that man! She'd played it mostly by ear, of course. But how easy he'd made it for her! With *him* pointing out the escape route she'd so desperately been seeking after his mention of the Sodium Fluoroacetate; *him* suggesting the blessedly mitigating circumstance that it was she, Pamela Sherwood, who had rung her husband; *she* who had tried not to *cause*, but to *prevent* her husband's death. Why he'd even told her the time of that telephone call—a call she'd never made, of course.

Oh, she'd willingly enough have faced the consequences of poisoning her husband, because above all things in life she'd wanted him dead. But now? If by some happy chance she were to be seen as guilty only of causing him a heart attack—well, she'd settle for that all right. Why not? He was dead, that was the main thing. And that Jane bloody Ballantyre—pox-ridden strumpet!—would have to seek some other demerara daddy now.

'You *were* kind, you know,' said Lewis as he drove the Jaguar out of Leominster Drive.

'How come?'

'Well, the photo—'

'"Stupid", do you mean?'

'—and the rail tickets.'

'You think so?'

'Yes, I do. You probably know you haven't got a reputation for being too generous with money—'

'No?'

'—but I reckon underneath you're a bit of an old softie, really. I mean, forking out of your own pocket for those tickets . . .'

Morse opened his mouth as if to reply; but decided against it. He *would* (he promised himself) inform Lewis about the expenses claim he had already submitted for £26—but not for the time being.

'Where to now, sir?'

'We're going to try to trace Peter Sherwood's mistress.'

'But—but haven't we cleared things up?'

'What? You didn't believe all that stuff we got from Mrs Sherwood, did you?'

'You mean—you mean *you* didn't?'

'Lewis! Lewis! Why do you think she refused to tell us anything about her husband's latest conquest?'

Lewis had no idea, and mercifully Morse continued.

'Because our dusky maiden is the only one who knows the truth in this case. And Mrs Sherwood doesn't *want* us to know the truth, does she?'

'Perhaps not,' mumbled Lewis, uncomprehendingly.

'So you ask me where we're going? Well, it's a longish shot, but not a hopeless one. The initials on the back of the photo were "JB"; she looked deeply tanned—'

'Perhaps she's just back from a topless two weeks in Torremolinos.'

'You know, Lewis, you don't often come out with such a splendid sentence as that.'

Lewis felt better. 'You mean she might belong to a local health centre?'

'Lying on a sun-bed, yes. And if Mrs Sherwood was able to find out a few things about her—'

'—she might not live a million miles from Leominster Drive.'

'Exactly so.'

'Sounds like my sort of job, sir.'

'Just what I was thinking, Lewis. So, if you'll just drop me off at the nearest pub?'

Late that same afternoon, in a luxury flat rather less than a mile from the Sherwood residence, a dark-haired, totally and fatally attractive young woman, wearing thinly rimmed, schoolma'amish spectacles, was still in an agitated frame of mind.

For she knew that she had killed her lover.

Had it been foolish to ring the manager of The Randolph? Certainly the questions he'd asked were disturbingly shrewd; yet her conscience had compelled her to do something. Yes, even she had a conscience . . .

It had been five minutes to six when she'd finally managed to park the car—up in Norham Gardens, rather further out than she'd anticipated. But at least a telephone booth had stood near by, and (as arranged) she'd dialled the hotel and been put through without delay. And virtually verbatim could she recall that brief— that *fatal*—conversation:

'Peter?'

'Jane!'

'Everything OK?'

'Will be once you get here. Room 231.'

'Is it nice?'

'Lovely double bed!'

'I can hardly wait.'

'I'll leave the door ajar.'

'Peter?'

'Yes?'

'I'm wanting you like crazy.'

'Jane! Please don't say things like that!'

'Why on earth not?'

'You make me—you make me so *excited*—'

That was when she'd heard a great crash, although the terrible truth had not immediately dawned upon her consciousness . . .

Who the two men were she now saw walking up to the block of flats, she hadn't the faintest notion. But they looked a well enough heeled pair, and the posh car parked at the kerbside hardly suggested a couple of double-glazing double-dealers. And when she answered the door-bell (yes, they had called to see *her*) she acknowledged to herself that she could really rather fancy one of the two men, the one whose hair looked somewhat prematurely grey. For in spite of her anxieties, she was already casting round (as Mrs Sherwood had suspected) for some replacement demerara daddy.

'Jane Ballantyre?'

She smiled invitingly. 'Can I help you, gentlemen?'

'You know, I rather think you can,' said the man whose hair looked somewhat prematurely grey.